"But . . . why?"

"I want you and I'm prepared to marry you to get you and keep you." There was a slight change in his tone of voice, a certain intensity in the eyes that now looked into hers.

Her head whirled. How she longed to say yes. But all the dreams a young girl dreamed of—a lover tall and handsome, big and bold, sweeping her away in a cloud of love—were shattered. A man had asked her to marry him, not for love . . . but to care for his child. In a way he would be her employer. She would be given food, shelter, and protection, for services rendered.

"Mister Carroll, I'll come with you and take care of your child, but I'd rather not marry you."

☙ ☙ ☙

ALSO BY DOROTHY GARLOCK

Published by
WARNER BOOKS

DOROTHY GARLOCK

Love and Cherish

WARNER BOOKS

A Time Warner Company

This book was originally published by Kensington Publishing, and was revised and expanded by the author.

WARNER BOOKS EDITION

This Warner Books Edition is published by arrangement with the author.

Cover design by Jackie Merri Meyer
Cover illustration by Donna Diamond
Hand lettering by Carl Dellacroce

Warner Books, Inc.
1271 Avenue of the Americas
New York, NY 10020

W A Time Warner Company

Printed in the United States of America

First Warner Books Printing: June, 1995

10 9 8 7 6 5 4 3 2 1

*This book is dedicated with love
to my real-life hero,
my husband of many years,
Herb L. Garlock, Sr.*

CHAPTER
* 1 *

*I*ndian summer lay shimmering along the Kentucky River. It bronzed the trees and filled the air with listlessness. It warmed the skin and tempted the mind to relax and dream vague, beautiful dreams. Beams of bright sunlight slanted down through the trees. The woods were alive with pleasant cheeps and chirps and the rustlings of hundreds of birds. A whippoorwill swooped overhead trailing his melodious repeated cry.

The afternoon was serene and beautiful.

The red-haired girl lifted her face to the sun, breathed in the warm scented air and followed the faint path through the trees toward the river. She had a light, free-swinging stride, and her small bare feet scarcely made a depression in the short grass. Gazing up through the high branches of the spreading oak trees, she studied the drifting clouds, then turned her head to look at the clear tumbling water of the river. Beyond there was nothing but dense forest and be-

1

hind her the hills glowed golden-red in the autumn sun.

She came to the river's edge, knelt and drank, then stood and gazed intently along the path she had just followed, her small well-shaped head tilted slightly as she listened for any unusual sound. Satisfied that she was alone, she quickly unbuttoned her dress, drew it up over her head, and hung the plain butter-nut-dyed garment on a tree branch.

Turning back to the river, she stood for a moment undecided, fingers touching the drawstring of her thin shift. Then, after a quick nervous glance over her shoulder, she stepped down into the water and waded out from the shadows of the trees into the sunshine. Here she stood, enjoying the feel of the hot afternoon sun on her bare arms and shoulders, trailing her fingers lazily in the clear water.

The sun was warm, but the water was cool. The girl scrubbed her arms and shoulders briskly and splashed water into her face. She ducked down until only her head and neck showed above the water, then rose and started back toward shore. The thin cotton shift clung wetly to her slender young body, outlining firm, high breasts with their shadowy dark nipples, a small waist, and gently curving buttocks and thighs.

Reaching the riverbank, she searched for a warm place in the sun. She found a huge boulder and leaned back against it to wait for her shift to dry. Her eyelids drooped though she struggled to keep them open. It was pleasant being alone here in this place where the air was pungent with the scent of the pine and spruce trees that lined the bank. The sun was warm. The silence was broken only by the chirping of the birds and an occasional flopping sound of a fish rising from the river. Exhausted from a sleepless, watchful night, she dozed.

Cherish came awake with a start the instant rough hands seized her. Loose wet lips pressed hers. In an agony of terror she stared into a whiskered, beastial face.

"Wal, now! What've I got me here?"

She gasped and struggled, but the man held her down effortlessly against the rock while his eager gaze roamed over her, taking in the beauty of her breasts and buttocks revealed by the still-damp clinging shift. He seized her hands when she tried to cover herself, and bent his face toward hers again. His stinking breath nauseated her. She rolled her head from side to side in an effort to escape his repulsive lips, and she managed to let out one loud, piercing scream before his dirty hand covered her mouth.

"Shut up, bitch!" he snarled. "Don't ya tell me ya ain't lookin' for somethin' undressed as ya are."

Terror gave her strength.

She kicked and clawed but he held on, breathing

rapidly, yellow teeth exposed in a leering grin, letting her wear herself out.

"Please . . . don't! Let me go—"

"Stop fightin'. Ya was waitin' for me. Ya been givin' me the eye all along, ain't ya?"

"No!"

"I seen ya. Ya know what I got in my britches, gal? Hit's been a rearin' for ya."

"Let go of me," she shouted. "Roy will kill you!"

"He ain't comin' back. Hear? I ain't givin' out nothin' for no pay. Ya'll pay fer yore grub on yore back."

So intense was his excitement that he failed to hear the call that came from the edge of the woods. It came again, closer this time.

"Pa! Whatcha doin', Pa?" The young voice rang with alarm.

The man sprang back and glared at his son.

Thirteen-year-old Jerd Burgess stood wide-eyed with astonishment, looking from his father to the girl. Almost as tall as his father, he stood with his big hands hanging from shirt sleeves too short for his long arms; his feet and legs protruded from pants too short for his lanky body. His eyes clung to the near-naked girl as she broke away and raced to the tree where she had hung her dress.

"Get back to camp!" his father ordered harshly.

The boy reluctantly tore his eyes away from the girl, who had slipped the dress over her head and was hastily buttoning the row of buttons that reached from neckline to waist.

"Ma wants ya. She wants ya, now." Jerd's voice was high-pitched with the strange excitement he was feeling at finding his father with the half-dressed girl. She was standing with her back to them, still fumbling with the buttons on her dress.

Jess Burgess scowled and spit in the grass at his feet.

"What she wantin'?"

"I dunno. She said fetch ya . . . now."

"A man ain't got no time to hisself a'tall," Jess grumbled. After a moment's hesitation while he looked from the girl to his son, he moved toward the path leading to the camp.

"What ya lookin' at?" he snapped at the boy. "Ain't ya knowin' a man's got ta dump his load from time to time?"

"Yeah, Pa. But, Miss Cherish is . . ."

"A slut is what she is. Ya'll keep yore mouth shut 'bout this, and I jist might let ya have a go at 'er. Ya'd like that wouldn't ya, boy?"

"Wal, yes, Pa. But—"

"Ya mind me, hear? Else ya'll be feelin' the strop on yore back," Jess growled threateningly as he passed his boy.

After his father left, Jerd took a step toward the girl. He wanted to tell her he was sorry, to explain that his pa had always been mean around young girls, that he knew she wasn't a slut. But his courage left him. He turned awkwardly and followed his father back to camp.

As soon as she was alone, the girl wrapped her arms around a young sapling and sobbed. She cried until she was drained and could cry no more. A cool breeze came up and passed over her, ruffling her hair. She turned and peered anxiously into the forest downriver.

The girl was Cherish Riley. She would be eighteen that autumn of 1779. Slightly built, she looked too frail to have coped with the long trek across the Smokey Mountains and the long ride down the Ohio River on the flatboat into the Kentucky wilderness. But cope she had, admirably so, until now.

Five days had passed since her brother had gone on ahead, scouting for a new campsite from which they could hunt and supplement their meager food supply. Cherish had waited with growing anxiety for his return. This morning she had awakened in black despair, certain that she would never see Roy again, that something terrible must have happened to him and that she was alone in the wilderness at the mercy of the disreputable Burgess family.

Blinking away fresh tears, she moved back toward the river. It was a pretty river, the Kentucky. It did not frighten her as the Ohio had done. She had been happy to see the last of that vast river with its endless convoys of flatboats carrying families and soldiers that Major George Rogers Clark was bringing into the country. She had been glad to leave it, but sorry that Roy had decided to join the Burgess family when they struck inland to make their way up the Kentucky to Boonesborough. The family was lazy, shiftless, and ill-equipped for the journey. But Roy, stubborn and full of pride, refused to take the advice of older and more experienced travelers to wait for a larger party before venturing into the wilderness.

With tears stinging her eyes, Cherish thought now of the home she had left behind in Virginia. The comfortable cabin had been nestled in the shadow of the big mountain. She had been born within its walls and had never lived anywhere else. She had swept its floor, tended it and kept it, had seen her parents die there. Her father had obtained his land title under Virginia law, but Pennsylvania claimed the country and, after his death, Roy had wearied of trying to get clear title to the land. After hearing about the free land in Kentucky, and the village at Boone's fort, he decided to go there.

It had not occurred to Cherish to object. Carefully she had sorted through their belongings. They would take the iron cookpot and her mother's pewter spoons. The axe, a hunting knife, and their pa's long rifle were necessities if they were to survive the trip. Along the way, Roy had said, they would pick up a hand gun. They would take two wool blankets, the small horde of silver, and a small bundle of seeds carefully tied in squares of cloth—squash, corn, pumpkin, turnip, and apple seeds. They would leave the feather beds, the rocking chair, the big loom, and the spinning wheel.

Now, walking along the bank of the Kentucky, Cherish thought nostalgically of the lilac and rose of Sharon bushes growing behind the stout little cabin with its stone fireplace. She thought of the graves of her mother and father and baby sisters on the hill where her father had planted the apple trees. The spring-fed creek at home had never ceased to flow, no matter how dry the summer or cold the winter. It had been a never-ending pleasure to her. She had drunk from it, bathed in it, and it had given her back her reflection.

She knelt now beside the Kentucky and freed her shimmering hair from its knot at the top of her head, letting it fall about her shoulders to her waist. Having no comb, she shook her hair and ran her hands through it to remove the snarls, then rewound it and slipped the thorn pins back in to hold it in place.

An evening fog was beginning to rise from the river in wispy patches. Reluctantly, Cherish turned back toward the camp, drawing on all her courage, unconsciously straightening her back as she made her way among the trees toward the smoking campfire.

On reaching the camp, she was relieved not to see Jess Burgess's gross body lounging beside the fire.

Motioning to a blanket-wrapped figure under the low roof of a makeshift shelter, she spoke to the woman squatting beside the fire.

"Is Unity feeling any better this evening, Mistress Burgess?"

"I'm thinkin' so. She et," the woman answered crossly, and hoisted herself heavily to her feet.

Mrs. Burgess was an older edition of her fifteen-year-old daughter, Unity. Fat and slovenly, she was forever grumbling and complaining about something. Unity had come down with a fever and was the reason why they had been camped here for almost a week.

"Don't think yore brother's comin' back, dearie," Mrs. Burgess remarked. "Been gone most five days now."

"He'll be back," Cherish replied with a confidence she didn't feel, and moved on to the brush shelter Roy had erected for her before he left.

She spread a blanket on the ground, sank down on it and unrolled the only other blanket to check her meager possessions. Everything was there—the extra dress, the shawl, shoes, comb and the chewed willow stick she used to clean her teeth when she had salt. Now all their foodstuffs were in the Burgesses' possession. She felt deeper into the blanket roll and touched the familiar shape of the hand gun, the powder pouch and shot. A small sigh escaped her. At least she still had the protection of the gun, if she should need it.

"Oh, Roy, how could you have been so foolish?" she whispered in despair as the full impact of her desperate situation suddenly hit her.

A poignant wave of homesickness overwhelmed her. Tears filled her eyes, and she longed with all her heart to be back in Virginia. She pressed her lips together to stop their trembling and vowed that somehow she would get back home. The cabin was lost to her forever, but if need be she would marry one of the neighbors. Of the three who had come courting, she hadn't been able to decide which one to accept. All three had been sincere enough, but dull and uninteresting. None of them had ever so much as touched her hand.

In truth they had been awed by the beauty of the girl—eyes the azure blue of a summer sky, hair the color of a maple leaf in autumn curling softly around a heart-shaped face, porcelain skin and cameo features. The fact that Cherish was totally unaware of the effect her beauty had on people was part of the charm that made her different from other beautiful women.

She was jarred out of her reverie by the sound of Mrs. Burgess's voice calling Jerd to bring water so she could start the evening meal. Cherish grimaced as she saw the woman reach into a sack with dirty hands and take out a handful of coarsely ground meal. She added a pinch of salt, wet the mixture with river water and quickly shaped it into small cakes. These she set on a flat stone which she moved into the heat of the fire.

Out of another pouch she took strips of dried meat; laid them on a piece of bark, poured water over them and left them to soften. When the meat was ready to cook, she stretched the strips across the prongs of a forked stick. Hunched by the fire, she held the stick over the burning coals, letting the heat dry and cook the meat. When it was done to her satisfaction, she pulled the meat off the stick and onto another piece of bark. Using the tail of her dress, she slid one of the pone cakes off the stone and onto the bark with the meat.

Cherish made no move to go to the fire, but Jerd hurried to stretch his meat on the stick and hold it over the coals.

"Best eat, dearie," Mistress Burgess called. "Ya'll need yore strength, 'cause ya'll have to tote yore brother's load now."

"I'm not hungry," Cherish lied. "I ate some berries this afternoon."

"Ya found berries and didn't bring poor Unity none?" The woman's voice was harsh and accusing.

"There were just a few and most were too ripe anyhow," Cherish explained, wishing she had used another excuse for not eating. She sat as far back in the shelter as possible and reached for a sack that held a few pieces of dried jerky. The meat was tough, but if she held it in her mouth for a while it would soften enough to be chewed.

Jess Burgess still had not returned to camp. Cherish dreaded the thought of facing him. She wouldn't dare go off by herself anymore and run the risk of having him catch her alone. She would have to stay in sight of Unity and Mrs. Burgess from now on. But she had a sick feeling that somehow Jess Burgess would find a way to get her out of the camp and away from his wife and daughter.

She would be ready for him, Cherish vowed. Taking a quick look to make sure that no one was watching, she unrolled the other blanket and took out the hand gun, the powder and shot. The gun was too large to conceal in her dress, so she made a sling from her shawl, placed the gun, powder and shot inside and looped the shawl over her shoulder. She sat back then, feeling a small measure of security.

CHAPTER
* 2 *

*I*t was dusk when Jess Burgess came back to camp. For one delicious moment hope sprang into Cherish's heart that Roy had returned when she heard Jess laughing and talking with someone. Her joy died quickly when he came into view followed by two heavily bearded men dressed in soiled buckskins. They had large awkward packs of furs strapped on their backs.

"Irm," Jess called. "Get some grub on."

Mrs. Burgess came out from under the brush arbor scratching her stomach.

"Where ya been?" she whined. "Who ya got there?" The small eyes in the fat face squinted against the smoke raised by the too-green wood that had been placed on the fire.

"We got us some callers. Fix 'em some grub."

"Grub's gettin' low, Jess," she complained. But the chance to listen to the men talk was irresistible, and she went without further protest to the meal sack and once again formed the soft, wet cakes.

The trappers left their shoulder packs at the edge of the camp, but placed their rifles on the ground near at hand where they squatted by the fire. They looked openly at Cherish. From the way they smirked at her, she guessed that Jess had been discussing her with them.

He passed a jug around and each man took a swig, wiping his mouth afterward with the back of his hand. A couple more rounds and the trappers were laughing and elbowing each other, having a great time regaling Jess and Jerd, who sat crosslegged near his father, with tall tales of their exploits in the wilderness. Mrs. Burgess passed out pone cakes and went back to sit beside her daughter. The jug made the rounds again . . . and again.

The talk became crude and the men grinned inanely across the campfire at Cherish, who, filled with a growing uneasiness, edged as far away as it was possible to go and still remain in her shelter.

The light was fading and so were Cherish's spirits. Numb with fatigue, she sat silently and listened to the talk. She knew instinctively that she must not fall asleep, that she must keep her wits about her if she were to survive the night.

Sometimes she actually found the conversation interesting. Jess was curious about the Indians. One of the trappers, older, heavy-set and with a scar near his right eye, had been in the area longer than the other one. He told about the Cherokee Indians being the finest thieves in the world.

"Why, they can steal yore pack right out from under yore nose," he said. "They can sneak up on a body and be not more'n spittin' distance before ya know it. That is, down wind." The trapper laughed loudly. "God, them Injins do stink."

"The only one I know of that beats an Injin in sneakin' is that Frenchie and his damn dog." The other trapper wanted to get in on the telling of the tale to the gullible Jess. "I swear he can move through the woods like a haint in a thicket. Injins don't pay him no mind, him bein' blood brother to some high muckamuck. Hit beats all, but they let him be."

Cherish was even more tired than she knew. She sat with her knees drawn up, arms hugging them. Gradually the men's voices became a hypnotic drone in her ears. Her head began to nod—she jerked awake. She nodded off again—then jerked awake. Finally she gave in. Resting her head on her arms, she fell asleep.

The snap of a twig woke her. She stirred ever so slightly, but did not raise her head. Jess had come to the edge of her shelter and stood looking down at her. Satisfied that she was asleep, he returned to the campfire. He leaned toward the trappers and began to talk rapidly, keeping his voice low. But not low enough. The drift of his conversation froze Cherish's blood.

He was talking about her.

"Ya can have her for a price," Jess was saying. "No more and no less'n a bag a powder, one a shot, ten pelts and that thar skinnin' knife."

"Yo're wantin' a heap."

"She'll keep yore bed warm on a cold night. Ain't sure, but don't think she been busted yet."

Cherish tried not to move, not to let them know that she was awake and listening.

"Ya ain't never seen no woman like 'er," Jess said. "Ya ort to see her standin' up in just her chimmy. Prettiest sight ya ever did see. Skin's white as milk." He paused to let them drink that in.

"How'd ya know that?" The younger of the pair was eager to hear more.

Jess laughed. "I touched it. Today. Down by the river. Kissed her too. Would'a done more, but my kid came bustin' in. She got lips sweet as sorghum."

Cherish writhed inwardly.

"I ain't ever had me no white-skinned woman."

"Hell, I'm thinkin' yore ma warn't even one. Think ya was had by a grizzly bear." The men laughed uproariously. "Iffn we get horny, we can buy us a woman from the Injins at the slave market."

"Not like 'er, Seth. They's usually broke down."

"We might get us a young'un. They catch 'em and sell 'em all up along the Lakes, those that last long enough to get thar. Some's real pert lookin'. Kind'a hard for us to get up there, though. Then we'd have to get 'er back past that Frenchie—"

"But this 'n's a real beaut!" Jess insisted.

"Hit don't make no difference in the dark." The older trapper shook his head. " 'Sides, she don't look big enough to tote much," he grumbled.

"She ain't big, but she's stout when it comes to totin' a load," Jess insisted. He added craftily, "But if you ain't satisfied, you won't have no trouble sellin' 'er."

"Ol' Mote'd have 'er wore down to a nubbin in two day flat. Huh, Mote?"

"Ya ain't no slouch even if yo're purt-nigh forty year old," Mote retorted, and the other man laughed as if he had been paid a high compliment.

Cherish's nerves screamed as she listened. She sat tensely, her head on her arms, waiting for them to stop talking so she could think about getting away.

"At your price we ort to see what we're a gettin'," suggested the younger of the trappers. He glanced toward the place where Cherish sat seemingly asleep.

"No," Jess said quickly. "Not in front of my old woman. She's hell on wheels when she's riled. Not that she cares 'bout the gal—thinks she's a snooty bitch—but would think it her duty, ya know." He jerked his head toward the place where Mrs. Burgess and Jerd had retreated long ago.

The fire had burned low. Cherish chanced opening

her eyes a slit to peek at the men. Actually she could smell them better than she could see them: a rank, greasy, rancid odor that she didn't think even the Kentucky River would wash away. She peered at them sitting by the fire. They stank and acted like animals. Except that animals, she thought with disgust, were more decent and a lot cleaner.

Almost sick with fear, she heard Jess tell them:

"I'll send 'er to the river come mornin' to get water. Take 'er from there. Don't pay no never mind to the ruckus she kicks up. She'll take real good to tamin', and come 'round to it right enough and be respectful-like." He leered and elbowed the younger trapper, who responded by making an obscene gesture with his hands. "Ya can drop yore load anytime ya want."

Revulsion washed over Cherish in such an engulfing flood that she almost fainted. She pictured herself being dragged along with a thong tied around her neck, for that was surely the only way they could ever force her to accompany them. Horrible pictures flashed through her mind as she imagined herself struggling like a poor animal slowly dying in one of their cruel traps.

With nerves taut as a drawn bowstring, she watched them bed down for the night, thankful that they came no closer but stayed across the campfire from her. Hot tears welled up in her eyes, filled them, spilled over and ran unheeded down her cheeks. She licked the salt from her lips and tried to swallow the lump in her throat. At last she lay down on her side, her face to the fire, misery seeping into every pore and bone in her body.

Tensely she waited for Jess and the trappers to fall asleep. She hoped that the warm night and the liquor would hurry the process. This was the worst of all, the waiting. She couldn't help thinking of herself and what future she could have after spending any time in the woods with those two pitiful excuses for men. What decent man would want her in his home after that? Every time he looked at her he would remember. It made her feel unclean, made her shudder to think of what lay ahead of her if she could not make good her escape.

The fire was dying down, its smoke drifting low. Cherish lay still, thinking hard. She would wait until the fire burned a little lower and try to count the snores of the men. She lay tense, not moving, listening intently.

She must not miscalculate. She must be sure. Yes, she could hear the three distinct snores. She hoped and prayed that one of them didn't belong to the boy, Jerd, or to Mrs. Burgess, or Unity. Picking up the blanket that held her possessions, she hugged it against her with one hand and quickly shaped the other blanket into a roll that would resemble her sleeping form should one of the men happen to wake and glance into her lean-to. Clutching the shawl-sling and the blanket, she began crawling, praying that she would make no more noise than the rustle of a leaf stirring in the wind.

One of the sleeping men grunted and turned over. Cherish didn't allow that to hurry her. She stopped until his breathing became even and regular. When she was sure that he was sound asleep again, she moved on, not more than a few inches at a time, shifting a hand or a knee, moving so slowly that it seemed to take hours to back out of the brush lean-to.

Finally she was out. Resisting the impulse to stand up and run, she continued to crawl like a baby creeping across a floor. She would move, then stop and listen, testing each time she placed a hand or a knee on the ground. She must not snap a twig, or make any unnatural sound. Heart pounding, she reached the path and silently crawled toward the river.

A plan was forming in her mind. She would head back toward the Ohio. With any luck she might run into a group of settlers who would help her get back to Virginia. She shouldn't think about that now, she reminded herself. Knowing that the trappers would track her, she had to keep her mind on the present. She had to get four or five hours' head start if she was to make good her getaway.

Reaching the river, she got to her feet. Her knees and hands were scratched and bloody. Not daring to stop long enough to put on her shoes, she struck off through the trees, running cautiously, putting as much distance as possible between herself and the camp. On and on she ran, keeping to the river. If she was unable to see it, she made sure that she could hear it.

Finally, gasping for breath, she sank down on the damp grass. Her feet hurt terribly. Lord, how they hurt! She wished she could stop and bathe them in the river, but there was no time. Shaking her head to clear it, she unrolled the blanket, took out her shoes and stockings and quickly put them on. It was painful to put her feet into the shoes, but she gritted her teeth and laced them up tightly around her ankles. Rolling the blanket again, she fitted it into the sling and eased it onto her back. Now her hands were free to ward off the tree limbs that continually hit her in the face.

She ran on into the night, often afraid; but the thought of what lay behind her overcame the terror of being alone in the wilderness. In the dark, knowing only that she must stay near the river, she feared that she would blunder into a bog. Once she did, and the muck rose up around her legs.

She stopped, frozen with terror. She was sure she was sinking, going to the bottom of the bog. Her fear turned to panic on hearing the sucking sounds as she tried to pull her feet from the thick mud. Terror seized her and she threw her head back to scream, but no sound came—and then her feet felt firm ground. She stopped to get her bearings. Holding her skirt high, she tried to wipe off some of the slimy mud with a handful of grass. Realizing the futility of the effort, she drew the skirt between her legs and, holding it in front of her, laboriously plodded on.

Her feet hurt terribly in the wet shoes. At times she felt as if she could not take another step. She longed to stop and rest, but she did not know if she would be able to get up again and go on. Every inch of her body ached, and she was getting light-headed from lack of food. She stopped long enough to draw out a piece of dried meat and put it in her mouth. She realized that if she let herself get weak she could not keep going.

Cherish didn't know exactly when daybreak came. Suddenly it was dawn—and she was even more afraid. Back at camp they would have missed her by now and be on her trail. She was exhausted, but she kept going. She prayed she would meet someone, but not a trapper. Oh, God, no! Not a trapper. Were there no decent people in this country? Family people . . . with children?

The time between dawn and daylight seemed like a dream to Cherish. She staggered on, her numb brain commanding her tired legs, and they obeyed. Her feet were in bad shape. Perhaps she should stop . . . but she was afraid. And oh, so thirsty.

An hour after sunup she came to a small stream running along the surface of the ground. Tracing it to its source, she found a small spring seeping from between layers of rock. She stood stone-still for several minutes, listening intently for any unnatural sound, before she allowed herself the luxury of bending down, cupping the cool water in her hands and drinking.

Ah . . . it was so good! She bathed her face and smoothed back the tangled hair that clung to her neck.

"You must have been awfully thirsty, ma'am." The voice came from behind her and she froze.

Fear ran tingling down her spine and chilled her heart. She dropped her hand into the sling and came up with the pistol as she turned.

Her heart beat wildly as she looked at the man. Even in her terror she found herself thinking how tall he was and that she had never seen such eyes as his: light gray fringed with black lashes. The man looked unconcerned.

"You'll not need that. I won't hurt you."

"Who'er . . . who'er . . . you?"

"Put down the gun," he said dryly. "You might shoot yourself, or me. Brown and I have been looking forward to getting a cool drink from this spring."

Cherish's eyes flicked down to the large brown dog standing motionless beside his master, its massive shaggy head tilted in an alert listening position.

"They're still a ways back, old boy," the man told

the dog. "We have time for a good drink before they get here."

At that, Cherish grabbed her blanket roll. "Who's coming?" she asked breathlessly.

"The two jaybirds who are trailing you," the man said easily. "They're about ten minutes away, I'd guess."

"Oh, no!" She gasped and darted away from the spring.

"Hold on." The man barred her way. "This is as good a place as any to face them."

"I've got to get away. That man . . . back there sold me to them. Please . . . I must go—" Tears filled her eyes. Her heart was beating so hard she could feel it in her throat.

"Stay," he said firmly. "They won't take you if you don't want to go."

"I don't! Please, don't let them—"

"Calm down. You don't have to face them alone. Brown and I are here." With one finger he motioned to the dog. They moved to the spring, leaving her staring after them in bewilderment.

The man was well over six feet, she guessed, broad in the shoulders, but lean and light on his feet. He wore no beard, but his tanned cheeks were shadowed with whiskers. Curly black hair clung to his head; it looked as if he had chopped it off at his neckline with a knife, for it squared off bluntly. The buckskin shirt and breeches he wore were clean, she noticed, and the large hand that held the barrel of the long gun was also clean.

Watching him, Cherish held her breath until her chest hurt, then exhaled. A tightness crept into her throat. *Am I foolish to trust him? I have the gun. His back is turned—*

He turned suddenly. "Better me than them," he said gently, as if he had read her thoughts.

She nodded in resignation, her eyes on his face.

"Sit down and wait for them," he said. "Brown and I will be over there, out of sight."

Cherish sat down obediently on a rock, then jumped up again.

"You won't go away?" she asked anxiously.

He smiled, and the change in his quiet face was miraculous. Creases fanned out from his light eyes and a dimple appeared in each cheek as his lips parted. His low chuckle gave her confidence and she sat down again.

"I promise," he said and stepped back soundlessly into the woods, the dog at his side.

Cherish could hear the trappers approaching. It took all her willpower to sit still and wait for them to find her when her nerves screamed at her to run and hide. They were cursing and grumbling as they entered the clearing—and stopped short when they spotted her sitting calmly on the rock. The face of the older man twisted into an angry mask as they came forward.

"I'm a-goin' ta beat the livin' daylights outta ya, gal," he snarled. "We been chasin' ya half the night."

"Ya ain't ort to make Seth mad. He be plumb looney when he's riled. Come on, purty thin'. Ya just give old Mote a good ride, 'an he'll treat ya right."

The words had no more than left his mouth when a huge, shaggy brown bundle came hurtling from the woods and landed between him and Cherish. Ears laid back, fangs bared, Brown hunched down ready to spring for the throat on command.

"What the hell!" Mote fell back and tried to get his rifle in position to fire.

"Don't do anything foolish." The dog's master stepped from the woods, his rifle cradled in his arms.

The trappers stared. A look of surprise mingled with the fear on their faces.

"The Frenchie!" Seth spat out the word.

"This ain't yore business," Mote sputtered.

"I say it is." The words were spoken quietly.

"She's our'n. Her . . . her old man gave her to us."

"You lie."

"Ya ain't got no call to say we lie. She's our'n I tell ya." Mote shifted his eyes from the man to the dog and then to his companion, who shrugged his shoulders and came to a decision.

"Come on, Mote," the older man said. "The gal's too stunted to be worth much anyhow."

"But Seth . . . we buyed her!" Mote protested.

"We can get our plunder back from the pilgrim."

"I ain't givin' up on her!"

"She ain't no good to ya with yore throat tore out, ya stupid mule's ass."

Mote hesitated, eyeing Cherish. "I was plannin' on havin' her and—"

"Shut yore mouth up," Seth said savagely. "Yo're goin' to get us kilt quicker'n scat."

"Ya ain't heard the last a this. That woman's mine."

"Then come get her." The words were softly spoken as the end of the rifle turned.

Staring at the end of the rifle and at the dog, Mote gave in.

"I ain't a-forgettin' this," he grumbled threateningly as he turned to follow Seth from the clearing. Eventually the sounds of their passage through the woods and their cursing the *goldamned Frenchie* faded.

Cherish was unaware that she had been holding her breath until she let it out. She almost slumped to the ground in her relief.

"Thank you, thank you." Her voice came out in a choked whisper.

The big dog came to her and looked at her with solemn eyes. She threw her arms about his neck and buried her face in the thick fur. The dog stiffened but stood still as Cherish's tears came in great racking sobs. Gentle hands loosed her hold on the dog. Gentle arms lifted her up and held her while the grinding sobs wrenched her slight body. She clung to the warm human being and his hands smoothed the tangled hair from her face. Finally her shudders ceased and she slept the sleep of utter exhaustion.

Cradling her in his arms, the man sat down on the grass. Where had this startlingly lovely creature come from? The dog padded over and stretched out beside him, eyeing him soulfully, head on his paws.

"Well, Brown, what do you think?"

The dog wagged his tail and inched closer.

"You liked her, didn't you? You didn't move a muscle when she put her arms around you. Smart boy."

His answer was a low whine.

"Maybe we won't have to go to Harrodsburg after all. Maybe we've found what we're looking for"—he glanced down at Cherish—"right here."

CHAPTER

* 3 *

The smell of burning wood roused her. Still half asleep, she lazily opened her eyes and found herself looking into the face of the brown dog, who was lying a few feet away, his big head on his paws and his eyes on her. Memory came rushing back and she turned on her side, pleasantly aware of a relaxed tiredness throughout her body.

She was lying on a bed of soft ferns that had been covered with a blanket. Draped over her was another blanket that smelled fresh and clean. She sat up, eyes searching the clearing for the man. He was squatting by the stream cleaning a rabbit. When she moved the dog made a small whining sound; the man glanced over at her.

Cherish judged it to be almost evening and was amazed that she had slept the day through. Tossing aside the blanket, she started to get up, then sank down again. Her feet were bare and clean. Embarrassment flooded over her. How could she have slept so soundly that the man could have removed her shoes and bathed her feet without her being aware of it?

She tried to stand, but with a small cry she sank back down on the blanket. Her feet were swollen and the cuts on the bottoms shot pain up her legs. The lower part of her dress was crusted with mud.

"I'll be away for a few minutes, if you want to change your dress." The man seemed to read her mind. He placed the three cleaned rabbits on a slab of bark and picked up his rifle and his axe. Indicating to the dog to stay, he walked into the woods.

Cherish crawled to the end of her blanket and pulled the small pile of her possessions toward her. The dress, seed packets, gun, powder and shot, the comb, soap and the clean chemise were wrapped neatly in her shawl. Quickly she slid out of her soiled dress and slipped the clean one over her head. After taking down her hair, she combed it and braided it in one long rope. She hurried because she wanted to try standing again before the man returned.

Setting her jaw against the pain she knew would come, she rose slowly to her feet. The pain was excruciating but endurable as long as she stayed on the soft fern bed. As soon as her feet hit the hard ground, it shot from the soles of her feet to her knees. She was unable to stop the groan that burst from her lips. Gritting her teeth, she snatched up the muddy dress, hobbled to the edge of the spring and plunged the dress into the water.

The man returned and leaned his rifle against a tree, then dropped a load of small sticks beside the fire. He came to her and knelt down. Tears of frustration shone in her eyes. He took the dress from her hands and washed it in the flowing water. Still not saying a word to her, he wrung out the garment and hung it over a limb near the campfire.

Unable to decide if she should try to stand or simply crawl back to the fern bed, Cherish stayed beside the stream. The decision was made for her. The man came and lifted her effortlessly in his arms. Holding her high against his chest, he carried her and gently lowered her onto the blanket.

"Thank you," she murmured.

Cherish fought to keep back the tears. Not since her mother's death had she known such gentle treatment—not even from her father and certainly not from her brother, Roy, who considered her more or less a millstone around his neck.

"What are you called?" she asked suddenly, as he straightened and turned to leave her.

Turning back, he looked down at her, the expression on his face one of quiet somberness. She wished that he would smile again.

"I'm called a lot of things. Some call me Frenchie. The Indians call me Light Eyes, but most folks call me Sloan." His voice was low and soft and his accent suggested that he was well educated.

"Thank you for what you've done for me, Mister Sloan." Cherish felt small and quite insignificant before this quiet but powerful man. "I'm Cherish Riley, sir, and I'm most grateful—"

"Just Sloan, Cherish Riley. Sloan Benedict Carroll." He turned away as if that concluded the conversation, then looked back at her. "When did you eat last?"

"I don't rightly remember," she admitted. "I chewed on some jerky last night while I was running, but—"

He stopped her. "You have a story to tell, Cherish, but first we'll get some food into you."

She sat quietly on the blanket, watching his quick, sure movements as he strung the three rabbits on a spit and hung them over the fire to roast. It looked so easy for him. With a sense of shock, she realized that she was trembling inwardly and that the trembling had nothing to do with the fact that her stomach was empty, or that she had come through a very trying ordeal. It was being here with this strange man, with Sloan Benedict Carroll, that was causing her heart to gallop so madly. She couldn't keep her eyes away from him.

"Is there something I could be doing?" she asked, hesitantly, embarrassed that she should be sitting there doing nothing.

"No. Stay off your feet until I can make some footwear for you." Nodding toward her shoes by the fire, he added, "I don't think you could walk very far in those. They'll be stiff as boards by the time they dry."

Something in his flat, dry tone disturbed Cherish. She hadn't stopped to think of the condition of her feet. She would have to walk out of this place to the Ohio, if she hoped to board a flatboat to take her home to Virginia. This man would help her, she was sure of that. Hadn't he already been her salvation? A shiver ran through her at the thought of what would have happened to her if she hadn't met him before the trappers caught up with her.

She started to speak and hesitated, uncertain how to begin.

"I don't know how to thank you," she said with a catch in her voice. She made a small appealing gesture. "I . . . I—" She let the gesture finish for her as her voice trailed away.

"You've thanked me. But no thanks were necessary." Taking a large tin cup out of his pack he walked to the spring, filled the cup with water and placed it on a flat stone near the campfire.

Cherish watched him with an apprehensive stare. Abruptly he looked into her eyes and caught the shadow of despair there. The silence between them was uneasy, and Cherish felt strangely out of her depth.

"Have you someone waiting for you? A man . . . a family?" His eyes had narrowed and were focused on her face.

She gave a choked little murmur and shook her head.

"Have you?" he insisted, unwilling to take the shake of her head for an answer.

"My brother, Roy, and I were going to Harrodsburg to homestead." She wiped her eyes with the bottom of her skirt. Her chin trembled when she continued. "We were traveling with some people named Burgess. Four or five days ago Roy went ahead to scout for another campsite and he . . . didn't come back." She couldn't bring herself to voice her fear that Roy was gone for good and that she would never see him again. Instead she added, "I have only Roy and some cousins in Virginia that I've never met."

The man nodded. He seemed, Cherish thought, about to say something, but whatever it was he changed his mind and turned instead back to his cookfire.

The meal was delicious, and Cherish ate hungrily. She thought Sloan's expression softened as he watched her and she smiled at him, but he did not respond. She took her cue from him and ate silently, keeping her eyes turned away from him.

When they finished, he placed one of the roasted rabbits on a piece of bark and carried it some distance away. Brown watched his every move but made no attempt to go to him until, with a slight movement of his hand, Sloan indicated he was to come.

While the dog was eating, Sloan went to the spring and returned with three more dressed rabbits and proceeded to hang them on the spit over the hickory fire. He refilled the tin cup he had used for tea and set it close to the flames.

"The water is to bathe your feet. We can't afford to let the cuts fester."

"That's a lot of meat," she said, gesturing toward the rabbits.

"I figure to have enough to last two days, maybe more, if it doesn't spoil. When that gives out we'll have to make do with the dried meat in my pack or set snares. I don't want to use my rifle as we go deeper into Indian country."

Cherish's heart began to pound. He had said "we." That meant he was going to take her with him to the Ohio!

It was dark by the time the meat cooled and Sloan packed it away. He picked up the cup of warm water, came to where Cherish sat watching him and sank down beside her. As matter-of-factly as if he were attending a small child, he raised her legs and placed them across his lap. By the light of the campfire, he examined her feet closely.

Nothing had ever happened in Cherish's life before to prepare her for such intimacy. She felt warm color flooding her cheeks and tried to look away, but her eyes were drawn irresistibly to the dark head bending over her feet. Unconsciously she shrank from him. Seeming not to notice, he placed one hand on the calf of her leg while he reached into his pack with the other and extracted a tin. With painstaking care he smeared a thick salve on the bottoms of her feet.

"Now," he said, looking at her for the first time since he had begun. "We need clean cloth for the bandages and your clean shift will do nicely."

"No!" she gasped.

"Oh, yes." He rummaged in her shawl for the chemise, drew it out and proceeded to tear strips from the bottom.

At the sight of his big hands handling her intimate undergarment, Cherish's cheeks flamed. She drew in her breath and closed her eyes tightly. She wasn't sure but she thought she heard him chuckle, and suddenly she was furious. Her eyes flew open.

"Don't you dare laugh at me," she stormed.

"So, the kitten has claws after all." He had a grin on his face when he turned to look at her.

"I just don't like to be laughed at," she said stiffly, grateful for the darkness, knowing her face must be beet-red.

"Accept my apologies, Cherish Riley, and tell me your story while I make some footwear for you."

Taking an animal pelt from his pack, he measured her foot and marked the skin with his knife.

Cherish remained silent, her confusion and embarrassment not allowing her to speak.

"Go on," he urged. "Tell me about yourself."

"Wh-what do you want to know?" She managed to get the words out, although they wanted to stick in her throat.

"Tell me about your home in Virginia. Did you live in the mountains?"

"At the foot of the mountains," she said. "In a cabin with a big stone fireplace and a spring at the back. I didn't want to leave my home, but after Papa died, Roy couldn't get clear title to the land. Besides, he wanted to come to Kentucky. He had no choice but to bring me with him."

The words came easily after that. Cherish found herself talking to Sloan as she had never talked to anyone before. She told him about her mother, a gentle-born woman who had fallen in love with her father—a farmer—and married him although he was beneath her station in life. She had taught Cherish to read and write and had instilled in her the manners of a lady. When she died, Cherish, only ten, had carried on in the ways her mother had begun.

But tension crept into her voice as she told about joining the Burgess family, about Roy going out to look for another campsite. She told of her anxiety when Roy failed to return, and about overhearing

Jess Burgess sell her to the two trappers. Then she told of her flight through the woods.

"It was five days yesterday since Roy left. Do you think he's dead?" Cherish finally voiced the fearful question.

By way of an answer, Sloan reached into his pack and brought out a leather pouch. He dropped it in her lap. She felt the weight of the bag and heard the clink of silver before she looked down at it.

"Would your brother have been carrying that?" he asked.

"Why . . . yes." She picked up the bag and examined it closely. "I sewed it for him myself. But where—?" Her frightened eyes met his. He reached out and clasped her two small hands in one of his.

"I took it off a man I buried yesterday," he said gently. "I found him floating in the river. From the look of things, he tried to raft across and capsized. A blow on the head either killed him or knocked him unconscious, and he drowned." He saw the trembling lips, the eyes swimming with tears, and his arms went around her, drawing her to him. "I'm sorry, Cherish."

Cherish wept. She wept for her young and foolish brother. She wept for the cabin in Virginia, for her mother and father. And she wept for herself now alone without close kin. The fire burned low and they continued to sit on the fern bed. It seemed odd to be sitting there, cradled in the arms of a man she had met just that morning, yet she had never felt so safe in all her life. How could she feel this way about this big silent man?

She drew away from him, suddenly self-conscious. He picked up her shawl and wrapped it about her shoulders to protect her from the cold night air.

"We have to talk, Cherish," he said quietly.

"Yes, I know," she whispered. "I'll use the silver in Roy's pouch to pay my passage back to Virginia."

"And go to the cousins you've never met?" he asked.

"No." She paused. After thinking for a moment, she said, "There are neighbors near our home who would take me in."

"With some cloddy youth who wants to marry you, no doubt," he said dryly.

"And if there is?" she said, resigned. "What else can I do?"

Silence hung between them for a long moment.

"You can't make it to the Ohio alone."

"You won't take me?"

"No," he said flatly.

"Not for this silver?" She held out the pouch.

"No."

She stared at him in disbelief, hurt by his blunt rejection.

"I guess I'll have to make it on my own, then," she said in a small tight voice.

"You try it and you'll meet up with men meaner than Mote and Seth."

"What else can I do?" she asked desperately, studying Sloan's face in the firelight.

"You can marry me."

At first Cherish wasn't sure she had heard him correctly. She tilted her head and stared at him, stunned.

"Does the thought of marrying me leave you speechless?" he asked with a touch of irony in his voice.

"I don't know you. You don't know me. Why would you want to marry me?"

He stared into the woods, being careful not to look into the fire, wanting to keep his eyes accustomed to the darkness. His gaze came back to her.

"I need a woman. A good woman to care for a child."

Cherish wished that he were not sitting so close to her. His nearness had filled her with a warm, tingling sensation she had never experienced before. Now a chill crept around her heart. Disillusion darkened her eyes, making them look enormous in her small pale face. It was not for herself that he wanted her. She didn't understand why the thought hurt and a choking lump had come up in her throat.

"How do you know that I'm a *good* woman?" she asked crossly.

His eyes twinkled and dimples appeared in his cheeks briefly.

"I would stake my life on it."

"Well, I'm not! I'm . . . a tart. So there," she snapped before giving thought to what she was saying.

He laughed. "You're no more a tart than I am. You're as good as you are beautiful and as untouched as the morning dew." He laughed again, then added, "With claws like a young pussycat."

The intense silence that followed seemed to press around her, as though it would hold her prisoner until she gave an answer. Her face was hot and her lips felt stiff. It took every ounce of control to keep her voice steady.

"Where is this child?"

"A two-week journey from here if the weather holds. Less if I were traveling alone."

"What kind of home?"

"A comfortable one."

"You will take care of me if I take care of your babe, is that it?"

"That's it," he said, looking her straight in the eyes.

"You don't need to marry me for that, Mister Carroll." Her voice was firm though her chin trembled, a fact that didn't escape his notice.

"I want to marry you," he said flatly.

"But . . . why?"

"I want you and I'm prepared to marry you to get you and keep you." There was a slight change in his tone of voice, a certain intensity in the eyes that looked into hers.

Her head whirled. How she longed to say yes. But all the dreams a young girl dreamed of a lover tall and handsome, big and bold sweeping her away on a cloud of love were shattered. A man had asked her to marry him, but not for love . . . to care for his child. In a way he would be her employer. She would be given food, shelter and protection for services rendered.

"Just like that . . . without love?" she asked, looking at him through tear-damp lashes.

"Who knows?" he said, misunderstanding her meaning. "You may come to love me in time."

A tremor ran through her. She knew then that she could not marry him, no matter how much she might long to. She could not bear to be *this* man's wife without his love. But what then? Go back to Virginia? She had no family, no home. And . . . she would never see him again. She didn't understand why that was such a devastating thought.

"Mister Carroll, I'll come with you and take care of your child, but I'd rather not marry you."

He had started to smile, but the smile vanished and he looked at her silently, as if he expected her to say something more. She did.

"I might not like it in the wilderness," she said desperately. "I might decide to go back to Virginia."

He nodded, his face expressionless. "Suit yourself," he said and got to his feet.

"Well?" Cherish waited. "Do we have a bargain or not?"

"We have a bargain . . . for now. You'd better get some rest. We'll hit the trail early in the morning." He moved closer to the fire, where he sat down and continued to work on her moccasins.

Cherish lay on her side watching him. Her heart ached, her mind whirled. At last the warmth of the blanket and the campfire, the security of his presence eased her mind and she began to drift off into sleep.

Suddenly, with a stab of fear, she thought of something.

"Mister Carroll," she called anxiously. "Do you think those men will come back?"

"They might," he answered, without looking up from what he was doing. "But I doubt it. Don't worry. Brown has their scent and he'll let us know in plenty of time."

Brown was lying much the same as he had all evening, his head on his paws, his eyes on Cherish. Now and then he raised his head, his large ears up and listening. Evidently satisfied that whatever he heard was nothing to be concerned with, he resumed his resting position. On impulse Cherish stretched out her hand to him. The dog crawled on his belly until she could reach him and gently stroke the rough hair between his ears.

"Thank you, Brown, for what you did for me today," she murmured. He responded with a soft whining sound as if he understood the words. Cherish looked up, found Sloan staring at her, and quickly withdrew her hand.

"Brown doesn't let many people touch him," Sloan said. "He must like you."

"I like him. I had a dog once. He wasn't as big as Brown."

"What happened to him?"

"A neighbor mistook him for a fox after his chickens and shot him. I never could understand how he could have made a mistake like that."

Sloan said nothing and Cherish reached out her hand again and let it rest on the dog's paw. Making the little whining sound, Brown put his nose under her hand and nudged gently. Smiling, Cherish resumed the stroking between his ears. The dog heaved a big sigh and closed his eyes contentedly. Sloan chuckled, shaking his head, and bent over his task.

The sounds of the night took over. Near the water a frog croaked earnestly and the crickets sounded startlingly loud in the darkness. Somewhere an owl hooted. Cherish snuggled warmly in her blanket on the soft bed, feeling strangely at home with the big dark-haired man and his dog.

CHAPTER

* 4 *

She woke with a start.

It was dawn. The campfire was out and nothing was moving in the camp. She reached out her hand and found the place empty where Brown had lain. A night bird called out with startling clarity, sending a shiver of dread up and down her spine. She had been told that Indians frequently used bird calls to signal each other. Her flesh crawled with uneasiness. She wanted to call out to Sloan, but she didn't dare for fear of calling attention to herself.

Had those two terrible men come back and killed Sloan as he slept?

Cherish was on the verge of panic when suddenly he was there, kneeling beside her. Her relief was so great she almost swooned.

"Oh . . . Sloan. I thought—"

He put his finger on her lips to silence her and leaned over until his lips brushed her ear.

"Someone is coming."

"Not . . . them?" she breathed anxiously.

"I don't know, but we'll take no chances."

The bulk of his body was warm and reassuring. He scooped her up in his arms, still rolled in the blanket, and carried her into the woods.

"What will we do?" she asked as he set her on the ground at the base of a large tree.

"We'll see who it is first," he said softly.

"Sloan!" Cherish grabbed his hand. "Don't leave me!" She was shaking.

"I must, but I'll be back." He loosened her fingers from his and said again, "I'll be back."

Fear closed in on her. She felt the nagging sense of danger she had felt during her flight from the trappers. Catching her lower lip firmly between her teeth to stop its trembling, she stared into the dim forest where Sloan had vanished.

He returned silently and dropped their packs down beside her. Kneeling, he looked into her frightened face.

Seemingly of their own accord her arms circled his waist and clutched him tightly. He let her cling to him for a moment, then, gently taking her arms from around him, he held her hands tightly in his.

"Don't be afraid. Brown will stay here with you and I'll not be far away." With that, he moved soundlessly away.

Brown, alert, moved into position beside her. His body was tense and his head tilted in the listening stance that was becoming familiar to Cherish. Worry for Sloan invaded her mind. She tried not to imagine something happening to him. In so short a time he had become the center of her life, a fortress to cling to in this vast, unpredictable wilderness.

Suddenly Brown's ears came down and his tail wagged slightly. Cherish had heard nothing. The dog moved closer to her. She reached out and wrapped her arms around his neck. Brown stood patiently. It was evident that he considered the danger, whatever it might have been, over.

Several minutes passed. Cherish heard a voice speaking words she could not understand and then a man's boisterous laugh. She caught the familiar sound of Sloan's low voice and sighed with relief. Whoever it was obviously was a friend. She leaned back against the tree to wait for her protector to return.

The morning light was filtering through the trees when Sloan came for her. She did not feel the pain she expected when she stood to meet him. Her feet were tender when pressed to the hard ground, but not with the agony she had suffered the day before. The sacrifice of her chemise for bandages had been worthwhile, even though she regretted the loss of the garment.

Before she could question Sloan about the visitor to their camp, he opened his pack and took out what looked like two leather pouches with leather draw-strings at the top. Kneeling in front of her, he lifted one of her feet, placed it in a pouch and gathered the top around her ankle and tied it. Cherish put her weight on that foot while she lifted the other. A smile of pure pleasure crossed her face. The bottom of the pouch was lined with soft fur. She felt as though she were standing on a feather pillow.

"Oh, wonderful! Thank you."

He stood looking down at her blankly, as if he couldn't understand her enthusiasm.

"They were necessary."

"I know that, but thank you for making them for me." Her eyes were shining, and her face glowed as if he had given her a precious gift.

His gray eyes narrowed and an odd stillness came over him while he looked down into the lovely face turned up to his. She was truly pleased, and over such a small thing. His hands came up and rested lightly on her shoulders, then moved slowly to encircle her neck. His thumbs caressed the soft skin at the base of her throat. He tilted his head toward her and, for one delirious moment, Cherish thought he was going to kiss her. But his hands fell away and he bent to pick up his pack.

Cherish swallowed her disappointment and looked down at his dark head. She wanted to stay with this man. She wanted to stay with him forever. When Sloan straightened, he had her shawl in his hands. He draped it over her shoulders.

"Who has come? It's obviously someone you know." Cherish struggled to keep her voice steady.

Sloan smiled that rare, miraculous smile that made her heart beat a little faster.

"Come on. You're going to meet a rare man."

Brown went ahead of them and entered the clearing beside the spring. With his tail wagging happily, he approached the bearded man squatting before a mound of dry leaves and twigs, trying to coax a small flame into a full-fledged fire.

"How-do, Brown." He spoke to the dog without looking at him and blew on the small flame. He carefully added a handful of dried leaves and twigs. "Catch and burn, drat it. That's it, just keep burnin', little fire." When there was a good, steady blaze he added larger pieces of wood and stood up. " 'Bout time you took a notion to burn, you stubborn critter. If I didn't need ya, I'd kick dirt on ya." He drew back a boot threateningly.

"Pierre, are you so desperate for conversation that you'll talk to a fire?"

"*Oui,* my friend. Pierre talk to the trees, to the sky, to the water." A startlingly white grin flashed in his dark beard.

Standing beside Sloan, Cherish felt secure enough to stare openly at the stranger. He was short, but with broad shoulders and a deep chest. Her papa would have said he was built low to the ground. His hair was black and framed his face with a mass of curls.

His beard was just as curly. Perched on his head at a jaunty slant was a fur cap.

As Cherish stared at him he stared back at her in frank admiration.

"Mon Dieu, Sloan! Where did you find this angel of a woman?"

His dark eyes examined Cherish boldly. She was disturbed, yet for some reason she did not understand, she was not offended by the way his glance roamed over her. He was looking at her as if he had forgotten Sloan's existence, all his senses completely involved with her. The heat of embarrassment soon rose up from her neck and covered her face. She inched closer to Sloan.

"This is Cherish Riley, Pierre." Sloan smiled one of his rare smiles. "And Cherish," the smile deepened, "this rake who is looking at you as if he has never seen a woman before is Pierre La Salle."

"Ah . . . Mademoiselle." Pierre's voice was hushed, almost reverent. He jerked the fur cap from his head and bowed low. "Mademoiselle, forgive poor Pierre, but your beauty makes a man's knees go weak. My eyes have enjoyed the feast so much, they do not want to see it end, for you are beautiful beyond imagination." He sighed deeply.

Flustered, Cherish managed a weak smile. "Thank you," she murmured.

Sloan dropped his pack to the ground and moved to help Pierre at the campfire.

"Pierre has offered to share his morning catch of fish with us."

Pierre put his cap back on his head, tilted it over one eye, and walked jauntily down to the spring. Sloan took the opportunity to speak to Cherish.

"Don't mind Pierre staring at you. Like all Frenchmen, he's a lover of beauty."

Cherish blushed. What he had said implied that he thought her beautiful too.

"If you want to be alone," he said next, "go a ways into the woods. Brown will go with you."

She nodded. She had been wondering how she was going to relieve herself. The woods held no terror for her now that she had Sloan and Brown.

After caring for her bodily needs, Cherish washed at the spring and rejoined the men. Pierre had prepared a breakfast of smoked fish and pone cakes. While they ate, he regaled them with the details of his encounter with Mote and Seth back along the trail.

"Ho, *mon ami*, the devil was on them. They look for pelts that hide from them." He winked at Sloan and shrugged his shoulders. "They look and they look and they curse and fight! Ho, it was a sight for the eyes. They have great distrust of each other. But Pierre know someone play a joke, no?" He slapped his leg and cocked his head at Cherish. "They fight like a dog over a bone, eh? Or beautiful woman?"

Cherish blushed. Her eyes were drawn to Sloan. He smiled slightly and, realizing that Cherish was re-

luctant to tell her story, told it for her, ending with
her being traded to Mote and Seth by Burgess after
her brother failed to return from a scouting trip. He
told of her courageous flight through the woods and
how he and Brown had heard her coming and had
waited at the spring.

"It be no wonder they be mad as hornets. They
lose such a treasure." Pierre kissed his fingers to
Cherish. "I, too, be crazy if I lose such a one."

Sloan glanced at Cherish's red face and rolled his
eyes upward as his friend launched into another long,
detailed description of Cherish's beauty.

"Pierre," Sloan finally said, "you're making Cherish uncomfortable."

"Forgive me, Mademoiselle." Pierre snatched his
hat from his head and held it against his chest. The
sorrowful look on his face made Cherish forget her
embarrassment, and she gave him her brightest
smile.

"I'm honored, sir, that you think me comely."

"Only comely! *Mon Dieu!* You've a face that put
an angel to shame."

"Pierre, do you want to hear the rest of this story
or not?"

"Of course." Pierre put his hat back on his head
and gave his attention to Sloan.

"I trailed Mote and Seth after Cherish fell asleep,"
he confessed. "I didn't like the idea of that pair hanging around too close, maybe waiting for another

chance to get her. Mote especially didn't seem to take kindly to giving her up."

Pierre's teeth flashed in his dark beard. "What man in his right mind *would* want to give her up, *mon ami*, eh?"

"I didn't have to track them far. Maybe they did figure on coming back in the hope of catching us unawares, I don't know. After they bedded down I waited until I was sure they were asleep, then stole their fur packs. I thought that might keep them busy for a while."

Pierre roared with laughter. "A while? It should keep them busy until spring, dumb as they be. They kill each other before they look up in tall tree."

"Do you remember the time you and I and John Spotted Elk were up on the East Fork and stole back the furs those renegades had stolen from us?"

"Ya, I remember. They take off down river to get back furs. Ha! They in trees not hundred paces from camp."

Pierre and Sloan began to talk about fur trading and Cherish let her mind wander. It was hard to believe that only a short day ago she had been in the depths of despair. Sloan had revealed nothing about himself, yet she was ready to go with him, to trust him completely. Strange how—

She came back to the present with a start when she heard Pierre growl a woman's name: "Ada!"

There was no doubt from the expression on his

face that, whoever the woman was, he disliked her immensely. From Pierre, Cherish glanced to Sloan and could see that he wasn't pleased with the turn the conversation had taken. He frowned and shook his head slightly, and Pierre stopped talking. He bent to poke at the campfire. Cherish couldn't be sure, but somehow she felt that Sloan hadn't wanted her to hear what Pierre was going to say about the woman.

"How long will you be away?" Sloan asked after a few minutes of silence.

"Who knows?" Pierre shrugged his thick shoulders.

"Come back and winter with us. John Spotted Elk and his people will be there sometime around Thanksgiving."

"I may go only as far as the Ohio, or I may take boat to Fort Pitt. See the sights, eh?" He grinned devilishly and wiggled his thick black eyebrows up and down. His teeth gleamed in the firelight against his black beard. "I may come to Carrolltown and pay court to Minnie Dove."

Sloan laughed. "You've already tried your hand at courting Minnie Dove. Didn't she chase you from her lodge with a fishing pike?"

Pierre looked wounded. "John tell his sister Pierre's heart not true." Then, he was laughing boisterously. "But I plenty fix that John Spotted Elk with honey on his blanket. Ho! He run for the river when the ants bite, and not a scrap did he have to cover him."

Both men laughed. Obviously they had shared many experiences together and with the man called John Spotted Elk. Cherish had not known many Indians, but the ones she had met were certainly not funloving as this one seemed to be. She wondered whether, if not for her, Sloan would have gone east with Pierre.

It suddenly occurred to her that this was her chance to get back to Virginia. Should she ask Pierre to take her as far as the Ohio and see her on a flatboat headed back east? Somehow she knew that she would be safe with him. She could pay her passage with the silver in Roy's pouch.

But, what then?

She saw that Sloan was looking at her. Was he thinking the same and waiting for her to give some indication of what she was going to do? Gray eyes locked with sky-blue ones. The expression on his face gave her no clue as to whether he wanted her to go or stay. The decision was to be hers. If she wanted to go with Pierre, now was the time to say so.

Unaware of the little drama taking place between the two, Pierre hummed softly to himself as he gathered up the last of the fish, wrapped it carefully in a large leaf and placed it in his food pouch.

Cherish reluctantly took her eyes from Sloan's. She looked down at the warm, sturdy moccasins on her feet, her mind awash with thoughts of this man's kindnesses. Her eyes met Sloan's again.

She smiled.

It was her answer.

Not a hint of what he was thinking showed on his face, but his shoulders relaxed. Reaching for the bark plate she had used, he put it with his and tossed it into the campfire.

CHAPTER
∗ 5 ∗

The forest was silver with the morning dew when they left the clearing.

"It's time we moved on," Sloan had said simply.

"Oui, mon ami." Pierre put out the campfire, scattered the ashes and covered the fire spot with leaves and twigs.

Cherish gathered her things together. Sloan took a strong strip of hide from his pack and ran this under the corners of her blanket roll. He tied the ends, making a long loop. Leaving it on the ground beside his pack, he wrapped her shawl around her shoulders and tied it loosely, forming a pouch over her chest. He placed her gun in the pouch, being careful not to touch her breasts.

"When you no longer need the shawl for warmth, we'll turn it around so that the pouch rides on your back. Have you used the gun?"

"I've not fired it, but I can load."

57

He took the gun from the pouch, checked the load and returned it.

"It's ready to fire. If you should need to use it, be sure to hold it in both hands and be ready for a kick-back."

"Do you think I'll need to use it?"

"You never know. It's best to be prepared."

He placed his own pack securely on his back and looped her bedroll over his shoulder.

"I can carry my own pack. This"—she motioned to the pouch on her chest—"is so light."

"It'll take on weight." He turned away, took up his rifle and headed into the woods. Brown followed.

Cherish adjusted the shawl so that the gun rode easily on her chest. She tried to match Sloan's long, free-swinging stride and learned quickly how to keep her skirts from wrapping around her legs. During the hour that followed she thought of what Sloan had said about needing help with the babe. She called to mind the tasks that would require. The work, she told herself, would be easy even if the babe was newly born. She had helped neighbors back home care for infants.

What had happened to Sloan's wife? Was he still grieving for her? *Of course he was.* Any decent man would grieve for a wife who died giving birth to his child. That Sloan was a decent man she had no doubt.

Cherish breathed in the sweet clean scent of the

spruce trees, listened to the soft shushing sound of her moccasins on the drying autumn grass and marveled at the silence with which Sloan and Brown moved. The floor of the forest was thickly bedded with old leaves. It was no wonder they could pass through with scarcely a whisper of a sound coming from their feet.

Pierre had taken a position at the rear of their small caravan and Cherish tried to maintain the same distance behind Sloan so as not to slow his pace.

Once Sloan glanced back, never breaking his stride. "Too fast?"

"No," she said, not wanting to waste breath saying more.

"We'll walk faster this morning while we're fresh, and slow a bit this afternoon until you get used to it."

To pass the time Cherish tried to call to mind everything she knew about caring for an infant. The feeding of a child without a wet nurse was difficult. Did he have a cow? Of course he had a cow or the child would have starved. She chided herself for thinking he would not have provided food for his child. Who was with the child now? Oh, she wished she had asked that question when he asked her to come with him.

Not until the sun was well up did Sloan change his pace. Presently they came to an oak grove bordering the river. Sloan stopped and dropped his pack. He motioned to Brown to go to the river and drink.

Cherish had long since turned the shawl around. Now, lowering it to the ground, she wandered down to the water.

"Tired?" Sloan asked.

"Not really. I'm mostly warm and thirsty."

"Feet holding out?"

"Yes, thanks to your wonderful footwear." She accepted a cup of water, downed it and returned the cup. "That was so good."

Sloan drank and returned the cup to his pack.

Pierre joined them. He had not said a word or made a sound since they had left the clearing by the spring. Cherish considered it remarkable that such a lively, boisterous man could remain silent for so long. She had felt his eyes on her often, but strangely she felt no resentment, was no longer embarrassed by his frank admiration.

"We'll go northwest until we hit Dry Bed Creek, take that to the Salt and follow it until we are almost home," Sloan told Pierre.

Pierre thought for a moment, then moved his big hands in a disapproving gesture.

"Mon Dieu, Sloan," he began and continued speaking rapidly in French, his eyes darting to Cherish, who recognized the word *enfant* and another she had heard before but did not remember the meaning of.

"Speak English, Pierre," Sloan said. "Cherish is no child. She has a right to know the dangers."

Pierre turned to her. "Mademoiselle, I tell my friend it may be mistake to go into Cherokee land. Cherokee are moving to winter quarters. The young bloods are restless, raiding and taking scalps. I say, maybe it be wiser to follow the Kentucky to the Ohio and take flatboat down river to Carrolltown."

Cherish said nothing, but her eyes went to Sloan.

"It will take weeks longer. You can't depend on getting a boat when you want one. If we are to be home before the cold sets in, we cut across and follow the Salt."

Sloan watched her as he spoke, judging her reaction. She felt a stirring of pride that he was sharing the decision with her.

"It's important to get home soon?"

"The babe has no woman with her." He stated the fact simply, his face giving none of his feelings away.

"I can walk," she said simply.

Cherish was sure she saw a glint of admiration in Sloan's gray eyes before he turned and picked up his pack.

For the rest of the morning the going was somewhat harder and their progress slower. Sloan picked his way unhesitatingly and surely, detouring around brush and fallen trees and avoiding boggy depressions. The river was off to their right, hidden by the forest where only an occasional bright ribbon of sunlight penetrated. Birds fluttered and chirped. Now

and then a squirrel scampered from branch to branch
and blue jays scolded them from the treetops. Cherish kept her eyes on Sloan's broad shoulders, her one
thought to match the pace he set.

The sun was only a third of its way across the sky
when Cherish's shoulders began to droop. The
weighted shawl felt increasingly heavy across her
chest. Once she glanced back at Pierre, his huge pack
on his back and his rifle cradled in his arms. He
grinned at her, his dark eyes shining. He was walking
easily, and she knew the pace was slower out of consideration for her. Deliberately she pulled her mind
off her discomfort, raised her chin, and settled into a
walking pattern.

By noon she was so tired she wanted to sink to the
ground, but Sloan pressed on, never speaking or
looking back. So when he did halt and drop his pack
it was so unexpected that Cherish simply came to a
stop and looked at him.

"We'll rest a spell and eat a bite." He sat down
under a large walnut tree. "I didn't stop for you to
rest," he explained, "because it would be harder to
keep on going. If you give in to it, you'll have to rest
every hour. If you put your weariness aside and press
on, in time the weariness will pass and you'll be
stronger."

Scarcely hearing his words, Cherish unshouldered
her burden, moved heavily to a nearby tree, sank
down and leaned back against the broad trunk. A

strand of her light hair had escaped its braid and was lying against her cheek. She swept it up with the back of her hand, then let the hand fall tiredly to her lap.

Sloan's face was turned to her, his light eyes narrowed slits between the dark lashes. She wasn't even sure he was looking at her until he spoke.

"Thirsty?"

She nodded.

"Me too."

He dug into his pack and drew out the cup. Motioning to Brown to come along, he went down to the river.

Pierre dropped his pack near Cherish and followed them. Vaguely, she thought she should go with Sloan, but she found it too much of an effort to get up. Her eyelids drooped. The silence of the woods closed in and lulled her senses. Groggily, she identified the various sounds she heard: the water rushing over stones hurrying on to some distant place, the rustling of dry leaves being worried by the slight breeze, flocks of birds gathering for the long trip south.

"Cherish."

She opened her eyes and sat up straight, embarrassed that she had dozed. Sloan held out a full cup of water. She took it, drained it without breathing, and returned the empty cup.

"Thank you," she murmured.

"More?"

She shook her head. "I'm usually not overly fond of drinking muddy river water, but that was good," she added with a smile. "The rabbit you cooked last night is more to my taste right now." She got to her feet, afraid that she'd not be able to move at all if she didn't.

For a moment she thought Sloan was going to smile, but instead he squatted beside his pack, took out the rabbit, tore off a leg and handed it to her. Pierre came from the river, whistling softly under his breath, and accepted a portion of the meat.

"Thank you, *mon ami.* Ah, it is good to sit down, *n'est ce pas,* Mademoiselle?" He sank to the ground with a deep sigh, rolling his eyes at Cherish.

Cherish didn't understand all that he had said, but she nodded in agreement.

Sloan took a portion of the meat and placed it on the grass for Brown before taking his own share. They ate hungrily, while Pierre chattered away between bites. Cherish listened with interest.

"I see John Harrod some days back. He tell me Daniel Boone came a-walking in days before. First his woman knew he was alive since he was taken by the Shawnee. He make friends, that Daniel. Make friends with old Chief Blackfish. *Mon Dieu,* Sloan, nobody know what to think. It is mystery why he is alive. His woman is going back over the mountains and is taking the little ones."

Both men were silent for a while, thinking.

"What do you think, Pierre?" Sloan asked.

Pierre cleared his throat and appeared to be studying the question.

"Who knows," he said at last. "Blackfish let Boone go, or he got a chance to run. Other prisoners were taken to Detroit—to the British—to be ransomed." After a moment's pause he went on. "There is much unrest in the Shawnee towns and with the Cherokee."

Cherish watched Sloan's face and waited for him to say something about the Cherokee, through whose land they would be traveling. When he remained silent, she dared not ask the questions on her mind, lest Sloan think she was afraid and insist on taking the long way around. She knew he didn't want to waste time.

The memory of riding the crowded, rocking boat on the Ohio was still too fresh in her mind for her to want to repeat that experience. The broad river of fast-flowing muddy water, studded with dead tree trunks, broken by islands of dreary sand, was an ugly and mysterious thing. She didn't care for water travel—sliding along past trees not changing in kind or color, the banks high in some places and low in others, but always the trees closing in the river. It was good to see open country, to walk in the woods, to cross a meadow and see the hills beyond.

She felt a thrill of excitement. There was so much

to see, such a lot of country to cross . . . and she would cross it with Sloan. She darted a glance at him. He was preparing to shoulder his pack, and the awesome width of his shoulders, the well-muscled legs straining in the tight buckskin made her suddenly catch her breath and look away. An unfamiliar tingling set her body trembling at the thought of being alone with him for days, or weeks, in the far-reaching wilderness.

He came to her, knelt and picked up one of her feet. He removed the soft, fur-lined moccasin and examined the bottom of her foot. Without looking up at her, he examined the other foot, then replaced both moccasins. He inclined his head slightly toward her and got to his feet.

"We've miles to put behind us before dark. Can you make it?"

She stood and tilted her head to look up at him. His gray eyes locked with hers, and for a moment, she was lost in their depth and couldn't speak.

"Yes," she said softly, but firmly.

She waited.

This time it happened. He smiled. Dimples showed in his cheeks and sent her heart pounding against her breasts.

"I knew you were hickory."

Cherish was suddenly wildly happy, and it showed in the glow on her cheeks and in her twinkling blue eyes. Her soft mouth parted as awareness of his masculine strength brought an overwhelming desire to lean forward and rest against him.

Sloan looked down into her wide shining eyes, and his expression changed into one of puzzlement.

"Ready?" he asked abruptly.

He settled the shawl pouch over her shoulders, motioned to Brown and walked away without a backward glance.

Cherish looked quickly at Pierre before following Sloan. He was watching quietly, waiting to fall in behind her, a knowing smile on his cheerful face. His black eyes sparkled mischievously and Cherish blushed a deep rose, but she tilted her chin up and smiled at him.

He gave a low chuckle of admiration and politely bowed his head, indicating that she was to precede him out of the clearing.

CHAPTER
* 6 *

The sun was going down. Thick shadows began to spread over the ground. Cherish was exhausted. The bodice of her dress was soaked with perspiration and clung to her bosom. Her skirt was limp and dirty. She had caught her hair on a low branch earlier in the afternoon and strands pulled from her braid floated around her face. Wisps of curls stuck to her cheeks.

Sloan led them through a dense growth of pines, needles of living green, each branch studded with rich brown cones. Sunlight, the last of the day, streaked through the branches, making ribbons of light on the ground. Flocks of birds settling in the upper branches of the trees were scolded by squirrels. The pungent scent of pine floated on the slight breeze.

The trail began to climb and run along a narrow ridge. The dense pine forest was on the left. The land on the right sloped down steeply to the river below.

A large brown bird glided lazily into the air, gradually circling down to the river.

Sloan stopped suddenly and Brown froze in his tracks, his big head up and watching. Cherish halted close behind Sloan and peered around his shoulder. Crossing the path ahead were two furry black bear cubs, an enormous black mother bear sauntering along behind them.

"Bears!" Cherish whispered.

"Lots of them here, Mademoiselle," Pierre whispered behind her.

"The little ones are lovely. The mother looks so calm and patient."

"She may look that way, *chérie,* but angered she is deadly. She could tear you to pieces with one mighty swipe of her paw."

Sloan turned around. "Pierre knows what he's talking about, Cherish," he said, low-voiced, but with a wide grin. "When Brown and I first met him, a bear had him treed and was just waiting for him to come crashing down. First he would yell like a stuck hog, then curse like a drunk river rat."

"*Mon Dieu,*" Pierre nodded. "It is true, *chérie.* I crossed the trail between her and her cubs, not knowin' they were there, and she thought I was to do them an injury."

"If that mama bear had understood French, you'd not be here today," Sloan teased. "I never knew there were so many French insults."

"If not for Brown here"—Pierre nodded toward the dog, still watching the trail ahead—"she would have had me for supper while this one did nothing but laugh."

"You'd have laughed, too, Cherish, if you could have seen him climbing that sapling with fifty pounds of furs on his back. The higher he went the more it bent toward the ground."

"Ho! 'Tis something I don't like to think about. Brown's barking scared her away. Brown was lucky she didn't know he was only a dog."

"Or mistake him for a Frenchman," Sloan said with a laugh.

He waited several minutes after the bears had disappeared from sight before he moved on out of the woods and across a park-like space with giant trees, then up a rocky ridge. Soon they left the ridge behind and the ground leveled out. The walking was easier even though the land had a roll and a swell to it. Evening insects were starting to hum and still Sloan didn't stop.

Cherish concentrated on his broad back, occasionally forgetting to ward off the branches that slapped her face as she moved after him. She prayed her feet and legs would not give out on her. Some hours back her feet had started to hurt. Now with each step she felt as though she were walking on sharp stones. She tried not to think about them or her other discomforts. She didn't allow herself to slow down or limp.

To keep her mind off them she envisioned a dish of warm cornmeal mush, laced with heavy syrup, and a cup of hot sweet tea.

The last rays of daylight vanished. The sky was a dull gray and a thick haze rose from the river. The trees pressed close in around them like tall dark sentinels. Abruptly Sloan turned toward the river, and they followed it a short way. The ground here was uneven, and Cherish was so tired that she stumbled several times in her effort to keep up with him. At last he came to a small clearing overshadowed by a steep cliff. He stopped beneath the overhanging rock.

The men dropped their packs. Cherish stood numbly by. Sloan picked up a large stick and signaled to Brown. They went inside the gaping hole in the cliff. Pierre poked around in the grass and leaves in front of the opening.

Cherish looked at him dully.

"Snakes, Mademoiselle," he explained. "Best to make sure, so close to the river."

She shuddered, but her exhausted body refused to budge from where she stood. Sloan came out of the cave, his eyes searching her face. It was impossible to keep her lips from trembling and she looked away from him, not wanting him to see the tears in her eyes.

He swung her up in his arms. Too tired to protest, she squeezed her eyes tightly shut and rested her head against his shoulder. He carried her into the cave and laid her down upon a bed of soft leaves. Miraculously, a soft blanket was wrapped around her, and she was instantly asleep.

It was dark when Cherish woke, but the campfire at the opening of the cave cast a wavering light on the two men sitting beside it. She felt stiff and sore and her throat was parched. A chill rippled over her when she sat up and the blanket fell away. The air was cold even in the shelter.

Brown lay close to her. When Cherish reached out and stroked his rough head, he whined appreciatively. The sound brought Sloan from the campfire. He had to stoop to enter the cave.

"Hungry?" he asked.

"Starved." Cherish smiled up at him. "My stomach thinks I've deserted it."

"Pierre has your meal ready, but first I want to tend to your feet."

He left the cave and returned with a container of warm water. As on the first night he sat down and drew her legs across his lap. He took off her moccasins and carefully looked at her feet, then washed them and applied the soothing salve as before. He rewrapped them and put her moccasins back on.

When he handed her the soft damp cloth to wash her face and hands, amusement glittered in his eyes. The fabric was a piece from her chemise. She met his eyes with a twinkle in her own before he left her to return to the campfire.

A pack had been pulled up close to the fire for Cherish when she joined them after she and Brown had gone into the woods so she could empty her swollen bladder. Oh, what blessed comfort, she thought as she sat down and held her hands to the warmth of the flames, to be in the company of men who were so thoughtful.

At that moment she felt the unreality of her situation more keenly than at any time since she had made her escape from the Burgesses. These two men, these strangers, had shown more consideration for her than she had received in all her short life up to now.

Out of the coals of the campfire Pierre dug what appeared to be a hard-baked clump of earth. A quick blow from his knife popped open the clump of baked clay and the tantalizing aroma of river catfish reached Cherish. Proudly Pierre served her the fish and a lightly browned corn pone. He stood waiting while she tasted it.

"It's delicious!" she exclaimed. "How did you catch it? I didn't think they would bite at night."

"Not catch, *chérie.*" He produced a long slim pointed stick, which he quickly stuck into the ground. "Spear. That is the way to get big fat lazy catfish."

Watching Pierre, Sloan chuckled. "Pierre is a lover, Cherish, not a hunter."

"*Mon Dieu*, Sloan," Pierre responded, pleased at the gentle teasing. "Cannot a man be both?"

Watching the two men, Cherish realized how deep the friendship between them must be to allow them to talk this way to each other.

"Of course," Sloan said, with a teasing look at Cherish. "When the time is right."

She felt the color rise up and flood her face. It was Pierre's turn to chuckle and he turned toward his pack singing softly, but distinctly:

And . . . so the brave hunter was caught, was
   caught.
And . . . so the brave hunter was caught, but
   not—
By the beast that he stalked, he stalked . . .

As the implication of the words dawned on Cherish, she felt a growing thrill of excitement that was quickly squelched when she glanced at Sloan. His expression was stern again, and not a trace of the teasing sparkle remained in his eyes.

He doesn't want to be caught. He needs me and is willing to sacrifice his freedom for his child. The thought passed coldly through her mind. Suddenly she had a fierce need to know all about the child and the place Sloan was taking her. She wanted desperately to ask about the woman Pierre had mentioned. Ada couldn't be the child's mother. No one would speak ill of the dead no matter how bad a person she had been.

To still the urge to question she filled her mouth with the warm corn pone and drank thirstily of the hot sweet tea. She knew that regardless of what he might tell her about the child, the woman, or where they were going, she would go with him. That he would let her go with Pierre to the Ohio River and back to Virginia if she asked, she had no doubt. But the thought of leaving him dismayed her, and although she craved more than casual affection, she knew she would stay and be grateful for even that much from him.

Before morning, Cherish understood the reason for the long march to the cave. Sloan had sensed the approaching storm. She awoke to hear rain pelting down and wind shaking the trees. Branches broke and plummeted to the ground. A flash of lightning illuminated the cave. She could see the sleeping forms of Sloan and Pierre wrapped in their blankets, heads resting on their packs. Faithful Brown lay beside her. She snuggled her hand under the warm fur of his head. He acknowledged the touch with a wet lick of his tongue, then rested his head on her hand. Cherish closed her eyes again and, feeling as safe as if she were in the log cabin in Virginia, gave herself up to the security of her warm blanket.

She woke again just before daylight and lay listening to the heavy stillness of the rain-sodden forest. In the predawn, when the first faint light tinted the east, Sloan got up. He covered her with his own blanket and started a small fire with dry sticks he had placed in the cave the night before. Setting water to heat for tea, he took out the rabbit, then rerolled his pack.

Cherish sat near the campfire and unbraided her hair. In the light of the small fire it looked like molten red gold as it cascaded down her back. She could feel Pierre's eyes on her and glanced at him with a quick smile. The look on his face made her blush.

She was running her fingers through her hair, trying to loosen the snarls, when Sloan produced her comb from the inside of his shirt and handed it to her. Both men now had stopped their activities to watch her. With fingers that were not quite steady, she deftly parted her hair in the back, made two braids and swung them forward over her breasts. She tied the ends with a bit of rawhide string Pierre cut from his vest. When she finished, Pierre heaved a huge sigh.

"Ah, *chérie,* never have I witnessed anything so beautiful. It warms my heart to see hair like the morning sun; so soft, so alive."

Confused, not knowing what to say, she murmured, "Thank you."

Not until they had shouldered their packs and were ready to leave the camp did Cherish realize that they were parting from Pierre that morning. Rather than follow the deep bow in the river, he would cut through the dense forest, meet the river again and follow it to the Ohio. Sloan and Cherish would walk the river bank until they found a place to cross and head west to where the Salt flowed into the great Ohio.

"Pierre, will we see you again?" she asked anxiously.

"*Oui, chérie.*" He winked at Sloan. "I will come to be sure this rogue be treating you as a beautiful woman should be treated." He kissed his fingertips to her.

Cherish didn't dare look at Sloan, but she heard his chuckle.

"You come to fill your belly with True's stew, gamble with Juicy and bake your feet before my fire."

Pierre's laugh was boisterous. He rubbed his stomach and smacked his lips.

"That too, my friend. Say a word to those two mangy old wolves for Pierre. I will be in Carrolltown I think before the river freezes and bring Christmas gifts to the beautiful Mademoiselle and the *enfant.*"

Sloan held out his hand. "Come winter with us and we will run our trap lines together like old times. You've put on weight, my friend, and should be able to outwrestle John Spotted Elk."

"Ho! But I love my neck too much to wrestle that Indian again."

The two shook hands warmly, then Pierre doffed his fur cap and bowed to Cherish.

"Such a beautiful bait he dangle before my eyes! It is an offer beyond my power to refuse." His dark eyes danced as he looked at her.

Cherish's cheeks were burning, but she managed a laugh and held out her hand.

"We'll look for you before Christmas," she said boldly.

"Before Christmas, Mademoiselle." He bowed over her hand, raised it to his lips and kissed it reverently. His mischievous eyes smiled into hers.

Smiling broadly, Cherish glanced at Sloan. His eyes had narrowed as he watched her and Pierre. Abruptly he signaled to Brown and, with a slight wave of his hand to his friend, started down the hill. Confused by his sudden departure, Cherish looked from Pierre to Sloan's retreating figure and back again. The Frenchman winked and jerked his head toward Sloan and the dog. Cherish turned and hurried after them.

After a few paces she paused and looked back over her shoulder. Pierre threw her a kiss and raised his arm in farewell.

CHAPTER
* 7 *

I t was a dull, gray morning. Along the riverbank the trail was narrow and steep. To Cherish's embarrassment, Sloan had to stop several times and wait for her to catch up. The wet grass dragged at her skirt and at times the ground was slippery, making footing uncertain and causing her to slow down. About an hour after they had started, the sun shone palely through the cloudy sky. It gradually ate away the gloom and opened up the distances.

They came to a rocky beach. Sloan stopped and shucked his pack.

"We may be able to ford here," he told her. "It's low for this time of year."

Dubious, Cherish looked at the river; it didn't look very promising to her. She waited beside Sloan's pack while he walked on along the bank, studying the river currents. Presently he came back.

"Well, Cherish?"

"Do we walk across?" she asked, trying not to sound worried.

"No way to cross but walk or raft. I think we can walk here." He pulled the buckskin shirt over his head. "I'll go first, but I'm going to strip. I don't fancy wearing wet clothes the rest of the day."

She stood in shocked silence and quickly averted her eyes as his big brown hands reached to unlace his britches. Unseen by her, he grinned at the straight back and the redness that covered her neck, but he understood that what he found natural, she did not.

He came to stand in front of her. Cherish forced herself to look at him and was relieved that he was wearing a leather breechcloth, Indian fashion. He was like some pagan god, she thought, sun-coppered, lean and powerful. His hairless skin was firm over the strong bones of his chest and shoulders. Nothing in Cherish's experience had prepared her for the strange excitement and pleasure she felt looking at his near-naked, perfect male body. His confident, unashamed masculinity left her breathless.

If Sloan was aware of her reaction, he didn't show it.

"Brown will stay with you," he said. "If I can walk across, it will save the time of building a raft."

She nodded wordlessly, taking the rifle he handed to her.

"Sloan!" she called as he moved out into the river. "Be careful."

He waded steadily on, not acknowledging her hesitant warning. Soon he was submerged up to his chest. He kept on, moving slowly, steadily. Suddenly he was struggling for balance and Cherish's heart leaped into her throat as he disappeared from sight only to surface several yards downriver, swimming strongly.

Sloan made several trips into the river before he found a route that allowed him to walk across, although at one point he was submerged up to his neck. He came at last, dripping wet, out of the river. Drops of water slid from his hair to his forehead and down his cheeks and into his dimples, for he was smiling. He had enjoyed the challenge.

"We can do it." His eyes sparkled and she knew he was reading her thoughts again.

Surely he didn't expect her to take off her clothes in front of him.

He placed a cold wet finger on her hot cheek and laughed.

"I'll carry our things across and come back for you. You can ride across on my shoulders."

"Oh," was all she could manage, and he chuckled.

No longer embarrassed by his nakedness, Cherish watched him balance his pack on his head and, choosing each step carefully, start out across the river. He swam back, using powerful strokes, and made the distance in half the time.

"One more trip and I'll come back for you," he

said. "Now, give me your pack and your moccasins. On the last trip I'll carry you and you can carry the rifle."

Brown watched his master intently as Sloan went—more confidently now—into the water.

He was in the middle of the river when Brown raised his ears, cocked his head in the familiar listening position and turned to face the woods. The dog growled deep in his throat, and Cherish's heart missed a beat as she realized Brown was alert to what he considered danger. She looked over at Sloan. He was neck-deep in the river, and although she wanted to cry out to him, she knew she must keep still.

Brown was tense. The hair stood stiff and straight on his back. Cherish clutched the rifle, her eyes trying to penetrate the darkness of the woods. Every few seconds she glanced anxiously toward Sloan's dark head bobbing in the water. She strained her ears, but could hear no sound. Brown was plainly agitated now. He turned his big head once in the direction of his master but stood his ground, legs stiffened for action.

Cherish's heart pounded so rapidly she was afraid she would be sick. She looked to where Sloan's broad shoulders and muscled arms were emerging slowly out of the water on the other side of the river. Faintly now she could hear voices. She waited for Sloan to turn and look in her direction, but he leisurely picked his way to where he had left his own pack on his first trip across. Cherish moved to the very edge of the water, waiting. Finally he turned and looked over at her.

She motioned frantically with her arms and the rifle. Sloan ran to the water and plunged in. Cherish turned then and gave all her attention to Brown and the woods, from which the voices now sounded quite clearly.

Above the soft sounds of the river rippling over the rocks and the swish of dry leaves, she heard a man's voice, loud and off-key, singing:

Come now, oh mighty King. Let me your
   praises sing.
Come now, oh mighty King. Come now, oh
   mighty King.
Come now, oh mighty King—

These seemed to be all the words the singer knew of the song, or cared to sing. With every repeated "Oh mighty King" the voice was louder.

Sloan was slicing through the water with powerful strokes. He came out of the river at the same time the singer and his party came out of the woods. Cherish went to him. He took the rifle and moved slightly in front of her. He spoke a word in French to Brown and the dog stayed in an alert position.

Sloan and Cherish must have been a startling sight to the newcomers. They stopped still and gaped at the wet young giant who could be either white or Indian and the beautiful red-haired girl who was definitely white but looked more like a porcelain doll than a flesh-and-blood girl.

There were four men, three women and two children—whose ages might have been eight and ten—in the party. Two of the men each led an ox, pulling a two-wheeled cart. That they were new to the country was obvious even to Cherish's inexperienced eyes.

The women wore black sunbonnets tied firmly under their chins, heavy woolen black skirts and fitted black jackets. The men were dressed to match in black wool pants, coats, and straight-brimmed hats that sat squarely on their heads. Not one touch of color showed on the group.

Cherish noticed that the women kept their eyes averted from Sloan, and she had to suppress a giggle at their embarrassment, forgetting her own of only a short time before.

A tall portly man with a remarkable flowing white beard stepped forward from the group and extended his hand.

"Brother, we—come—in—peace." He paused after each word as if he clearly believed that they didn't understand English.

Sloan gave another command to Brown in French. The dog relaxed and came to stand beside them. Then Sloan took the hand offered him and spoke in his soft, educated voice.

"It is obvious, sir, that you are in no position to do anything else."

The other man raised bushy white brows and looked at him sharply.

"Ah, yes . . . er," he stammered. "Aninus Mackanib, minister. My flock and I are carrying the Presbyterian gospel into the wilderness."

"Sloan Benedict Carroll," Sloan said politely, "and Mistress Cherish Riley."

The minister glanced at Cherish fleetingly, then back to Sloan, as if she were of no importance.

"We are going to Harrodsburg, at the invitation of Mister John Harrod, himself. Ah, it is indeed gratifying to be allowed to bring the message to the poor lost heathens in this godforsaken place."

Cherish was fascinated by the man's booming voice. That he loved to talk was certain, for he didn't introduce the members of his "flock," and none of them uttered a word.

"I would suggest, sir, that if you and your people wish to reach Harrodsburg with your hair in place you go about it quietly. In another week these woods will be alive with Cherokee going south."

"We are wrapped in the cloak of God, my friend. We have no fear for he is with us."

"Are you a marrying preacher?" Sloan asked.

The minister's big head came up. The white whiskers cleared his chest as he boomed his reply:

"I have joined more maids and men together than

any preacher west of the Saint Lawrence River. I have sent hundreds on their way to live in wedded bliss in the eyes of the Lord and man. They have promised to cleave to each other and to let no man put them asunder."

He paused to take a breath and Sloan said, "Excuse us for a moment." He pulled Cherish a short distance away and stood with his back to the group. "Cherish, this is our chance to wed. We may not get another chance until next spring."

"No." She shook her head. "I told you that you don't have to marry me. I'll take care of your babe."

"You don't want to marry me?"

"Marriage is forever. What if after a while . . . you don't want me anymore? I've known of women who married in order to have a roof over their heads and were miserable. Later you might find someone you *really* wanted to marry and you'd be stuck with me."

"Cherish!" He put his hand on her shoulders. "Don't you know what a prize you are?"

"You think so now because you need me."

"Maybe I want to bind you to me so you won't leave and go back to Virginia."

"I won't! I promise I won't leave until you want me to go."

"Is this the way you want it to be? You'd have more security if you were my legal wife."

"I'm satisfied with the arrangement."

"All right. But I give you warning. I found you and I intend to keep you."

He smiled at her then, and for a moment she was tempted, conscious of his nearness and her growing yearning; but she made no sign.

The preacher was looking at her speculatively when they returned to stand before him.

"The folk at Harrodsburg will be glad to see you," Sloan told Mackanib smoothly. "Sometimes it's a year or more before they see a marrying preacher." He turned to Cherish. "We must be going. We have miles to cover before nightfall."

She nodded, filled with an aching misery, already regretting her decision.

The women in the group were clustered together, talking in low tones and casting disapproving glances at Cherish. She decided they looked like a flock of black crows and had to suppress another giggle. She raised her chin defiantly. Sloan, taking in the situation at a glance, leaned over and whispered to her.

"Do you think that those old hens can stand the shock of seeing your bare legs?"

Her face turned red but her eyes danced with a wicked gleam.

"Shall we try it and see?"

"Take the back of your skirt, bring it up between your legs and tuck it into your waist band," he ordered.

Without hesitation, Cherish did as she was told and stood with her legs bare to the knees. She was rewarded with a horrified gasp from the women. Sloan handed her the rifle and knelt down. With the grace of a queen stepping upon her throne she swung first one leg and then the other over his shoulders. Holding her legs to steady her, he stood.

Cherish looked down at the shocked white faces staring in open-mouthed astonishment. As Sloan moved toward the river with her on his shoulders, she inclined her head.

"Good-day," she said politely.

She could feel the laughter in Sloan as she wrapped her bare legs around his chest, her feet digging into the back of his rib cage. Cherish never looked back but gave all her attention to helping Sloan keep his balance on the slippery river bottom. She heard a murmur of indignant voices and then the booming voice of the minister trying to quiet his flock.

The water came up to Sloan's shoulders and the bottom part of her dress dragged in it. Brown swam alongside. It was plain that the shaggy dog was not fond of the water and was hurrying to get to dry land.

The water receded again as Sloan neared the other side. At last he walked out onto the shore and knelt down so that Cherish could dismount. She climbed off his shoulders and wrung the water out of her skirt. Aninus Mackanib and his flock were still standing in a tight group, watching.

"We've given them something to talk about all winter," Sloan said. "Shall I grab you by the hair and drag you into the bushes? That's what they're expecting."

"Oh, Sloan, did you see their faces? They're sure that I'm a fallen woman."

"I saw the men ogling your bare legs. The old preacher gave them a look too."

"Will you think I'm wicked if I say it was fun to shock them?"

He laughed. "Not at all. I enjoyed letting them think I'm a savage." His face settled into a sober expression. "In some ways the savages are more civilized than we are. I hope the poor fools make it to Harrodsburg."

"Is there a chance they won't?"

"There's always a chance. They'd be good pickings to a couple like Mote and Seth."

"And the Indians?"

"It's according to what tribe they meet. They'll not know the pilgrims are 'wrapped in God's cloak,' " he said with humor.

"Oh, I hope they'll be all right."

"It's out of our hands."

Sloan dressed quickly and shouldered their packs. Cherish picked up her share of the load, and they turned their backs on the river and the group watching, and headed into the woods.

CHAPTER
* 8 *

Despite the heavy clouds hanging overhead, Cherish felt . . . light. Different. Stronger. Walking behind Sloan, she felt as if she could follow him to the ends of the earth. During the late afternoon she became tired, but not as worn out as she had been the day before.

It was almost dark when Sloan stopped beneath an overhang of rock that came out of the hillside offering a few feet of shelter over their heads. He motioned for her to wait; and before he shucked his pack, he walked out a short way in each direction and looked around.

"I think this is the best we can do."

Lightning flickered in the western sky. Cherish had been so intent on putting one foot before the other in order to keep pace with him, she hadn't realized that he had been looking for some type of shelter from the approaching storm.

Sloan gathered wood for a fire while she walked

down to a narrow stream. Hidden from view, she relieved herself, then bathed her face and hands in the clear running water before she filled the big tin cup from Sloan's pack.

The fire gave off only pale smoke, hardly visible in the late evening light. Sitting beside the bright-flamed fire, Cherish was engulfed by a feeling of safety; but her eyes were wary when she looked beyond the small circle of light. Although she was not frightened of the forest at night, her flight from the trappers had given her a respect for it and a caution that was already a part of her.

They ate cold rabbit and drank the hot tea in companionable silence. They lingered beside the fire, soaking in the warmth, the forest closing in around them like a great dark blanket. The fire made a home, a hearth spot in the wilderness. Sloan sat at the side of the fire and avoided looking into the flame, as did Brown. The dog lay with his head pointed toward the darkness.

Cherish remembered her brother telling her that a man who looks into a fire cannot see for several seconds when he looks away, and those few seconds could cost him his life.

When they finished eating, Sloan walked with her to the creek, where she pulled off her moccasins and lowered her feet into the stream. The water stung only a little and she touched the healing cuts with her fingers. She let the water flow over her feet, then dried them on the hem of her dress before slipping back into the soft moccasins.

Sloan fed a few small pieces of wood into the fire when they returned and she sat down on the blanket, her legs suddenly weak with an awareness of this man.

"I'll smother the fire after I've seen to your feet," he said over his shoulder. "We'll need to be more cautious from here on."

"Because of the Indians Pierre warned us about?"

"Them and a few other things."

"The fire doesn't give out much smoke."

Sloan sat down beside her, slipped off her moccasins and turned her feet up to the light of the fire.

"That's because it's apple wood," he told her. "It makes a thin smoke that isn't easy to spot from a distance. I always use it or hickory when I camp."

His offhand manner of handling her feet and legs did nothing to ease her confusion. She didn't understand at all why her heart should beat so fast.

"We don't need to worry about anything sneaking up on us in the dark," Sloan was saying. "Brown's ears are the best I've ever known a dog to have."

She didn't say anything, and suddenly she realized that Sloan was making conversation to put her at ease. But it wasn't working and she began to tremble.

"Are you cold?" he asked.

"Yes, no . . . I guess I am," she murmured.

He finished with her feet and folded the end of the blanket over them.

"Are you afraid of me, Cherish?" he asked suddenly, his voice gentle. "Are you afraid that I'm going to pounce on you and demand something of you that you're not willing to give?" He placed firm fingers beneath her chin and turned her face toward him. His eyes were bottomless as they looked into hers. Her lips trembled with the frustration of words she could not utter.

"I believe that you've made up your mind that the reason I wanted to marry you was to give me the right to use your body for my own gratification."

"No . . . no . . . I didn't want to be bound to you . . . unless it was because we—"

"—Were in love with each other?"

She nodded wordlessly.

"I also believe that you have made up your mind that the coming together of man and woman is somehow shameful and degrading—something a woman must endure and it is easier for her if she likes or loves the man."

She opened her mouth to deny it, but before she could he continued.

"Remember this. When the time comes for you, it can be something beautiful if you make it so." He bent his head and briefly touched her lips with his. The kiss was sweet, gentle, undemanding. "You'd have to want it as much as I before I'd ever touch you. If not, it wouldn't have any real meaning for either of us."

There had been no opportunity to prepare for this moment. Her senses were swirling from the thrill of his kiss. Cherish wished she had the words to tell him that the thought of being with him, mating with him, did not frighten her. But already he was drawing away, his face sober, his tantalizing eyes veiled by his dark lashes as he scooped dirt onto the fire. When he spoke again, his soft words came out of the darkness.

"When I asked you to marry me, it was for your own protection as much as anything else. An unwed white woman in this country is like a crust to a starving man. And one with your looks could start a major uprising." He chuckled a little to himself. "I was on my way to Harrodsburg because I heard that there was a young woman there who was recently widowed. I need a woman to care for the babe, so I thought I would look her over and, if she were suitable, marry her and bring her back. I couldn't believe my luck when I met you on the trail."

Cherish sat very still and tears suddenly stung her eyes. It all sounded so cold and impersonal. A woman was what he needed, any woman would do.

Rescuing her from the trappers had saved him a trip to Harrodsburg.

The thought was bitter, and she was fiercely glad now that she hadn't let him know that she regretted her refusal to marry him. At least a small portion of her pride was saved.

With an empty ache in her heart, she shifted her position, drawing her legs up and wrapping her arms around them. She rested her chin on her knees and stared into the darkness, her unshed tears stinging her eyes and such a feeling of homesickness slicing through her that she winced. She had left behind everything that was known to her—for this. But then she glanced sideways at Sloan. She could see only the outline of his strong face and knew again that she could not have done anything else. She had chosen to be with him rather than some unknown man in Virginia.

"Tell me about your child," she said, forcing a calmness into her voice she did not feel. "You said it was a girl. How old is she? How long has your wife been dead?"

"I was wondering when you were going to ask," he said quietly. "I was beginning to think you were the least curious woman I had ever met."

"I thought you'd tell me when you were ready."

"To answer your questions, the child is a girl of almost two years. She is my child, although she is not of my seed, but my brother's. And in answer to your last question, I have never had a wife."

His tense short answers hurt her. Her eyes sought his face, but it was turned away.

"But . . ." She had to know. "But the mother. Where is she? Dead?"

"Not dead. Gone," he said harshly. "She left the babe when she was less than four weeks old."

"And your brother?"

"Died shortly after she left." His voice was low and full of emotion. "He didn't have the desire to live after Ada went away. His lungs were bad, and he worked himself to death. He chopped wood all day, every day, for a week. The snow was red with the blood he coughed up."

Ada. So that's who she was—his brother's wife! The feeling in his voice was so intense, Cherish could have cried for him. She could find no words of comfort to say, so she remained silent. The silence lasted for a long while and finally she said, "It must have been difficult taking care of a baby that young."

"No. You would be surprised." She sensed a smile in his voice. "It was quite easy at first. Ada left her black slave behind when she went away, and we found an Indian woman for a wet nurse. Then Pierre brought us a cow." To her surprise, he laughed then. "I never asked how he came to have a cow. At the time I didn't want to know."

"But you said there's no woman with her now."

"There isn't. The Indian woman went back to her tribe and the slave, Vinnie, died a few weeks ago."

"Then who is taking care of her?"

"Oh, she's in good hands," Sloan said quickly. "If

the two old goats I left her with haven't killed each other by now." He reached over and wrapped the end of the blanket about her shoulders. "Old Juicy has probably got more half-breed babes scattered around than any mountain man this side of the Ohio. And True," he continued, "had a couple of young ones of his own once. Lost them and his wife when the fever infected the bay area where he lived."

The lightning forked now, seemed to be closer, and they could hear a distant rumble of thunder. A gust of wind swept through the clearing.

"We could be in for a storm before morning," Sloan said.

Cherish's thoughts were not of the approaching storm.

"Then there was no great hurry for you to find someone."

"Juicy and True can care for her all right, but I want her to know the ways of a well-brought-up white woman. It would be an easy thing to find an Indian maid to come and take care of her, but she would grow up knowing only the Indian way. While it is a good way, I want her to know her own culture. Can you understand that?"

Cherish nodded even though he was not looking at her.

"What is her name?" she asked.

"Orah Delle. Orah Delle Carroll. It was my grandmother's name—my father's mother. My own mother was French. Her name was Claudine."

The statement seemed to require no response from her. It explained why he spoke the language so well and why some called him Frenchie.

After a silence she asked, "How long have you been out here?"

"Six years. I came out from Virginia, liked it and built my home in a deep bend of the Ohio. I furnish supplies to settlers, trade with the Indians and send my furs back upriver."

"I heard Pierre call it Carrolltown."

He laughed. "It's been called that. To my way of thinking two cabins, barns, storage sheds, and a lodge doesn't make up a town." After a pause, he said, "My home is not fancy, Cherish, but it's comfortable."

She wasn't sure if he expected an answer to that, so she said nothing.

He got up, stretched, and walked a distance out into the darkness. Without him the campsite took on a ghostly atmosphere. Cherish rolled her shawl into a pillow, laid her pistol beside it, folded the blanket over her and lay down, her back against the stone wall.

Brown crawled on his belly until he was near enough for her to reach out a hand to him. He licked it gratefully before giving a big sigh and closing his eyes.

Sloan returned and flung his blanket on the ground, angled out from hers.

"It'll rain before morning. This ledge won't be much protection unless the wind shifts to the southwest." He lay down, stretched out on his back, his head pillowed on his arms. Only his head and shoulders were beneath the ledge.

Cherish's breath bubbled through her parted lips when she thought of his kiss. Why had he kissed her? Was it just an impulse? She had never before felt the pressure of a man's lips on hers. It had been over so fast, yet she could almost feel the touch. Had he kissed her as if comforting a child? If that were the case, he'd not have kissed her on the mouth.

Gradually the ground began to make itself known to Cherish. It was not covered with fern or even a bed of dry grass. It was hard and lumpy. She shifted positions trying to find a place between the lumps. Finally she lay still, her body aching from the unaccustomed demands that had been made on it.

The moment she closed her eyes the forest began to crackle and pop. Her eyes flew open. She wondered how she could have thought the wilderness a silent and peaceful place. Each new sound left her tense and waiting for another. She thought she heard a footfall, and immediately Mote and Seth came to her mind in frightening detail. She thought she could even smell the rancid stench of them—sweat, spoiled meat, smoke, rotting teeth—

In desperation she lifted her head and looked at Brown. At her slight movement, he opened his eyes, closing them again when she lowered her head.

An owl hooted. Startled, she lifted her head again. Brown licked her hand. She looked across at Sloan, but he was breathing evenly and did not move.

Cherish was sure that with the hardness of the ground, her body aches, and the sounds of the forest she would never sleep. Yet, even as she thought this, she drifted off.

CHAPTER
* 9 *

C herish moaned and flung out her arms. She wanted to open her eyes, but her lids felt as if two lead weights were pressing down on them. She tossed her head from side to side, gasping for breath. Something hard took her shoulders and shook her. She struggled to sit up, but her bones were too heavy and her body felt like one giant ache.

As if from a distance, she heard Sloan's voice. "Wake up, Cherish!"

She fought her way out of the uneasy sleep and managed to push herself into a sitting position. Her neck hurt, her mouth was dry, and strands of her hair had pulled out of her braids and stuck to her cheeks. Drugged with sleep, she finally became adjusted to the darkness and could see that Sloan was kneeling beside her on the blanket.

"Are you awake?" he asked.

"I'm awake."

"There's a storm coming. We've got to be ready for it."

A flash of lightning lit up the clearing. Instantly, Cherish scrambled to her feet.

"What shall we do?"

"We've got to keep our foodstuff and the gunpowder dry." He began stuffing everything in his pack except their two blankets. "We don't have much time. Stay here."

"Sloan . . . but—"

"No buts. Stay here." Sloan barked out the orders.

Lightning forked out, overhead this time. Cherish was almost knocked down by a gust of wind that swept through the trees. Panic seized her and she dived for their few possessions. She grabbed her shawl and her moccasins as Sloan returned, almost floundering under the weight of a log which he placed against the rock wall. He picked up the rifle and shoved it into her hands.

"Hold this. Put it under your skirt if necessary to keep it dry." Then he was gone.

The wind came howling through the trees again, sending Cherish's skirt swirling up around her waist. The wind felt cold on her bare thighs. She knocked down her skirt and looked around for Sloan. The lightning came again, followed by thunder. She saw him coming toward her, bending against the wind, carrying another log. He shouted at her, but she couldn't distinguish the words. He placed the log beside the other one, grabbed his pack and placed it on the logs.

"Sit on it," he shouted and left her.

Panic clutched her. She called after him: "Come back! Come back!" The words were lost in the roar of the wind.

Her breath came in rasping sobs now. Her hair, loosened by the wind, whipped across her face. Large drops of rain came, pressing her hair to her head and her dress to her shaking body. Thunder rolled and branches snapped off the trees.

She neither saw nor heard Sloan until he was beside her, staggering under the weight of yet another log, which he dropped and kicked up next to the others. Now there was a platform of sorts. Cherish helped him to adjust the packs. He shouted at her, but she could not understand what he was saying. He lifted her and set her down on the logs next to the packs.

The thunder and lightning came together now. The wind tore at her hair and an icy rain began to fall. Sloan sat down beside her and pulled the two blankets around to cover the packs as well as themselves.

"We're safe here," he said, adjusting a blanket over their heads. He enveloped her in his arms and pressed her head to his shoulder. With the heavy downpour came a wind that tore at the blankets. Sloan's back and bowed head were to the wind. The blankets, arranged like a tent, shed the rain that pounded them.

Cherish was aware of the hiss and crackle of lightning as it played in the tops of nearby trees.

"Don't tremble so. We're safe here."

She was surprised to hear his voice so close to her ear. She leaned gratefully against him, her breasts pressed tightly against his chest and her face buried in the hollow of his throat. He held her so tightly, in a protective, sheltering way, that she could feel his heart beating. Her arms encircled him. She liked the feeling of being so close to him. She couldn't remember being this close to another human being except her mother, and that was so long ago.

She liked the smell of his skin. It smelled like woodsmoke. The whiskers on his chin scraped her cheek. She liked that too. If they had married they could be this close every night. She blushed at the thought.

The storm raged on. Lightning splayed down and struck. Trees split and would have burst into flame, but the deluge of rain quickly extinguished the sparks. The wind tortured the trees, bending them, stripping their limbs and uprooting the weakest among them. Beneath the logs the water puddled, and Cherish understood the reason for keeping the packs off the ground.

It seemed as though hours had passed and still the rain came down. The storm was moving away; the thunder and lightning were less frequent, but the rain continued to fall. Away from the wind, Sloan folded back the edge of the blanket. Grayness crept into the clearing as daylight struggled to establish itself.

Cherish was wonderfully warm. Being small she fit snugly into the arms of the big man holding her. She rested in sweet comfort against him while the rain curtained them and bestowed upon Cherish her first real sense of belonging, enriching her faith in this man with whom fate had joined her in this unpredictable, untamed wilderness.

The fury of the storm finally passed, but the rain continued. Cherish wondered if Sloan's arms and back were cramped from holding her. She moved her face away from the warmth of his neck and smiled up at him. He smiled back and she forgot the rain hitting the sodden blanket and the puddle of water that surrounded them.

They were a mere breath apart, so close she could see her reflection in the depths of his eyes. She was like a creature mesmerized, her bright hair tumbling about her pale face. His intent gaze moved from her eyes down to the soft parted mouth. Her gaze fastened on the firm lips and she scarcely moved as he breathed words she strained to hear.

"You are beautiful!"

There was controlled power in the way he moved his head. Before she knew what was happening, he brought his lips tasting of rain down upon hers. With a sensual deliberation, his mouth took hers, careful not to crush the feeling from her lips, but to teach them, second by second, to respond and vibrate to the warm caressing movement of his. The feeling became so intense that her entire body pressed with a will of its own to his in sheer delight.

Never before had she been so tremblingly alive. Never in her life had her senses known such excitement. His mouth was an urgent, provoking pressure upon hers, arousing her. She quivered against him, awakened by an overwhelming sensation that she had not known existed.

His mouth left hers reluctantly. He looked at her, eyes glowing, sensuous and beckoning. There was not a whimper of protest in her when he drew her to him again—so close that he hurt her against his hardness—and once again stilled her trembling lips with his. His lips explored hers in desperate search. It was as if he were a man dying of thirst and drinking from a well of cool sweet water. He kissed her until she uttered a little groan, not of fright, but of longing for she knew not what.

Then, just as she was melting into a mindless dream, he shattered it. With two strong hands on her shoulders he put her from him.

"My God!" he said, as if he were being tortured. "You're so desirable it's frightening!"

Cherish sat still, dazed, aware of a coldness seeping in where she had been so glowingly warm before. Did he think she had led him on, encouraged his kiss? Was he sorry he had given in to the temptation? With shaking fingers she pulled her shawl up and around her. Sloan turned and looked down at her. He was in control of himself once more, although his eyes were still sultry as they dwelt on her.

"Looks like the rain is about to let up," he said, as if nothing out of the ordinary had happened between them.

Even as he spoke, Cherish noticed a lessening in the downpour. The rain had definitely eased. She looked out from under the blanket, too full of new radiance within her—and at the same time too disappointed—to speak.

Sloan reached down and touched one of her bare feet tucked under her skirt. It was almost numb with cold, but she hadn't noticed until she felt the warmth of his hand. She fumbled in her lap for the moccasins she had placed there to keep dry. With his large hands Sloan rubbed her cold feet until the warmth returned. Only then did he let her put on the moccasins.

The rain soon splattered into nothing, and the sun broke through. They got to their feet and stood swaying on tortured legs. Cherish pressed the water from the bottom of her skirt while Sloan wrung the water from the dripping blankets. Cherish's body ached with cold, but the glowing warmth inside her, the wonder she had shared with Sloan if only for a moment, was too precious to allow the misery in her body to dampen her spirits.

The sky after the rain was cloudless, and the sun shone brightly. They stood in front of their campsite and looked at the destruction caused by the storm. Out of a hollow log at the edge of the woods a shaggy brown bundle extracted itself. Brown shook himself vigorously and trotted toward them.

"Look at that!" Sloan laughed. "Snug as a bug. I knew that old boy would find a dry spot for himself." He reached down and scratched the big head. Brown whined, painfully happy to be united with his master again.

Sloan gave the dog another friendly pat and walked over to where their belongings sat on the logs. The rain had not even dampened the rawhide covering. Everything was dry except for the clothes on their backs and the blankets. Sloan opened the pack and took out her dry dress. He handed it to her and she stepped behind the protruding end of the rock to shed her wet dress and slip on the dry one.

Sloan whipped the wet blankets to remove as much water as possible and spread them on the bushes in the sun. Cherish hung her wet dress on a branch, then shook her hair loose from the braids. She combed it with her fingers and let it hang down her back to dry.

Sloan took the last of the cooked rabbit from his

pack and stood regarding it thoughtfully. He handed a piece of it, along with a corn pone, to Cherish.

"Are you hungry enough for this?" he asked.

She accepted the food. "Even this looks good this morning." She took a bite of the tough meat and chewed slowly.

He watched her, soberly, and started eating his own portion.

"I was going to try to catch us a mess of fish, but the creek is too high. It must have rained a flood up north."

When they had finished the meal, he sat down to clean the guns, while Cherish turned the blankets, then paced back and forth, letting the sun and the breeze dry her hair.

Several times Sloan stopped what he was doing to watch Brown intently as the dog raised his ears and stared into the dense, still-dripping forest. Sloan's brown hands moved faster with the work of cleaning the rifle. When he rose to his feet, a remarkable transformation had come over him. His calm relaxed expression had changed to one of fierce alertness.

"Stay here," he told Cherish. "I want to look around." He checked the load in the handgun and thrust it into her hands.

Cherish stifled the question that formed on her lips and nodded numbly. In the space of a moment her contentment had changed to dread. Sloan motioned for Brown to stay with her, but it was clear that the dog wanted to go with his master, for he followed him to the edge of the clearing and then stood and waited until Sloan was out of sight.

Returning to Cherish, Brown looked into her face, half-wagging his tail as if apologizing for not wanting to stay with her. Grateful beyond words for the dog's presence, Cherish put her hand on the shaggy head, and together they waited.

CHAPTER
* 10 *

With flintlock in hand and a knife and a tomahawk in his belt, Sloan pursued a course leading alongside the creek. At intervals he would stop and listen. The sounds of the woods were no mystery to him; they were more familiar than the voices of men.

He turned abruptly from the trail he had been following and plunged down a steep hill. Here he crossed the creek on a large windfall and took to the cover of the willows that grew densely along the bank. Striking a deer trail, he began to run in easy long strides that covered a mile in short order.

Coming to the edge of a rugged bluff, he paused, then veered on down the trail to walk slowly along the edge of the creek that had wound around the hillside. Just as he had expected, he struck the trail of the Indians where they had crossed the water. There were moccasin imprints in the wet sand, some still smooth and intact. They told him the Indians had passed that way since the rain had stopped.

The tracks led along the stream and into the woods. Like a shadow, Sloan passed from tree to tree, from bush to bush; cautiously, but rapidly, he followed the Indians' tracks. He went on and on. An hour of this found him in the dark backwoods where tangled underbrush, windfalls and gullies blocked his path and made tracking impossible.

Sloan hesitated. He wanted to make certain that the Indians were heading south and would not cross their trail again, but he had gone much farther than he would have liked from the clearing where he had left Cherish. With sudden decision, he turned and retraced his steps, anxious all at once to be back where the girl waited perhaps frightened by his long absence.

Cherish focused her eyes on the spot where Sloan had disappeared into the forest. Silence closed in around her, as deep and impenetrable and threatening as any she had ever known. Panic stirred in her. Common sense told her that Sloan was an experienced woodsman, unlike her brother, Roy, who had been new to the hazards of the wilderness. He would come back for her, wouldn't he? Of course he would. She scolded herself for her doubts.

Yet, she was alone in the strange world of towering trees and wild things, and—judging by Sloan's abrupt departure—some danger yet unknown to her.

A wave of fear washed over her. It was so fierce that her skin began to prickle, her scalp to crawl, her heart to pound, and her breath to quicken. She stood where Sloan had left her, holding the pistol, her eyes alert for any movement, her ears alert for any strange sound.

When Brown came and lay down beside her, a little of her panic drained away, only to rise again each time the dog tilted his head and lifted his ears.

Time passed slowly as Cherish moved from her position beneath the overhang only to turn the blankets in the sun. Her hair dried and she put the pistol down long enough to twist the shining tresses into a long braid. The sun was directly overhead. She would have liked to sit in the warm sunshine and let it bake the stiffness out of her joints and heal the rawness that scratched in her throat, but she was reluctant to leave the shelter of the trees. Still she waited—tense, watchful, fighting growing fear—praying for Sloan's return.

Such relief flooded over her that she began to tremble when Brown began to whine, wag his tail and dance in place. She knew that Sloan was near. When he entered the clearing, she batted the tears from her eyes.

Sloan motioned for her to stay where she was.

And scarcely looking at her, he gathered up the blankets—dry at last—and began assembling their packs.

"Found Indian sign," he told her simply. "We must move from here."

Cherish, so wildly happy to have him back with her, only nodded and hurried to help him.

When the packs were ready Sloan squatted down before her and unsheathed his hunting knife. Before she could guess his intentions he had split her skirt, front and back, from mid-thigh to hem.

"We'll make britches for you so you can move unhampered," he said before she could voice a protest. He wrapped the sides of the split skirt around her legs and wound a thong from her knee to her ankle to hold it in place.

She mourned the loss of her dress, but the makeshift britches were warm against her legs, and she was surprised when she moved about how comfortable it was to not have her skirt flapping in the wind. Sloan hoisted his pack and the blanket roll to his back. He adjusted her shawl over her shoulders, checking the pistol before he placed it in the sling.

"I figure to make quite a few miles. We'll have to move fast. Can you do it?"

She nodded, her expression as sober as his. "Don't worry. I'll keep up."

He grinned then, and touched her chin with his fingers.

"All right. Let's go." He swung off ahead of her

down the slope and into the trees, Brown after him. Without looking back, Cherish followed. She was glad to be traveling again. She kept her eyes on Sloan's broad back and on Brown trotting at his side. Once, Sloan stopped, wet his finger and held it up to determine from which direction the wind was coming. He frowned.

"Wind's at our back," he said, and started off again, stepping up the pace.

Cherish considered the remark as she hurried after him and finally concluded that Sloan thought the danger was ahead and that Brown wouldn't get the scent because the wind was behind them.

The forest floor was thick with old leaves and sodden with morning rain, and they passed through the woods with scarcely a whisper of sound. Overhead the tall trees met. The sun came through only in scattered patches. Cherish took note of the trees along the creek. She could pick out the ash and the beech, the walnut and the birch and gum. The broadest and the tallest were the oak. They towered over the others, their broad branches discouraging any undergrowth.

Sloan kept to the edge of the creek, making good progress, and Cherish's spirits rose. She walked lithely, moving easily in her new "britches," feeling free as air in spite of the strain of constant watchfulness. To breathe the forest smells and to see Sloan and Brown moving ahead of her, safe for now, filled her with quiet joy and crowded fear from her mind.

Sloan didn't stop until they were well above the place where the Indians had crossed the creek and then only long enough to take his tin cup and some dried meat from his pack. He cut a strip and handed it to Cherish.

"We must keep going," he told her. "No time to rest. There are at least forty thousand Indians between the Kentucky and the Ohio, and they're not sitting peacefully in their lodges."

Cherish bit off a piece of the tough meat and let it soften in her mouth before she tried to chew it. Sloan dipped water from the creek and offered her the cup. She motioned for him to drink first. He drained the cup and refilled it. Cherish had to take the meat from her mouth before she could drink.

They traveled all afternoon without stopping, following no trail that Cherish could see. They had veered away from the creek and now walked steadily up and along a ridge through underbrush and scrub growth, down a ravine and up a hillside, twisting and turning through briar patches and thickets. Cherish lost all sense of direction and time. She concentrated only on staying on her feet and keeping pace with Sloan.

Cherish was not aware when Brown had moved on ahead and taken the lead. She was deep in thought as they made their way through a stand of walnut trees.

The thick trunks were almost hidden by dense undergrowth. Her destination was uppermost in her mind. To keep her mind off her exhaustion, she tried to imagine what Sloan's cabin would be like and how she would be perceived by his friends.

Suddenly an arrow came silently from the right of them, lodged in the top of Brown's head and dropped him instantly. Before Cherish could react, in sound or movement, Sloan pushed her backward toward a thicket. Her ankle turned and she almost fell, but she caught herself and kept going until she was surrounded by dense forest. Breathing hard, she slipped behind a huge tree and peered back in the direction from which they had come.

Sloan was not in sight.

Cherish was terrified. She could hardly breathe for the fear that choked her. Her hands shook as she took the gun from the sling and waited. She could see no one and hear no sound but the pounding of her heart. Passionately, she longed to be near Sloan. She screamed inside for Sloan but remained stone-still and absolutely quiet. She began to remember all the things she had ever heard about Indians—about their meanness, their cruelty and their treachery, their cunning and . . . their bravery.

When she could stand it no longer, she cautiously moved out from behind the tree and glided swiftly to another farther on, eyes staring, ears straining for the slightest sound. She paused, then moved to another towering oak. Seconds—or was it hours—passed before she slipped quietly on, strangely calm now, determined to find Sloan and to help him.

Cherish was peeking around the tree, planning her next cautious advance, when she saw the apparition that leaped from behind a tree ahead of her toward an unsuspecting Sloan. The Indian had a powerfully built body and his muscular arm brandished a tomahawk.

She was so stunned she couldn't cry out. Sloan turned to meet the charge but had no time to raise his gun and fire. In swift reflex, he stepped back and swung around the butt end, smashing the warrior in the face. Bones crunched. With a shrill scream, the brave fell back and lay still, his hand spread across his face as if to hold back the blood that spurted between his fingers.

With a blood-curdling screech another warrior sprang at Sloan. His war-painted face was like a hideous devil mask. With no time to turn his gun and fire, Sloan fell backward to the ground to avoid the vicious swing of the brave's tomahawk. Then with a trick taught him by his friend John Spotted Elk, Sloan thrust both feet upward. The sudden blow caught the Indian in the stomach and sent him reeling. Agile as a cat, Sloan leaped to his feet, slammed a shoulder into the Indian's chest and grabbed the arm that wielded the weapon.

The impact threw the two men to the ground, the

Indian on top. Buckskin-clad legs wound around the wiry brown torso and bucked and heaved. The cords in Sloan's neck stood out as he pushed desperately against the body pinning him. The tomahawk flashed up but was blocked by a blow that shoved the arm to the side. Sloan's fingers dug into the Indian's throat, forcing his head back, causing him to gag and suck wind.

Leaping to his feet, Sloan yanked out his tomahawk, and without hesitation, without mercy, his powerful arm swung down and the sharp blade split the Indian's skull. Without a moan, without a quiver, the Indian sank limply to the ground.

Cherish had scarcely drawn a breath when she saw the brave with the bloody face rise to his knees, then to his feet and leap toward where Sloan was crouched. The wounded Indian, half-blinded by blood squirting into his eyes, lifted his arm for the killing blow.

Cherish screamed inside, in her shocked terror unable to make a sound. Then she remembered that she was holding the pistol. As if in a dream, she felt her fingers pull and tighten as she swung the gun into position. She heard the shot, smelled the smoke, and stared at the blossom of blood growing on the Indian's chest. He moved crazily about, like a puppet dancing on a string, then fell down, still twitching.

Cherish stood, dazed, clutching the pistol. Sloan glanced at her and at the Indian she had killed. He never uttered a word. He pulled a knife from his belt and, placing his foot on the dead man's cheek, seized his hair and yanked the skin up from the head. Cherish watched in sick horror as he cut it swiftly all around with the sharp tip of the knife. A powerful tug ripped the scalp from the head, which rolled to the side and lay in a widening pool of blood.

The pistol dropped from Cherish's hand and her stomach convulsed. She bent from the waist and vomited.

Rage consumed Sloan; his breath rasped harshly in and out as he quickly took the scalp of the second Indian. Blood smeared his hands, stained his sleeves and moccasins. His own blood trickled down the side of his face from a cut on his forehead. He turned to Cherish, the bloody scalps dangling from his hand.

"Goddamn bloody Huron!" He spat the name out, as if he had something filthy in his mouth.

Cherish recoiled from him, shock and disgust plain on her face.

"How could you do . . . that?" she whispered hoarsely. "You're no better than . . . they are!"

The anger of battle was still in him. He glared at her silently for a long while.

She shivered at the killing rage she saw in his face.

"Wasn't killing them enough?" she asked. "Did you have to mutilate them too?"

Still he said nothing.

"Sloan?"

"An hour with them and you'd have prayed to die."

"Yes, but . . . you didn't have to do . . . that—" Her voice trailed helplessly.

"They would have done it to me."

"But they're . . . savages! For you to be so brutal—"

"It's a brutal land." The anger left him, leaving his face stern. "It's a brutal land, Cherish," he said again. "A man does what he has to do to stay alive. As for the scalps, that is to let them know that when they tangle with Light Eyes they can expect no quarter. I've survived this long because the Indians and scum like Mote and Seth fear and respect me."

Cherish looked at him numbly.

Moving swiftly, Sloan picked up the pistol, slipped the powderhorn from the straps of his pack, reloaded the gun and thrust it into her hands. He made a quick survey of their surroundings, slipped his knife and tomahawk in his belt, picked up his flintlock and moved back to the trail. With her eyes averted from the bloody dead bodies, she followed him and found him squatting beside Brown.

In the horror of the past few moments Cherish had forgotten the dog. Now, with a little cry, she ran to him.

Sloan looked up at her. With something like wonder in his voice he said, "He isn't dead!"

The arrow had penetrated the skin on the top of Brown's head; the tip had slid along the skull, knocking the dog out. The arrow, embedded in the loose skin, gave the appearance of horns, with an equal amount of the shaft protruding on each side of the head. Brown's eyes were open, but he was dazed.

The smile on Sloan's face reflected his joy at finding Brown alive.

"The bastards," he murmured. "They spent their one sure shot on you, old boy, because they knew that together we would be too much for them."

Sloan cut a notch in the shaft of the arrow and broke off the end. Holding his knee against Brown's neck, he yanked the spear from the loose skin. Brown, becoming more alert, thrashed and struggled, but Sloan held him firmly to the ground, talking softly to him.

"Stay still for just a minute more, old boy. You're going to be all right. Take more than a couple of Hurons to get us. Of course, we had a little help from Cherish. We might not have made such a bad bargain there after all," he continued, speaking as if Cherish weren't there to hear. "She'll do to winter with once she gets the hang of things. Come on, get to your feet, boy. Let's see if you can travel."

Brown got shakily to his feet and stood swaying. He shook his big head and moved around, coming back to stand close beside his master.

"Sloan, why didn't they shoot you with an arrow?" Cherish spoke as the thought came to her.

"They wanted to take me back to camp with my hands bound and a thong around my neck. There will be much praise for the man who captures Light Eyes."

"More than if they killed you?"

"If they had killed me they would have had to carry my body a couple hundred miles. He had the blunt end of the tomahawk turned. He was going to give me a tap on the head to knock me out."

"Would they have taken me with you?"

"They would have raped you and then killed you," he said bluntly.

"Oh." Cherish drew her breath in sharply. "Then . . . killing him was what I needed to do."

Sloan smiled. "You're about the spunkiest woman I ever met . . . outside my grandma," he said slowly.

The surprise statement and the glimmer of admiration in his eyes caught Cherish unawares. Momentarily she forgot the dead Indians in the clearing and the two bloody scalps lying now at Sloan's feet. Before she could respond, however, Sloan's mood had changed.

"We've been here too long already," he said briskly. "That shot was heard for miles." He stooped and picked up the scalps. "I'll get rid of these. Whoever crosses this trail will know that Brown and I were here. They must believe that I took these with me. Wait here."

Cherish drew the pistol and waited nervously as Sloan disappeared into the woods. This time she didn't have long to wait before he returned, materializing noiselessly out of the forest.

"I found a hole in a hollow tree and dropped them in," he told her.

He had been to the creek, too, for his dark hair was wet and his face and hands free of bloodstains. The cut on his head had been washed and the cold water had stopped the bleeding. He picked up his pack and the blanket roll.

"We'll need to move fast and move all night."

Cherish replaced the gun in the sling and, with unsteady hands, smoothed the tangled hair from her face.

"But can Brown travel?" she asked, looking at the dog doubtfully.

"He'll have to," Sloan said gently and moved out. Brown, on slightly unsteady legs, took his customary position beside his master.

CHAPTER
* 11 *

When they resumed the march, Sloan set a rapid pace. Cherish trudged resolutely behind him as usual, but there was a difference. Each time a bird called out, each time a shrub rustled, a squirrel scolded, she started nervously, certain an Indian was about to leap from the bush. Hours passed. Cherish became bone-achingly weary, but hardly aware of it, her fear overshadowing everything else.

The sun disappeared. The scarlet fingers of dusk faded and the moon rose swiftly to cast a mellow light over the wilderness. With night came a creeping cold. The moon slowly climbed the cloudless sky, but Sloan showed no sign of stopping. He stayed as close as possible to the outer line of trees, keeping in the shadows. He walked more slowly than during the day, but just as steadily.

Cherish was miserably tired and hungry, but she would not ask him to stop. She took shorter, quicker steps, hoping the exercise would keep the chill from her body. She worked her hands constantly to keep them from getting numb. Occasionally she cupped her hands over her face and breathed into them to warm her nose. She moved, kept moving, through the damp and now frosty grass and grew colder with each step.

Just as Cherish was beginning to think that she could not take another step, Sloan stopped and dropped his pack. He knelt down beside Brown, examined him closely, then turned to Cherish.

"Are you all right?"

She nodded her head tiredly.

Watching her, eyes narrowed, Sloan said, "It's best if we go on, if you can."

He took the pistol from her and shoved it into his belt, untied the shawl and draped it over her head and around her shoulders. She snuggled her hands gratefully into its soft folds and hugged it to her. Sloan rummaged in his pack and brought out the cup and some meat scraps. The meat he placed on the ground for Brown.

"Rest a spell," he told Cherish. "I'll get some water."

Too weary to care, she stood and waited, hardly aware he had gone. When he appeared before her, the cup brimming with the water, she looked at him dully and accepted the cup with both hands. While she drank greedily, Sloan took a small sack from his pack. When she returned the cup, he gave her a handful of dried berries and picked up his pack.

"Brown's enduring the trip," he volunteered. "It's good that it's a cold night. Keeps his head clear."

Cherish concentrated on her scanty meal. She chewed slowly to make it last as long as possible, and she automatically fell in line behind Sloan when he moved out again.

The moon disappeared, leaving the forest dark with predawn blackness. The shawl wrapped around Cherish's head and shoulders and the split skirt wrapped around her legs protected her somewhat, but still she was damp and cold. Her tired feet bothered her more than anything else. They were bruised from rough spots she had been unable to avoid.

It was after sunup and they were climbing a steep cliff. Cherish's hands were torn from grabbing at trees, bushes, rocks—whatever she could grasp to help herself up. She prayed her strength would hold out. When at last she pulled herself up to the last ledge, she saw that they were in a grassy clearing above the creek and that Sloan was laying down his load. A great longing swept over her then to lie down, snuggle in a soft blanket and sleep. She felt as if she could sleep forever. Her legs trembled, and her head ached with long dull throbs of pain.

Watching her, Sloan unrolled her blanket and spread it on the grass. He motioned her to him.

"You sleep. I'll keep watch."

She drew the shawl from her head and sank down wearily on the blanket, her eyes searching his face, not daring to lie down . . . not yet. Her eyes burned, and she had to open them wide to keep them open.

"You're tired too."

"You sleep. Then you can take a turn watching." Gently he pushed her down and folded the blanket around her. "You've done well," he said. "You kept up with me and made not one word of complaint."

She heard no more.

The next thing she knew, Sloan was shaking her awake. She stared groggily up at him for a moment, then consciousness returned and she realized that the sun was low in the west.

"Why didn't you wake me sooner?" she demanded, sitting up quickly and wrapping her shawl around her shoulders.

"Because you were tuckered out," he said simply. "Besides, I had a chore to do." He grinned and motioned toward his pack. With an elaborate bow, he announced formally, "Your dinner is served, madam."

A variety of nuts and dried berries lay on the pack alongside the cup filled with water.

Cherish's mouth formed a startled O.

"A feast!" She smiled her thanks, smoothing her hair back with the palms of her hands.

"We have a little cornmeal left. We'll save it for mush when we can have a fire. Break the nuts with the stones"—he nudged two flat stones with his foot—"and try not to smash your fingers."

"Did you eat?"

"Yes, and I squirreled away some of the nuts for later."

Sloan sank down on the blanket and stretched out, his flintlock by his side, and pillowed his head on his arms.

"Wake me when dark begins to fall." He closed his eyes for a second, then opened them to peer at her. "And wake me if you see or hear anything." He closed his eyes again and was instantly asleep.

Brown came and lay down beside Cherish. She ate the food and drank the water Sloan had set out for her. The rest and the food had cured her headache but not her sore and tired muscles. While Sloan slept, she tidied herself as best she could, combing her hair and rebraiding it. She removed her moccasins and massaged her feet, then stood and flexed her arms and shoulders to drive the stiffness from her joints.

She felt good keeping watch over Sloan, letting him rest. And—she could look her fill of him as he slept. This was the man who had saved her from the trappers and cared for her during the storm. He had fought Indians as much for her as for himself. It didn't seem possible that this was also the man who, burning with rage, had scalped the Indians. She was still horrified by that action, though she understood why he had done it. He had survived life in the wilderness by his ability to turn as savage as his surroundings when the need arose. That ruthlessness would keep her safe.

As darkness began to settle over the clearing she went to him and knelt down. She spoke his name softly only once and he came instantly awake. He looked up and met her smiling eyes. His face relaxed and he stretched his long frame.

"It's almost dark," she said.

"I see it is, sweet spunky woman."

Suddenly his long arms snaked up and encircled her, pulling her down beside him. Wrapping his arms about her, he wrestled her over on her back and leaned above her, grinning like a small boy pleased with himself. Her arms involuntarily went around him and she snuggled against his chest, savoring his warmth, his male scent, his strength. Her spirits soared on wild wings as he nuzzled his face against the side of her neck.

"It's time to leave," he said against her throat. "I wish we didn't have to go. I wish I could lie here all night with you in my arms."

"Sloan . . . I wish it too."

"Do you, sweet girl?"

His lips traveled across her face, and when they reached her lips he gave her a quick kiss and sprang to his feet. Reaching for her hand, he pulled her up, looking at her for a long minute before he turned to assemble his pack.

It all happened so fast Cherish wasn't sure it had happened at all, but the song in her heart gave lightness to her feet as she followed him down the hill.

They followed the pattern of walking at night and sleeping during the day for the next two days and nights, then switched again to walking in the daylight hours. They rarely spoke, for they were always alert to danger. Cherish began to feel that she was a part of Sloan and he a part of her; and as she walked along behind him, she knew that she would rather be here with him, facing danger and possible death, than in any place in all the world.

Cherish had been constantly tired during the first few days and nights of travel, but gradually she toughened until she could carry her own blanket roll without suffering extreme fatigue. She developed an awe of the wilderness, marveling at its beauty, respecting its unpredictability.

Ten days after they left Pierre beside the Kentucky, the sun failed to shine and the wind changed, blowing with frigid breath out of the northwest. By evening the air was so cold that Sloan stopped and wrapped Cherish's blanket about her, saying nothing, then moving on, watching the rolling sky. They came to a game trail which made the going easier, but the air was colder and hinted to Sloan of impending snow. It was the last part of October and a premature blizzard was not uncommon in the Ohio valley.

They stopped for water when their path brought them within yards of a running stream. Sloan let Cherish rest for a moment. When he rose again, she rose doggedly and followed him. He wanted to move faster but was reluctant to push her strength to the limit. Suddenly the wind died and quiet fell in the forest, along with the first intermittent snowflakes. Within an hour the flakes were falling fast, huge, fluffy, and thick. The wind picked up again, driving the blowing snow. Cherish was not frightened, but she felt increasingly anxious as the snow whipped around them.

Before darkness set in, Sloan took her arm and led her off the trail in search of shelter. The falling snow made it difficult to see, but he finally found a huge tree that lay on its side with a depression large enough for them to shelter under its trunk. With his knife, Sloan stripped the surrounding pine trees of their lower branches and layered them in the depression. He cut larger boughs and propped them along the sides of the log. Inside the shelter he spread Cherish's blanket and motioned for her to enter. Leaving several large boughs within reach of the entrance, Sloan crawled in after her, and Brown snuggled in beside him.

Sloan pulled the boughs over the opening and stripped off his buckskin shirt. They were both thoroughly chilled. Cherish huddled in her shawl shaking uncontrollably, clenching her jaws tightly to keep her teeth from chattering. Her hands and legs were numb with cold. Her stomach rumbled and she swallowed miserably. She was almost weak from hunger.

"You'll be warmer without that wet dress," Sloan said gently.

She glanced vacantly at him, as if she hadn't heard.

"Come. I'll help you." He reached out to remove her shawl.

She remained silent, but turned away from him.

"Cherish," he said firmly, "your dress is wet from the snow. Take it off. We'll wrap ourselves in the blankets and our body heat will help us keep each other warm."

She twisted away. "No!" she said harshly.

"Yes! If we want to live through this night we must keep warm." He grabbed the shawl then and started to unbutton her dress.

There was no response from her at first, nothing. But suddenly she turned on him, beating her fists against his arms and chest. At the same time she began to cry. There was surprising strength left in her, and he let her pound away at him while he removed the dress.

"Leave me alone!" Her voice rose with emotion. "Don't touch me." She was close to hysteria. He was helpless to reason with her. She went on in an anguished outburst, "I'll die anyway. It might as well be now. I can't take anymore of this godforsaken wilderness. I can't . . . I can't—"

The tears ran down her cheeks. He reached out to draw her trembling body into his arms, and his touch broke down the last vestige of control. She began to sob hysterically. Sloan straightened the covers over them and held her while she cried. Her body was taut as a bow string, her limbs so icy cold that he feared they might be frostbitten. He held her tightly to him, rolled her over onto her back and partially covered her chilled body with his own, trying desperately to impart his body heat to her.

"Relax against me. I'll get you warm."

"No!" she sobbed. "I'll never be warm. Never!"

"Yes, you will. I promise you will."

His hands moved down her thin body. He rubbed first one cold thigh and then the other. Gently he stroked her from shoulder to knee, hoping to quiet her as well as to warm her. Gradually the tension began to leave her, and he felt her muscles slowly relax. She lay quiet for a long time. At last she reached an arm up, encircled his neck and buried her face in the warm curve of his shoulder. He rolled off her then, pulled her to him and tucked the blankets firmly about them. She didn't speak or move and finally she fell asleep.

Cherish woke slowly and lay listening to the soft sound of Sloan's breathing against her ear. Her back was pressed tightly to his chest, her head lay on his arm, and his arms and legs were wrapped around her. She was deliciously warm! Heavenly warm! Memory returned and she squirmed uncomfortably, thinking of her actions earlier. Sloan's arms tightened around her.

"Are you warm?" he murmured.

"Oh, yes! Sloan—?"

"Mumm—?"

"I'm sorry."

"For what?"

"You know—"

"Forget it," he whispered, raising his head so that his lips touched just below her ear. "You've done real well. I was beginning to think that you had no woman's weakness at all."

"You saved my life and I thank you."

"You saved mine and I thank you."

She giggled. "We're being silly."

He brushed away a tendril of hair that clung to her cheek. Cherish could feel his lips smiling against her skin. Not wanting to disturb the magic of the moment, she remained silent.

Presently she asked, "Is your back cold?"

"Brown's snuggled up to my back."

She laughed softly, then held her breath. Her heart began to pound, and she was sure he must feel it beating. A warm tide of tingling excitement flooded her. She was suddenly cold, then hot and trembling.

Her mind whirled giddily, for although she had never seen a man when he was aroused, she had seen stallions in rut and she had no doubt about what was pressing against her buttocks. Warmth began to spread down her breast and across her belly and loins and thighs. Warm languorous pleasure, the sensitivity of the flesh. Sloan stirred and slowly turned her toward him.

As innocent as any young female animal that responds by instinct, Cherish pressed against him. She lifted her face to meet his kiss, her trembling lips parting as his mouth possessed hers. His kisses were suddenly savage, fierce. Time seemed to verge on eternity before he released her lips, only to capture them again. His hand slid down her back and pressed her hips tighter against him. The fire in his loins was raging and he trembled violently. Cherish tore her mouth from his, her body cringed away in sudden alarm.

"Are you afraid?" Sloan fought down his desire and lay quietly.

"I can't help it!" Her anguish was apparent in her voice. "I want you to . . . to . . . but I'm afraid."

She tilted her head back and her eyes searched his in desperation, fear growing that he would turn away from her now.

He pulled her to him.

"I frightened you," he said huskily. "It's been so

long for me that I forgot what it must be like for you." His lips pressed soft kisses on her face.

"You said it would be beautiful," she whispered. "But all I've ever heard about it is the pain and the . . . shame. Am I shameless for wanting you? Is it wrong for me to want, Sloan? Tell me."

Sloan smoothed her hair and drew his mouth along the line of her jaw. His parted lips touched hers briefly before he answered.

"Why should it be shameful? The coming together of a man and a woman is as natural as the sun rising. You've never been kissed, have you, love?"

"Not the way you kiss me."

He put his hand to the back of her head and pulled her to him. As their lips came together, he parted his, forcing hers apart as well. He could feel the charge of passion that leaped between them. For a very long time they held the kiss, before they separated.

"I love your kisses, Sloan."

"There's more, love, much more."

Cherish felt the thunderous beating of his heart against her nearly naked breast and the trembling in his arms as he held his passions in check.

"As for the pain," his voice was hoarse and his breathing ragged in her ear, "if your desire is strong enough you'll not mind the pain. It is possible you'll have none, but if you do it will be only the first time." He took a deep breath, trying to forestall his desire. "Don't let your fear make you unresponsive. I want you to like doing it as much as I do, but in all honesty, I must tell you it may not be possible the first time."

He drew back and his eyes searched her face. She was wide-eyed and he smiled at her innocence.

"That doesn't mean you won't enjoy it. If not this time, surely the next. Like everything else, it isn't always perfect. Do you understand?"

Her face was tantalizingly close. She trembled against him. Her reply was to press her warm lips to his cheek.

"Forget everything you've heard." His voice was thick with emotion. "Give yourself up to me."

He caressed her with his lips and stroked her body with his hands, pushing away the chemise. He bent his head to kiss the soft firmness of her breast and felt her body go rigid at the boldness of his touch.

"It's all right, sweetheart. I'm loving you. Love me, honey. Love me. It will make it better for both of us."

With something like wonder, she felt along his lean ribs and the hard-muscled waist. Their breaths merged and became one as his open mouth sought and found hers. His hand moved farther down her body to her hips and her thighs. There, his fingers began stroking, kneading, massaging. When she began to respond to his caresses, his fingers moved to her secret place.

Cherish's world careened crazily beneath the urgency of his caress. She was swept along in a violent storm of passion and lost her last touch with reality. The naked hunger that caught her was both sweet and violent. She felt his hands beneath her buttocks lifting her up and she opened her thighs to him.

Sloan came between her legs and entered a little way into her. There he stayed and kissed her without hurry, himself feeling the most wonderful of all touches as the membrane guarding her virginity thinned and yielded to his throbbing phallus. Cherish let out a low whimper of pain that was lost in his mouth. Then there was only the giving and the sharing. They were one, belonging, possessing and a thousand twinkling stars blending together.

In the interval of extreme pleasure Sloan put everything aside, save this headlong quest for fulfillment for her and for himself. He forgot the Indians, the cold, the long trip ahead, and only thought of their hunger to be satisfied. The ecstasy hung in explosive potential, easily attainable, but he postponed it to prolong the delicious agony of the quest.

Finally it happened. They reached the peak, but there was much more than momentary pleasure. The strength of his passion for her left him shaking. She had touched the deepest innermost part of him. As he held her tightly to him, he could believe they were the only two people on earth. For the moment they were one.

When it was over, Cherish lay warm and secure in

his arms, knowing a strange peace she had found nowhere else. There had been a little pain but no sense of having sinned because she had found pleasure. It was beautiful, beautiful, just as Sloan had said it would be.

She sighed contentedly and kissed the side of his neck where she nestled. He raised his head and studied her carefully. He stretched out a finger and leisurely traced a line down her neck and over the swelling curve of her breast. Her soft mouth parted with yearning, and he leaned down to her and kissed her waiting lips, touching his tongue to hers. Her eyes grew dark, like two bottomless pools staring up at him, and her face glowed as radiantly as the sun on a clear day.

Relief flowed through him and he pulled her head up and kissed her long and tenderly.

"What do you think, sweet spunky woman?" he asked softly. "Do you feel like a shameless doxy?"

She laughed against his face and twisted her fingers in his hair without answering. He chuckled and nibbled at the soft flesh of her shoulder. His hand descended to cup her small breast, then glided over her smooth hips. His wandering caresses made her quiver. His kisses on her mouth were warm, devouring, fierce with passion. She felt the bold urgency of him against her and thrust forward in eager anticipation. Then he was a flame within her, consuming her, taking her way beyond herself. Waves of unbearable pleasure flooded her as they were caught up together in a surging, swelling tide of rapture.

Cherish heard his harsh breathing in her ear and his hoarse, whispered, caressing words.

"Sweet, sweet woman, will I ever stop underestimating you?"

She was silent for a long while, filled with unbounded happiness. She pulled his head down until it rested on her shoulder. Her lips traced his eyebrows and the lines on his forehead. Finally she whispered, in a voice filled with wonder, "In my wildest dreams I didn't imagine it would be like this."

"You don't dread doing it again?"

"No. Not with you. Did you like doing it with me?"

"You silly, sweet girl!" He laughed, kissed the curve of her throat and ran his hand lovingly down the full length of her until she caught it and held it tightly beneath the fullness of her breast. "We'd better get some sleep. We've got a ways to go tomorrow."

She sighed. "I don't think I'll ever sleep again. I feel so good."

He chuckled and kissed her lightly. "Well, try, sweetheart."

Obediently she turned over, snuggled close to him and was soon asleep.

CHAPTER
* 12 *

A tickling on her face roused her. She opened her eyes slowly. Sloan was leaning over her, brushing her face and nose with the end of her braid. She focused her eyes on his face and a smile curved her lips.

"It's time to get up, sleepy-head. I've got a surprise for you."

She reached out to him and discovered he was fully dressed in his buckskins and was lying on top of the blanket covering her. Happiness was reflected in her face when he bent down to kiss her. As their lips touched, her arms came up and closed tightly about him. All shyness between them was gone. In its place was an intimacy so precious that Cherish could scarcely believe it. Sloan was aware of it, too, for he held her close in his arms for a long moment, unwilling to break the spell.

"Get dressed, lazy-bones!" he ordered. "Come and see what Brown and I have got for your breakfast."

Laughing, Cherish threw off the blanket—and caught her breath sharply as cold air hit her warm body. Gritting her chattering teeth, she dressed quickly, tying the split skirt about her legs and slipping her feet into the fur-lined moccasins and securing them around her ankles. She smoothed her hair back and wrapped the shawl over her head and around her shoulders.

The air was cold, but the wind had died down and it had stopped snowing. Sloan had scooped the snow from a spot sheltered by the branches of the fallen tree and had built a small fire. Near the fire lay two roasted rabbits and a mug of hot steaming tea. He smiled at the look of pleasure on her face.

"Brown and I ran them down in the snow," he explained.

Cherish patted the dog gently, carefully avoiding the wound on his head.

"A few days ago I thought I could never eat another bite of rabbit, but now . . . oh, Sloan, I'm so hungry!"

She sat on a log and ate, savoring every bite of meat and every drop of hot sweet tea. Sloan squatted and watched her.

"It's risky to build a fire," he admitted, "but we need hot food. I don't like the looks of the weather." He hesitated, then added: "If we can keep going we should be home in three days."

Cherish stopped eating and looked at him, noting his serious expression.

"We'll make it," he assured her. "The closer to home we get, the less likely we are to run into hostiles."

"I'm not worried, Sloan," she said quietly, finishing her tea. "But shouldn't we be going?"

Five minutes later, the packs ready and shouldered, the fire smothered with snow, they left the spot where Cherish had known the happiest moments of her life.

The snow was only a few inches deep and walking wasn't too difficult, but the air was damp and cold. Sloan followed the creek until late afternoon, then veered off. As usual, they seldom stopped and hardly ever spoke. When night came suddenly, they huddled together, their backs against a broad tree trunk, the two blankets binding them close. Cherish was so tired she fell asleep instantly, her head on Sloan's shoulder. Brown, beginning to show the effects of the wound and the travel, sank down beside them, lending them his warmth.

By first light they were on their way again after eating sparingly of the remaining cooked meat. Sloan slipped Cherish's head through a hole he cut in the center of her blanket. It was getting increasingly colder; and while he had suffered cold before and could steel his mind to it, he was worried about her pinched face and the vacant look in her eyes.

If all worked well, this should be their last night on the trail. They should reach his cabin by late tomorrow. Sloan explained this to Cherish, thinking it would raise her spirits, but she only nodded and smiled weakly at him. At one point he carried her over a small stream, stepping lightly on the slippery rocks, and marveled at how light she was even with the heavy blanket. No wonder, he thought grimly. His own stomach felt the sharp pangs of hunger.

After a hard day's travel, they found a steep bank with an overhang for shelter. The light was almost gone with just a faint afterglow remaining. Sloan dug back into the bank with his knife, scooped the soft dirt out with his hands and made a nest of the blankets for Cherish. She was asleep at once.

A short time later, when Sloan placed his hand on her shoulder and called her name, she woke and sat up, and the blanket fell away. The cold shocked her into alertness.

"Hot tea, Cherish, and meat and mush."

She took the cup from him. "I'm too tired to eat."

"Drink the tea," he told her. "Then eat slowly—you've got to keep up your strength."

She eyed the cornmeal mush and lifted her eyes to his.

"Where's yours?"

"I've already eaten. Now eat it all and the meat.

We'll have more meat by morning. I set a few snares."

He rubbed the back of his hand gently against her cheek. She took his fingers and pulled his hand around to her mouth. Then, only half aware of what she was doing, she leaned toward him, her soft mouth slightly parted. Her lips touched his and clung, gently tasting the sweetness of his mouth.

They lay in each other's arms that night, but did not make love. They were both so weary from the day's journey that as soon as Sloan put out the fire and called Brown to them, they sank down in the nest of blankets and slept.

Flakes of ice from the trees fell on Sloan's face the next morning as he checked the traps. He had caught one rabbit; it was roasted and the tea made when he woke Cherish.

"We should reach home this afternoon." That brought a sparkle to her eyes, but then Sloan added, "It will be snowing again soon, I'm afraid."

She said dully, "More snow?"

"I'm afraid so. But we can make it."

"But can we make it by night?" Despair tinged her voice.

"If we keep moving."

Suddenly she blurted out: "I love you, Sloan! Somehow I want you to know. I've never loved anyone but my mama and my papa." Her face crumbled and tears rolled down her cheeks.

Sloan reached out and gathered her into his arms, resting his cheek against her hair. She clung to him fiercely for a moment, the released him and stepped back, her face composed, her eyes averted from his.

"Are you all right now?"

"Yes. I'm all right." She looked at him then, forcing a little smile. "We'd better be moving."

Silently Sloan adjusted the shawl and slipped the blanket over her head.

They had been walking for about an hour and hadn't gone nearly as far as Sloan had hoped they would when the snow began to fall. A sharp wind came up that seemed to push them backward, and the snow gradually increased. They stopped only long enough for Sloan to wrap Cherish's head in her shawl and for him to pull down the flaps on his fur cap.

They walked another mile. It was getting more and more difficult for Cherish to keep up. Once she fell down, but she got quickly to her feet before Sloan turned around. A chill unrelated to the weather rippled through her—a dread that she was losing her strength, that she would be unable to keep up and would be a hindrance to Sloan, that they would die in these swirling drifts of snow because of her.

"I've got to get hold of myself," she muttered.

With a new spurt of determination she trudged on, but the storm increased its fury and the wind blowing against her gradually slowed her down again.

Her weariness was bone-deep. Peering at the forest through a haze of physical exhaustion, she began to imagine strange shapes moving in and out of the trees. For the first time her courage faltered. She tried to force her mind away from her misery and onto other things, but the other things faded quickly as the physical pain she was suffering pulled her back to the present.

"I must keep moving," she said aloud. "I must keep my blood flowing. I must not let Sloan down."

A little later Sloan heard a faint sound and turned to see Cherish sitting in the snow. He let her rest a few minutes, then helped her to her feet. She clutched the blanket around her, her face grim.

"Can you go on?" he asked gently. The hand that reached out to cup her chin was warm and brown and strong. She nodded but refused to look at him.

He stayed beside her, an arm about her waist. They went several more miles before he stopped again. They ate the last of the meat, and Sloan placed a small ball of snow in her mouth to quench her thirst.

"Not too much," he cautioned. "Just enough to wet your mouth."

He started off again and she followed. They walked for another hour before she stopped.

"I can't go on." She whispered the words, tears glistening in her eyes.

"You can," Sloan said firmly, "and you will."

"Go on without me . . . please!" she begged.

He stood looking at her, the light eyes regarding her steadily with growing disgust.

"I would never have taken you for a quitter!"

"I'm sorry. I'm just too tired." She shook her head numbly.

"You could go on if you wanted to. You just don't have the guts to put forth the effort. Maybe you should have gone back to Virginia and lived the soft life. You're gutless, Cherish. Soft and gutless."

She reacted instinctively, unaware of what he was trying to do. One small foot lashed out and slammed into his shins. At the same time she balled her fist and hit him a solid blow in the face.

"Guts!" she shouted, tears of fury streaming down her face. "What do you think I'm made of? You . . . you . . . backwoods dolt! Don't you think it takes guts to come to this hellish wilderness? Don't you think it takes guts to follow an uncouth savage like you to God knows where?"

"Evidently it takes more guts than you've got," he said haughtily.

"I hate you. Oh, I hate you!" she raged, then stopped, too angry to continue, and glared at him with blazing eyes.

"I don't care that much for your hate." He snapped his fingers, then raised his brows and sneered at her. "I still say—no guts!"

Cherish closed her eyes tightly. The rage burning inside her made her cheeks flame. Opening her eyes, she saw Sloan's back. He had started off again without waiting to see if she could follow.

Her rage boiled over.

"You . . . you bastard!" she shouted. "You can't take hearing what you are . . . you uncivilized lout! There's not a Carroll alive who can hold a candle to a Riley! And not one dead either. Hear me? You'll be sorry you said that to me. You'll be sorry." She scrambled after him, her fury carrying her onward, muttering to herself: How could I have thought I loved that brute? I hate him. He doesn't care anything for me. All he wants is a nursemaid. But I won't do it now. Not after this. I'll take the first boat that comes along. I'm not going to stay with him— I'm going home where people are civilized. Home to Virginia. Oh, why didn't I go with Pierre? He'd never say such things to me. I know he wouldn't.

They hadn't gone a mile before her anger burned itself out and shame took its place. *How could she have been such a fool? What was the matter with her? Was she losing her mind?*

Step after agonizing step, she trailed in Sloan's tracks. Shame eventually gave way to indifference. Her mind went blank and she followed automatically.

The snow was getting deeper. Sloan dropped back to walk beside her. He carried his flintlock cradled in one arm and put the other around her waist to support her. She only half-acknowledged him, but he felt her body stiffen with determination. They went on, Brown leading the way now. By late afternoon the storm had intensified, and they could see no more than a few feet in front of them.

Cherish stumbled and fell, pulling them both down. She looked up dully when he tried to lift her to her feet.

"Can't we rest? I'm so tired."

His own body was weary and he knew it was a mistake to linger, but he sat and held her while they rested. Brown came back and lay down beside them, whining softly. When Sloan felt himself getting dangerously drowsy, he got to his feet and pulled her to hers.

The howling blizzard swept down out of the northwest, making it almost impossible for Cherish to stand alone. The brief rest hadn't helped. She fell again and again and begged him to go on and leave her. Sloan realized that every delay lessened their chances of reaching home and safety. Finally he had no choice but to sling her over his shoulder and carry her.

He made better time that way for a while. But gradually his own strength began to decline under the double load. It was getting darker and, as night approached, colder. He began to wonder if he had missed the trail to the homestead, but, no, Brown was leading the way and would make the right turn when they came to it.

Sloan struggled on, his arms numb and his legs weak with fatigue. Cherish hadn't moved since he had hoisted her to his shoulder. His apprehension turned to near panic; perhaps he had pushed her too far. He thought of sending Brown on ahead for help, but abandoned the idea. He needed him to find the cutoff trail. And there was the possibility that only one man might be in the cabin and he would never leave the babe alone, not knowing how long he might be away.

Sloan stopped to rest, easing Cherish gently down into the soft snow. She didn't move as he peered into her snow-encrusted face. He wiped it dry with the end of her shawl. She was either asleep or unconscious. Either was a deadly sign.

Wrapping the blanket around her, he lifted her again to his shoulder. It was hard to carry her that way, but he knew he would be unable to get her onto his back. He half-smiled remembering how she had lit into him, cracking him on the jaw. The anger he had deliberately aroused in her had brought her two or three miles. Those miles just might make the difference.

The cold was beginning to tear at his lungs. He was having difficulty breathing deeply. Again and again he turned his face into the blanket covering Cherish and took several deep warm breaths.

He staggered on, following Brown, who looked back at his master every few yards to be sure he was coming. Sloan could only guess how many miles they had covered and how far they had yet to go.

His weary mind dwelled on the cabin and its warm fire, on a huge bowl of stew and a warm bed. Once he veered off to the right, and Brown stopped and barked until Sloan righted his direction. After that he kept his eyes on Brown and didn't allow his mind to wander.

Abruptly, all his strength left him and he slumped down in the snow. He knew he must get up, but would he have the strength to lift Cherish? As he sat holding her the thought came to him that he should leave her, go on alone and bring True or Juicy back for her. Anger at himself for thinking it stirred his muscles. He raised himself onto his hands and knees.

"She's right to call you a bastard," he muttered. "She'd freeze before you got to the cabin and back."

He gathered her to him and knelt there swaying on his knees. Struggling to his feet, he picked up the limp girl, but he fell again after going only a few feet. He got up and stood reeling. Suddenly he caught the faint elusive whiff of wood smoke. He sniffed it again, and relief flooded through him. He staggered after Brown, Cherish on his shoulder. When he saw the faint glow of light from the cabin window, he called out: "Go, Brown. Go get Juicy."

The dog didn't hesitate. He shot ahead, barking with every leap. Sloan reeled after him.

It seemed hours, but could only have been minutes, before Sloan heard Brown barking again. Then a fur-clad figure loomed in front of him.

"My God, Sloan," a voice rumbled out of the darkness. "Ya done gone and scared the wits outta me, sendin' that dog in thataways. Whatcha got thar?"

Sloan tried to speak, but no sound came from his frozen throat. He tried again. The third time he managed to get out: "T-take h-her, Juicy—"

The bear of a man cradled Cherish in his arms as if she were a babe. He carried her toward the cabin, talking all the way. Sloan staggered beside him, and Brown, happy to be home, circled them.

"This mite yer woman? Ya ain't got much, iffn' ya was to ask me. A fresh-whelped pup'd weigh more'n this."

"She may be in a bad way," Sloan said, regaining his strength and with it his voice. "I've carried her for the last five miles."

"Well, now, her jist might take on a bit a weight that fer."

He called out when they reached the cabin, and the door swung open. A tall man stood away from the entrance so they could enter. He gaped at them.

"Shut yer mouth, True, ya long skinny jaybird, and take this here young'un. She pert nigh froze."

He shoved Cherish into the arms of the astonished man and turned to where Sloan slumped in the doorway. His black-haired face split into a grin.

"I ain't never seed ya so tuckered, Sloan." The booming voice filled the cabin.

True lowered Cherish to a bunk and covered her with a faded quilt. He straightened to glare at the big man with the loud voice.

"Now ya just shut yer mouth. Ain'tcha give no thought to the babe? Her'll be wild when her sees Sloan an' him pert nigh wore out. Want to be a-rockin' her all night? Git on, now. Git Sloan a swig of that thar licker yer allus a-sneakin'."

Sloan followed True to the bunk, suddenly feeling stronger now that they were safe within the walls of the cabin. He leaned over Cherish to listen to her heart beat.

"Is her live?" True asked.

"Yes, and we've got to get her out of these wet clothes. Get blankets. Juicy, get stones out of the fireplace and wrap them for the bed."

Sloan began undressing her, his frozen fingers fumbling with her clothing. True brought the blankets, piled them on the end of the bunk and took over the undressing.

"Why'd ya get such a skinny one fer?" he asked while removing her dress. "Ya ort ta have got ya one that'd keep ya warm on a cold night."

Sloan grimaced. "This one will do just fine. Wrap her up, you old goat, and quit looking."

Juicy came to stand beside the bed. They covered Cherish with the thick blankets and Juicy slipped the wrapped stones under the covers against her feet and thighs.

"Ain't she 'bout the purtiest thing ya ever did see?" His booming voice was hushed, almost reverent.

"She's sightly," True agreed. "I thought the babe's ma was a fair looker, but this'un puts 'er to shame."

Sloan was relaxed in the presence of these men. He could say things to them he would never say to anyone else.

"She's not only beautiful, but she has pride, spirit and courage. She'll make a good mother for the babe." He looked down at the sleeping girl. "She may be only a little thing, but she's all woman."

His two friends glanced knowingly at each other over Sloan's bent head.

There was nothing more they could do for Cherish now but keep her warm. Sloan stood before the fire and stripped off his clothes. True brought him dry ones, and he dressed with shaky slowness.

"How long's it been since ya et?" Juicy asked.

"We've been on short rations for a week." Sloan didn't mention that he had given Cherish the larger portion of the food, keeping only enough for himself to keep up his strength.

"Why didn't ya say so?" Juicy demanded.

"I was just getting ready to." Sloan sank down in the fur-lined chair before the fire and held out his hands and his stockinged feet to the flames.

"We warn't lookin' fer ya fer a few weeks yet," True said. He handed Sloan a cup of hot tea laced heavily with rum.

Sloan knew they wouldn't ask why he came back several weeks early and with a beautiful young girl. They had expected him to return with a middle-aged widow, perhaps with a couple of children of her own. He couldn't help but enjoy keeping them in suspense a while longer.

"Yes, I did get back sooner than I expected. Hurry up with that stew, True. I'm starving."

True swung the iron pot out from over the fire and filled a bowl with bubbling stew.

"This's been cookin' two days an' is jist 'bout right."

Juicy let out a snort. "Ain't no stew done till hits been boiled more'n a week, ya scuddle-brained crow-bait. Hain't I told ya an' told ya that?"

"I don't keer what ya told me, ya ol' son of a grizzly b'ar. I been studyin' on hit, an' hit says clean pot ever three, four days. How're ya goin' ter clean the pot with stew in hit?" True's voice got louder as he got madder.

Bickering came as naturally to these two as eating. Sloan had been entertained many evenings listening to them. His eyes twinkled now as he watched them. They were more than friends, much more.

He had met them when he was new out from Virginia. Thanks to them he had survived his first winter on the new frontier. They were with him when he surveyed and bought the homestead, and they gave it his name. They were with him when his brother arrived with his new bride. They helped care for the babe when the mother abandoned it, and they helped him bury his brother. His affection for them went deep, as he knew theirs did for him.

Sloan finished the stew and asked for a second helping. True brought it to him, smirking at Juicy.

"Ya starve a man long enough an' he'd eat a sick dog," Juicy muttered. "Take Brown thar, he'd ruther have that raw meat I gived him."

Brown lay stretched out on the floor, his nose where the cold wind came in under the door, eyes closed, no longer feeling the need to keep watch over his master.

Sloan ate the stew and went to check on Cherish. He thought he saw a little color creeping back into her face. Sitting down on the side of the bunk, he put his hand under the covers and felt her legs. They were still cold, and he rubbed them until he could feel a little warmth returning. Her feet against the covered hot stones were warm enough. It was a good sign. He breathed a sigh of relief; she would be all right.

He turned to True. "How's the babe?"

"Her's jist as feisty as a ring-tailed coon in the spring. Hit was fer certain the tyke missed ya."

Sloan stretched his arms high above his head.

"I'm going to get some sleep. Sit with her." He nodded toward Cherish. "She may be frightened when she wakes up in a strange place. Her name is Cherish—Cherish Riley."

"Cherish?" Juicy said. "Who's ever heard a name like that?"

"You have, now." Sloan grinned. "And I'll bet a gold piece that you'll be eating out of her hand in less time than it'll take to tell about it."

"Wal, now, I dunno as ta that," Juicy retorted. "Ain't seen no woman yet I can't turn me back on. The all-fired purty ones don't usual have no brains. Can't see this'n be no different."

"Well, if you feel that way, I guess True will have to do all the watching over her."

"Thar ye go. Ye just hold on a dadburned minute. I never said I ain't gonna take keer of the little ol' bag a bones. I jist said—"

Sloan laughed and clapped his friend on the shoulder. "I know what you said, Juicy. Lord, I'm tired. Call me if she wakes up."

He went to the far end of the room, climbed into a bunk and gratefully pulled the warm blankets over him. He fell instantly into the first truly peaceful sleep he had had since leaving the homestead more than three weeks before.

CHAPTER
* 13 *

C herish was in a dreamless state halfway between sleep and reality. She heard a voice asking for water. An arm raised her head and a cup was placed to her lips. She drank deeply and opened her eyes. She saw the fire in the hearth and the candle on the table.

"Home," she whispered. "I'm home."

A black-bearded face drifted into her line of vision. She reached out and her small hand was engulfed by a huge calloused one.

"Papa! Oh, Papa—" She closed her eyes and was floating, floating in the warm bed.

Juicy looked anxiously at the girl's face. "What'a ya think, True? Reckon we ort ta call Sloan?"

"Naw." True placed the palm of his hand on Cherish's forehead. "She ain't got no fever. She jist plain tuckered out. Pore little ol' mite. Her jist ain't built for trailin'." He shook his head. "She's jist as purty as a covey a' quail, an' her'd make jist 'bout as big a mouthful."

"Ain't no use of us both missin' sleep," Juicy said. "I'll sit an' I'll call ya."

True turned away. "Ya call me an' I'll sit."

Cherish woke hours later. The first thing she saw when she opened her eyes was Sloan sitting in a chair by the bed, a doll-like child on his lap. The child's head was covered with a mass of dark curls and she was staring at Cherish with wide light-gray eyes. The resemblance to Sloan was so strong that Cherish's mind fought frantically to recall Sloan's words. He had said the child was his brother's—hadn't he?

The little girl had her thumb in her mouth and was rhythmically bumping the back of her head against Sloan's chest. He was gazing over the child's head at some distant point in the room.

Cherish peeked at him through her lashes. He didn't look like the same man she had met in the woods beside the Kentucky River. The blue shirt he was wearing was made of a soft, beautifully woven material. It fit his broad shoulders and chest exactly. The sleeves of the shirt were full and gathered at the wrist. His face was clean-shaven but showed lines of fatigue. The child on his lap wore a dark-red dress of wool linsey. Peeking from beneath the skirt were leather fur-lined shoes that laced high on the small legs.

Cherish moved her hands from under the cover and Sloan's eyes swung to her immediately.

"So, you finally woke up." He smiled. "I've been having a hard time keeping this scamp from jumping right on top of you." He removed the child's thumb from her mouth. "How do you feel?"

Before she could speak, her stomach made a gurgling sound, reminding her of its emptiness.

"All right . . . except I'm terribly hungry."

"Good." He set the child on her feet beside the bed. "Sit up and I'll bring you a bowl of True's stew."

Cherish sat up and smiled tentatively at the child, who stared back at her without the slightest flicker of an eyelid. Cherish could not get over the child's startling resemblance to Sloan. She wondered if he and his brother had looked much alike.

"I think you have her treed, Cherish. I've never seen her so quiet." Sloan placed a board with a large bowl of stew on it across Cherish's lap. "Come to think of it, she's hypnotized. She's never seen a woman like you before."

"What do you mean . . . a woman like me?" She spooned the stew into her mouth hungrily.

"I mean a white woman. No, I mean a pretty white woman with red hair. We have people from the river stop from time to time, but, well, no one like you." He gently removed the child's thumb from her mouth again. "She's never seen hair like yours or such white skin."

Cherish emptied the bowl. "That was so good. My stomach must have shrunk," she laughed. "I'm full."

"Your things are in the other room," Sloan said. "I'll take in warm water so you can wash. You probably want to be dressed before Juicy and True get back."

Hesitantly, Cherish placed her feet on the floor. Pulling and tugging at the blanket, she managed to get it wrapped about her. She was surprisingly weak when she got to her feet, but she walked steadily across the floor and into the adjoining room. Sloan followed her with a copper kettle and poured hot water into a large china basin.

Orah Delle came with him, her tiny hand holding tightly to the buckskin of his britches. When he poured the water, her arms circled his leg and she peeped around at Cherish.

Cherish held out her hand. "Orah Delle, would you like to stay with me?"

The child hid shyly behind Sloan.

"Don't you want to stay with the lady and get acquainted, sweeting?" Sloan put down the kettle and picked up the child. He sat her on a chair beside the washstand. "It'll take her a while to get used to you," he told Cherish.

As soon as he was gone, Cherish looked around the room. It was not as large as the main room, but, as in the other, the chinks between the logs had been filled with clay and the walls covered with white birch bark. A large stone fireplace was set into the wall at the end of the room and a log crackled and popped on the grate. Cherish didn't think she had ever been in a nicer room, but what caught her eyes were the furnishings and the glass window, unusual in a wilderness cabin.

A walnut chest with four large drawers and two small ones stood near the window. On the washstand was an elaborately decorated pitcher and bowl set. A massive wardrobe stood against the wall opposite the chest. The rest of the furnishings included a rocking chair by the fireplace, the straight chair—from which Orah Delle sat quietly gazing at her—and the bunks. There were three of them, their heads nailed to the unbroken wall. The middle one was child-size with rails on three sides; the other two were long and narrow, the head and one side against the wall. All looked comfortable with filled mattresses and woven coverlets.

Cherish stared at the bunks. Involuntarily her eyes closed and she recalled the haven Sloan had made for them during the blizzard. He had not meant that to happen. She knew that now. A desperate weariness enveloped her and she began to tremble. She must not forget: Sloan wanted a nursemaid . . . nothing more.

Ashamed, she opened her eyes and turned away

from the bunks. She was being unfair. Sloan had explained his position clearly. He needed a nursemaid for the child—Cherish glanced at Orah Delle. What had happened between them on the trail simply hadn't meant to him what it did to her. It couldn't.

Her belongings lay on one of the bunks. She shook out her spare dress, examined the shift and decided it was wearable, although part of it had been torn away to be used for bandages for her feet. She found towels, soap, and cloth by the washstand. After stripping off her clothes, she washed herself from head to toe. Dressed again, she unbraided her hair and ran her fingers through it to remove the snarls.

She had almost forgotten the child was in the room and was startled when the small hand tugged at her skirt. Staring up with large solemn eyes, the little girl timidly held out a large silver-handled hairbrush. Impulsively, Cherish knelt and gathered the small body in her arms.

"Why, thank you, lovey. That's just what I need. But how did you know? Let's sit here in the chair and we'll brush it together."

Holding the child's hand, she led her to the rocking chair. As soon as she was seated the little girl climbed into her lap and snuggled against her. A rush of sympathy came over Cherish. She hugged the small warm body, marveling again at the silky dark curls, the wide gray eyes with their fringe of dark lashes that were so like Sloan's. *So like her beloved Sloan's.*

Cherish brushed her hair and let it hang down over her shoulders and breasts. With an impish smile on her face, Orah Delle reached out and wound the shiny hair around her chubby fist.

"I know a game we can play," Cherish said. "Here . . . you sit on my knees and I'll hold your hands. We'll play like you're riding a horsey." She positioned the child and grasped her hands. When she lifted her knees up and down, Orah Delle bounced. A giggle burst from her rosebud mouth. Encouraged, Cherish began to sing.

> Ride a little horsey go down town,
> Ride a little horsey go down town.
> Ride a little horsey go down town . . .
> To Get Orah Delle a dolly . . . oh!

The small face was transformed with laughter. It rang merrily through the room. Each time Cherish sang the song she ended it with something different for Orah Delle—a dog, a toy, a sweet. When Cherish's legs got so tired she could no longer bounce her, the little girl threw her arms about her neck and hugged her tightly. The longing for a mother's love was so evident that Cherish had to squeeze her eyes shut to hold back the tears.

"I'll be a good mama to you, my baby," she said

impulsively. "I'll be your mama and you'll be my precious little girl."

The child leaned back and looked up into her face. "Mama. Mama . . . Mama . . ."

A sound drew Cherish's attention to the doorway. Sloan stood there with such an odd look on his face that she couldn't tell if he was pleased, angry or indifferent as he witnessed the scene.

She hesitated, then asked, "Is it all right? Do you mind if she calls me Mama?"

He came further into the room. His expression still told her nothing and she began to feel acute embarrassment.

"If that's what you want. True's been telling her I had gone to get her a mama." He reached down and lifted Orah Delle from Cherish's lap. "You'll have Cherish worn out, sweeting."

"Mama," the small voice insisted. "Mama."

"All right. Mama. You'll have your new mama worn out." Sloan was smiling when he said it.

"Papa . . . Papa!" Orah Delle threw her arms around Sloan's neck.

"I was beginning to think she didn't talk. She's not said a word but she . . . laughed," Cherish finished lamely.

"Oh, she talks. Between True and Juicy's mountain lingo and mine, I think she's confused." He nuzzled Orah Delle's neck and she giggled.

Cherish felt a faint pang of jealousy and was immediately ashamed. The little girl was obviously starved for love and companionship. Cherish was sure she could love the child and be loved by her, even if she couldn't be loved by Sloan.

She stood and began coiling her hair, then remembered that she had no pins to hold it up. She groaned and released the shimmering mass. It fell like a waterfall about her shoulders and down her back.

Sloan gazed at her, his expression giving away nothing.

"I forgot that I lost my hairpins." She tried to keep her voice light. In the back of her mind she remembered her mother saying that no respectable woman would let a man other than her husband see her with her hair loose.

Sloan went to the wardrobe and opened the double doors. Attached to one of the doors was a long mirror. Cherish saw for the first time in her life her full reflection, head to toe. At first she failed to recognize herself. When she did, she looked away in embarrassment.

Sloan pulled out drawers—one of sewing supplies, and another filled with small garments for the child. A third drawer contained lengths of dress goods, ribbons and tatted laces. Another had spun wool rolled in tight balls ready for knitting. Cherish had never seen such an array of tempting items.

"Use anything here you need."

Her eyes went round with surprise. "Oh, my. I couldn't do that."

"Why not?"

"I just couldn't," she repeated, shaking her head. "They're . . . it's just too fine."

"I insist, Cherish," Sloan said sternly. "This is your home now. I want you to feel comfortable in it and to use anything that's here as if it were your own."

"Thank you," she said in a small voice, then added. "If I use anything, I'll use it . . . sparingly."

"I'm not poor. You don't have to be miserly." He rummaged in a drawer. "There's a lot of things here, but I don't think you'll find any hairpins."

"It doesn't matter," she said quickly. "I'll braid my hair again."

"I'll whittle you a couple of pegs to get you by for now. True is the best whittler in the country. In no time at all he'll have you supplied with fancy combs and pins."

"I couldn't ask him to do that. But I would like some pegs. Back home, Mama and I used thorns Papa cut from the thorn tree. I lost mine the night I ran away from the Burgesses."

Sloan came close to her and gathered up a handful of her bright hair.

"Leave it down for now. I'm going to enjoy seeing the looks on the faces of two old goats when they see it. I'm sure their mouths will drop open a foot." His eyes were concealed by dark lashes and she couldn't read their expression to know if he was joking or serious.

They stood looking at each other. Sloan fingered her hair. Orah Delle, sitting on his arm, reached out to feel it too.

The sound of the cabin door opening, followed by the heavy stomping of boots on the plank floor, broke the spell between them. Cherish's heart was dancing wildly in her breast and her cheeks were flushed as she followed Sloan, carrying Orah Delle, out of the room.

The two men who entered took off fur robes and hung them on pegs beside the door. One, with a shiny black beard that rested on his chest, was the largest man Cherish had ever seen. As tall as Sloan, he was at least three times as big around. His bright blue eyes twinkled as he looked at her. It was impossible to tell if he was young or old.

The other man was tall and terribly thin. His face had a razor sharpness to it and his eyes were sunk deep in his head. From the lines in his face Cherish guessed that he had suffered immense pain. He must be the one Sloan said had lost his family to the fever.

Cherish hung back, suddenly realizing that she was standing before Sloan's friends in her stocking feet, wearing a faded, wrinkled dress, her hair hanging down her back. She was completely unaware that she was a vision of loveliness such as men dream about but seldom see. The fact that these men didn't say anything increased her discomfort.

Sloan moved to her side, and made a courtly bow.

"Gentlemen, may I present Mistress Cherish Riley?" He glanced at her and winked. "Cherish, meet my two good friends, Juicy Deverell and Truman Beauchamp, better known as True."

Cherish stepped forward and held out her hand. The two men stood as if they were glued to the spot. Sloan nudged Juicy, whose huge hand then swallowed Cherish's small one.

"How do you do, Mister Deverell," she said and smiled up at the man who towered over her. "I woke up once in the night and you were sitting beside me. It was good of you to give up your sleep to care for me."

"Ma'am," Juicy's voice was as soft as if he were speaking to a small bird. "Twarn't nothin'. Twarn't nothin' a'tall."

"Well, I do thank you."

Cherish turned and smiled at the tall, thin, serious-faced man. She gave him her hand.

"Mr. Beauchamp, your stew was delicious. I've never tasted anything so good in all my life. Will you tell me what all you put in it?"

"Harrumpt!" The derogatory sound came from Juicy.

True ignored him and bowed over Cherish's hand.

"I'm glad to meet ya, ma'am," he said in a soft, slurring voice. "I'd be more'n glad ta do it."

"There's so much I need to know. I've never cooked at a fancy fireplace and I've never even seen a baking chamber as fancy as this one. If you'll be patient with me until I learn, I'll be a help to you."

Sloan, holding Orah Delle, stood behind her. He pressed his lips together to keep from laughing. The two men had eyes only for Cherish. As he had predicted, she had completely captivated them without even trying or being aware of it.

"While you stand there jawing and gawking," he said, "I'm going to whittle some pegs for Cherish's hair. She lost her pins days ago."

"Ya ain't no good at whittlin'," Juicy protested.

"Yo're worse," True said quietly.

"Well, somebody's got to do it or her hair will catch on fire when she leans over the cook pot." Sloan caught Cherish's eye and winked.

"I'll do it," True said, taking out a long thin-bladed knife and going to the wood box.

Cherish sat in the fur-lined chair by the fire. Orah Delle came and climbed into her lap. The room's white birch-bark walls were adorned with various trophies of the hunt. Several beautiful fur pelts were stretched and nailed to the walls, as were bows, arrows, tomahawks and knives. The wide-spread antlers of a noble buck occupied a space on the wall, as did a sturdy shelf that held a wooden clock, its pendulum swaying gently back and forth. Flat stones were set in the masonry of the fireplace to serve as a mantel that held candles and gun clutter. An iron-doored baking oven was built into one side of the fireplace. On the other side of the room was a low chest and above it were pegs for hanging clothes.

There were three bunks nailed to the other two walls. Above each, readily available to the sleeper, were slanted wooden pegs holding long flintlock rifles. Farther along on the wall in which the fireplace was built were shelves stocked with tableware and food containers. The shelves, which reached almost to the ceiling, expanded into a work table with legs extending to the floor.

A long trestle table and two benches took up the space in the middle of the far end of the room. Set at random angles were wooden armchairs, a tiny stool, and a crudely made rocking horse for the child. The room had two glass windows, one at the front and one on the side.

True shyly handed Cherish two slender wooden skewers. Scraped smooth with the edge of his long knife, they were pointed on each end so that they resembled knitting needles. Cherish thanked him, then stood, bent over, and worked her hair with her fingers until it hung loosely from the top of her head. Whirling it around in a coil, like a rope, she straightened and swirled it around on the top of her head, fastening it with the two pins. Suddenly aware that all three men and little Orah Delle were watching her, fascinated, Cherish turned brick-red, sat down and took the child on her lap.

"That's quite a feat," Sloan said, breaking the silence. "We were wondering how you were going to get all that hair up with only two pegs."

"My mother learned how from her mother, and her mother from her mother and so on. I always did it up that way in front of my pa and my brother. I just didn't think about . . . that it might be unseemly—" Her voice trailed off and she squirmed with embarrassment.

"Hit were 'bout the sightliest thin' I e'er did see. Warn't it, Juicy? Warn't it purty to see how she done it?"

"That's for certain. Purty ain't the whole of it. 'Twas more sightly than a b'ar pawin' honey outta a holler tree."

Cherish saw that Juicy's eyes were crinkled at the corners and knew he was laughing. She laughed then.

"Thank you. Thank you both."

CHAPTER
* 14 *

When the sun went down, the wind came up and whipped the snow around the cabin. Beside the warm fire, Cherish sat with the men, Orah Delle asleep on her lap. Sloan told True and Juicy about meeting her on the trail, about Mote and Seth, about finding her brother, Roy, in the river.

He told about meeting up with Pierre.

"Pierre said give you a hello and that he'd try to be here by Christmas."

"I knowed he was out thataway. Don't it jist beat all ya crossin' paths like ya done?" True was whittling again. His long fingers and the knife was forming a piece of white wood into something that looked like a curved two-pronged hairpin.

"Ain't so surprisin'," Juicy said. "Iffn there be a skirt in five mile, Pierre'd know of it."

Cherish failed to see the warning glance Sloan gave Juicy before he resumed his story about the greenhorn minister and his flock heading for Harrodsburg. At this point Juicy had plenty to say.

"Harrumpt!" he snorted. "If that ain't the beatin'est I ever heared of. I jist betcha a two-bit chaw of tobaccy they lost their hair a'ready. I can't figure out John Harrod a-tellin' 'em ta come on without no guide or nothin'."

"Harrod's awfully anxious to make a town," Sloan said seriously. "A preacher and a church will draw people."

"Harrumpt!" Juicy snorted. "Preacher ain't goin' to draw no folks iffn his skin's hangin' on a tree and he ain't in it."

Cherish's worried eyes were going from one man to the other and Sloan decided it was time to change the subject.

"Pierre told me that Daniel Boone's back in Boonesborough. He said that Chief Blackfish let him go after he ran the gauntlet. The men captured with him were sent to Detroit to be ransomed by the British. A lot of folks think there is something fishy about Daniel being the only one to come back. Some say he plans to turn his fort over to the Shawnee. I don't believe it for a minute, but some folks would find fault with the Lord if it suited their purpose."

"I jist can't think folks 'ud be that stupid . . . harrumpt!"

"Daniel is insisting on a trial to clear his name."

Sloan went on to tell about killing the two Hurons, including Cherish's part in it.

"I was surprised by the Hurons," Sloan admitted. "It was the Cherokee I expected. I'm not worried overly much about an attack here. They're too afraid of the Shawnee. Have you seen anything of John Spotted Elk?"

"Ya," Juicy nodded. "He an' his sister an' the ol' chief was a campin' ta other side of the river. Had a big mess of Injins with 'em. John and that thar Minnie Dove came by one noon. That Minnie Dove was claimin' ya was here when I said ya warn't. Threatened ta cut off my nose with her knife." Juicy stopped to laugh. "John got so mad he boxed her ears, 'cause she acted up so." Now Juicy laughed uproariously. "She's got 'er a powerful cravin' fer ya, Sloan."

Cherish felt the heat rise and flood her face. It hadn't occurred to her that Sloan might have romantic attachments. By the sound of it the girl was in love with him. With a name like Minnie Dove, she was probably a half-breed. Cherish hid her hot face in the silky curls of the child asleep in her arms.

"That gal's 'bout the feistiest Injin gal I ever did see," Juicy rattled on. "'Course her blood's jist half Injin an' that thar would count for some of it. An' John Spotted Elk dotes on her too."

True moved his pipe from his mouth and said quietly, "Shet up, Juicy."

"Harrumpt! Now just why'd ya go an' say that? Oh, wal, hit don't matter nohow."

A small silence followed. Juicy was uncomfortable. He knew he had said something he shouldn't have, but he didn't know exactly what.

Sloan got up and took Orah Delle from Cherish's arms.

"This has been an exciting day for this little girl. Come, Cherish, and I'll show you where to find her things."

Together they undressed the child. Sloan brought out a bag-like garment with a drawstring at the top and bottom and slits at the sides for the baby's arms.

"The slave woman made this. It keeps her real warm."

Cherish held the sleeping child up while Sloan slipped the garment over her head.

"What do you do about—?" Cherish fumbled for the right word. "You don't take her outside for—?"

"No." Sloan opened the door on the washstand and brought out a large china chamberpot. "Both of you use this. It can be emptied in the morning." He went to one of the bunks and punched the mattress with his hand. "True said he put a feather tick on this bunk and there are plenty of covers. I'll see to the fire."

"Thank you."

"Well . . . goodnight."

"Night, Sloan."

Cherish didn't move. Sloan hesitated a second or two, then walked out of the room, closing the door softly behind him. Cherish heard the chair creak as he lowered his weight into it. She heard his voice as the three men resumed their conversation.

She sat down on the edge of the bunk, suddenly filled with anguish. So this was the way it was going to be. Never again would he take her in his arms and hold her and kiss her. Perhaps he loved the Indian girl, Minnie Dove. Perhaps he wished that what had occurred between them on the trail hadn't happened.

She lifted Orah Delle and sat her on the chamber pot. The child whimpered sleepily when her bare flesh met the cold china rim, but she discharged water when she was told. Cherish put her back into the bed and tucked the covers around her. She stood back and looked down at her for a long moment, wishing fervently that she were really her child . . . and Sloan's.

The fire lit the room with a faint glow when Cherish blew out the candle. She removed the skewers from her hair and carefully placed them on the walnut chest. She slipped out of her dress and, not bothering to braid her hair, crawled into the bunk. All her life she had heard about sleeping on a feather tick, about how they were soft as a pillow and that a person sank down and down until you thought there was no bottom. Tonight, however, her heart was too heavy to appreciate the luxury. She pulled the covers up to her chin and lay wide-eyed, listening to the drone of voices from the next room.

She slept . . . and dreamed that she was floating, swimming in the creek back home in Virginia. A man's bronze arms matched the movements of her own as she sliced through the tranquil water. The man turned to her—it was Sloan. His white teeth flashed as he laughed with her. Soundless words came from his mouth as he rose and arched his muscled back to dive beneath the water. She hurried to follow him into the deep where they came together, arms and legs entwined, sinking deeper and deeper—

She awakened. Sloan's face was close to her own. She blinked and moved her head, thinking the vision would vanish. But he was still there. His lips hovered over hers, whispering.

"Is there room for me, love?"

With a soft welcoming cry she reached up to draw him down to her, her heart flooding her body with warm gladness.

"Oh, Sloan. I'm glad you came!"

"I couldn't stay away." He lifted the covers, slid in beside her and gathered her to him. "I lay thinking about you . . . wanting you," he whispered before finding her lips and kissing her with gentle persistence.

"I wanted you to come—"

"Did you, love? Did you?" He found her lips again, moving over them slowly, touching them with his tongue. "Are you all right? Are you rested enough? I can just hold you—" His hands moved on her, the shift was swept away and there was nothing between them.

"Love me. Love me like you did that night I was so cold."

"I will, love. I will. This time it won't hurt you. I promise."

"It was a wonderful sweet hurt," she whispered against his mouth.

"You sweet woman—"

Their lips met and met again, each kiss sweeter than the one before. His arms curled around her, his hand caressed downward along her spine to press her hips closer to his. His breath was a warm tickling in the curve of her neck. His lips touched there, then moved back to her lips again . . . tasting the softness, the sweetness, playing, warming, rousing her until her arms crept about his neck. She caught her breath as a wild flooding ache shot to the center of her being. As wonderful as the kisses were, she felt an urgency for more.

Sloan moved his hard, demanding body over her soft yielding one. He entered her gently, moving slowly at first, then faster and faster with a heat that melted them into one. Cherish clung to him, feeling as if she were in another world. Gradually she came to feel like a child on a swing going up and up . . . higher and higher.

Her need was as great as his, their passion full-grown, overwhelming. He filled her body, her heart and mind. He was there to stay; there would never be room for another. Rational thought slid away and they fell into the warm elusive pit of ecstasy.

They lay in silence. She ran a hand down his back when he moved to lie at her side. He buried his face in her hair. Her body nestled against him, a warm soft thigh resting casually between his legs, one arm flung out across his chest. She stirred sleepily as his hand began to caress the small of her back. Lazily she stretched, like a contented kitten. A throaty purr escaped her.

Sloan laughed. "You liked that?"

She purred again and rolled her head back to look into the smiling gray eyes.

"I'm not supposed to, am I?"

"Ah, sweet. Of course you are. God didn't mean for just the male to enjoy the mating."

She pulled his head to her breast. In the flickering firelight his hair shone with the sheen of black satin against her white skin. Her hair spread out across him in shimmering molten waves.

"I was afraid." She hurried on before she lost her courage. "I was afraid you'd not want me again. I thought that what happened before was just . . ."

"Just what?" When she didn't answer, he said, "Animal lust? No, sweet thing," he whispered. "It was more than that. Much more."

"I hoped that it was." Her voice trembled a bit.

He rolled her onto him and with strong fingers worked the muscles in her back.

"Are you still afraid?"

"No," she said simply.

But even as she lay in his arms, warm and contented, she felt a recurring stir of old uneasiness. There was still so much she didn't know about him. So much she would have liked to ask but didn't dare. She wondered about Orah Delle, who looked so like him, and about the child's mother, Ada, who had abandoned her. Above all, she wondered about the Indian girl, Minnie Dove, who loved Sloan too.

The time sped past.

For three days now the sun had shone brightly, melting the snow left over from the blizzard.

Cherish and Orah Delle sat on a tree stump and watched the men work. True and Juicy were building their own cabin. They had felled the trees and notched the logs during the summer. The work on the construction had been slow while Sloan was away because one of them was always with the child. But the work now was progressing faster with the three of them working. The walls had gone up in two days. The roof and fireplace were taking longer. The men worked from first light until dark, racing to finish while the good weather held.

The new cabin would be the sixth structure in the

small settlement. As she sat watching the men work, Cherish could not keep her eyes from straying to a boarded-up cabin nearby. It was a larger version of the one that Sloan lived in. Both were weathered and had rock fireplaces at either end, but rough shutters covered the windows of one while glass windows in the other shone in the sunlight.

The cabins were set about a hundred yards back in the timber above the river where it turned to form a deep bend. There in the cradle of the horseshoe bend the little settlement was a small touch of civilization in the wilderness. Between and behind the two cabins was a smokehouse and beyond that a barn that housed the cow. The other building was a lodge the Shawnee used from time to time, Sloan had told her. Attached to this structure was a storehouse, which held supplies not only for this settlement, but for others farther downriver.

On the highest piece of ground in the bend, overlooking the river and inside a split-railed enclosure, Sloan's brother was buried. Cherish had walked up there one afternoon while Orah Delle was napping. A smooth thick slab of wood marked the grave. The words, neatly carved, read simply:

SLATER BUCHANAN CARROLL
1752–1777
25 YEARS OLD
Father of Orah Delle Carroll

Cherish wanted to weep for the young man, already ill, whose young wife had run away and left him with a wee babe. She would have liked to ask Sloan more about him, but he hadn't mentioned his brother again after telling her he was Orah Delle's father. The only time she had mentioned the cabin, she immediately wished she hadn't. She had wondered aloud why True and Juicy couldn't use it.

Sloan's face had gone still. He had said, "Why should they? It isn't theirs," and walked away, leaving her shaken.

The land in the river bend was referred to by True and Juicy as Carrolltown, but True explained to her that the land was owned by Sloan, bought with money he received from the sale of the family plantation left to him and his brother when their father died. Sloan had no intention of starting a settlement such as Boonesborough, or Harrodsburg, and encouraging other settlers to come. True said, in fact, that the Shawnee had sold him the land with the understanding—and with the assurance that they would be allowed to retain their lodge and continue hunting on their old hunting grounds. Sloan considered it a good bargain, because the Shawnee were good neighbors. They also kept other marauding Indians away, providing better protection than a fort.

Several weeks had passed since Sloan had come staggering out of the blizzard with the half-frozen girl in his arms. They had been weeks of adjustment to a whole new way of life for Cherish.

At first Cherish felt almost like an intruder. She took stock of the contents of the wardrobe and the walnut chest in the bedroom. Her fingers itched to sew on the lengths of fabric she found in the drawers and to knit the fine wool yarns. She spent two days cleaning the room thoroughly. Evenings, before the fire, she mended the child's clothing. Her own dress was worn and she longed to make another, but for the time being, it would have to do. Her only footwear was the moccasins Sloan had made on the trail.

One evening Juicy brought out a skin of soft leather, and two evenings later he slipped a pair of dainty slippers on her feet. She was so delighted she kissed him soundly on the cheek. To Sloan's delight, Juicy, for once, was speechless.

When the weather settled and the men began working outside all day, Cherish tackled the job of cleaning the big room. She found a large wooden basin turned upside down under the work table, carried it to the fireplace and filled it with hot water from the teakettle. By rubbing a chunk of hard lye soap between her hands, she built up a light foam, then laid the soap aside, for she had been taught never to rest it in a pool of its own drippings, or it would melt away wastefully.

First she carefully washed and dried all the table-

ware they had not previously used, handling the
pewter plates, cups, and eating utensils lovingly. She
scrubbed the dusty shelves and replaced the tableware, then washed the trestle table. When it was dry
she rubbed beeswax into the wood and polished it
until it shone.

True had taken her into the root cellar a few morn-
ings after she arrived. She found potatoes, carrots,
cabbage, pumpkins and sacks of corn there ready for
grinding. There was a keg of molassess and several
more of rum, plus some jugs of corn liquor she suspected were for Juicy's use. On a shelf in the coolest
part of the cellar were crocks where the milk and
eggs Sloan had bought from a passing freighter were
stored. Cherish had never seen so much food in one
place, and True told her there were slabs of bacon,
sides of venison, smoked turkeys, even bear meat in
the smokehouse.

Cherish was astounded.

One evening, just before she went to bed, she announced that she was going to wash clothes the next
day.

"That is if the sun is shining and the day is reason-
ably warm."

"What fer?" Juicy asked.

"Because there won't be many more days when
we can dry the clothes out of doors," she told him.

"Hit's a good idee," True said.

Sloan nodded agreement. "We'll get out the boiling pot and get you set up the first thing in the morning."

Later that night, when the cabin was still with only the pop of the logs burning in the fireplaces to break the silence, Sloan slipped into bed beside her. This was the moment she looked forward to eagerly every day.

Holding her in his arms, he kissed her long and leisurely before whispering into her ear: "I don't want you to use up all your energy in the daytime. Save some for me."

She laughed against his face and placed her lips to his ear.

"I can't sit around all day and wait for you."

"Why not?" he murmured. He ran his hand down the length of her, feeling all the curves and warm places that only his hands had ever touched. "I want to sit in front of the fire every evening, with you on my lap, not doing anything but looking at you and touching you—here . . . and here . . . and here!"

She wound her fingers in his hair and gave a gentle tug, pulling his head toward her parted lips. His mouth was on hers, open and exploring and caressing, and hers answered it. Her hands were on him, eager and instinctive, with none of the shyness of their first coming together. He covered her when she was ready for him, and there was bigness and hardness and motion met by her unrestrained response. His breath mingled with her breath, his moans with her moans, blending together as they reached their tempestuous completion.

When it was over, he fell away from her for a moment before he gathered her again tenderly into his arms and held her, stroking her hair. The clock on the shelf in the other room chimed, and he continued to hold her. He kissed her mouth, her breasts.

"I can't seem to get enough of you," he whispered huskily, nuzzling his face in her hair. "I've never felt like this and I really don't know what to do about it. I don't want to love you. I've seen what love can do to a man. Love is having your heart and soul twisted, tied and knotted and . . . stomped on."

Cherish was shocked at the bitterness in his voice. *What* had done this to him? *Who* had done this to him?

"Sh . . . sh . . . we don't have to think of that now," she whispered, kissing him and caressing his face with her fingertips. "It's enough that you want me like this. We can be happy together like this, can't we? I love you, but I'll never try to hold on to you if you should want me to go away."

His hold on her tightened. "I can't think of a thing in this world that would ever cause me to want you to go away." He moved his lips down her face. "I've got a bear clinging to my back, honey. Someday maybe I'll shake it off and be able to truly love."

"You truly love now, my dearest one. Love comes in many shapes. You love Orah Delle and you loved your brother. You love True and Juicy in a different way."

"You amaze me with your goodness, sweetheart."

Long after he had fallen asleep, Cherish lay awake in his arms and thought about what he had said. Was it his brother's disastrous experience, or was it something else that so tortured him? She cradled his head on her breast and stroked his hair. Would the time ever come when he would be able to tell her that he loved her? She prayed that it would, that he would appreciate love for what it was: the most binding and yet the most giving force in all the world.

CHAPTER
* 15 *

Cherish was up and dressed the minute she heard the men moving about. The lamp was lit and the fire blazing when she came into the room. Sloan and True were at the trestle table drinking mugs of steaming tea.

"It's going to be a good day for your washing. Come have coffee and mush, or would you rather have tea and cold rabbit?"

The smile Sloan gave her spread a warm light into his eyes and she found herself beaming with pleasure. She met his eyes and her pulses leaped in excitement. Her slightly flushed cheeks made her blue eyes seem all the brighter, clearer. Juicy was watching her with a wide smile and twinkling eyes.

Her mind groped for something to say.

"Landsakes! Don't mention rabbit."

"What's she so red-faced fer, Sloan?" Juicy tilted his head and peered at her in puzzlement.

"I don't know, unless she got sunburned lazying around out there in the sun watching us work."

"By George, that's it. She's done nothin' I knowed of but dawdle 'round fer the last week or so."

"Dawdle!" Cherish snorted. "Just for that, Juicy Deverell, you can wash your own socks."

"Now, little missy, don't be gettin' yore back up. I didn't mean *dawdle,* what I mean was ya been smoodlin' 'round."

"Smoodlin'? What does that mean?" Cherish stood with her hands on her hips, glaring at the big man.

"Tell her, Juicy. What does smoodlin' mean?" Sloan urged, his broad smile showing the dimples in his cheeks.

Juicy turned on Sloan. "With all the school larnin' ya got and ya don't know what smoodlin' is? Harrumpt!" He got to his feet and pulled on his coat. "Iffn that don't beat all," he muttered and hastened out the door.

Sloan laughed at Cherish's dumbfound expression. He got to his feet and bent and kissed her hard on the mouth.

"Guess we're just a couple of dummies."

"Sloan, what—?"

"I think he meant smooching. What we're doing right now." He kissed her again.

"Do they know that we—?"

"—I'm sure they do."

"Oh, my! Oh . . . my!"

"Don't worry about it, sweetheart. There's a whole new set of rules out here in the wilderness."

"I love you . . . or I wouldn't have welcomed you to my bed."

"I know. Sit down and eat. True's coming in with an armload of wood."

Streaks of light lit the eastern sky when True carried the big iron boiling pot up from the barn. After partially filling the pot with the water he brought from the spring in two wooden buckets, he built a fire under it. Sloan produced a bench, which he set against the wall of the cabin. He made another trip to the barn and returned with two wooden tubs that he set on the bench.

Cherish was amazed. "I thought I would do my wash in the river."

"Ain't no call ta do that," Juicy said, setting down two more buckets of water. "Washin's 'ard enough, I allus say."

"You want more water, Cherish, sing out. We'll be down at the new cabin." When Sloan passed behind her, he ran his hand lingeringly down her back, from above her waist down over her hips, in a quick, sweeping, proprietorial move that left her shocked and breathless.

By the time Orah Delle was up and dressed and had eaten her breakfast, the water in the iron pot was boiling. After cautioning the child to stay away from the fire, Cherish set to washing clothes. The white things went first into the hot suds. They were punched down into the roiling water with a wash stick again and again, then draped over bushes and along the rail fence to dry.

Cherish washed her shawl, her blanket and the dress with the split skirt, which had been carefully mended. She washed several shirts for Sloan, pressing them to her face quickly before dipping them into the suds. Seeing the gaping holes in Juicy's and True's stockings, she made plans to knit each of them two pairs. She could knit a stocking in an afternoon and evening, if she set her mind on it.

When the washing was done and spread out in the full sun, she took her suds and scrubbed the main room and everything in it, including the mantel shelf and the hearth, the furniture, bunks and shelves, until the room was soap-smelling clean. Then she poured the water out, well away from the cabin, so that Orah Delle wouldn't be tempted to wade through the mud it made. She did all this and still by noonday she had carrots, cabbage, and smoked meat in the cooking pot and corn pone in the baking oven.

"What's that thar I smell?" Juicy sniffed as he came into the room. "That gal washin' things again? Ain't healthy, Sloan. Yer just gotter do somethin' 'bout her. She'll have everythin' washed down to a nubbin."

"You just get yourself on in here, Juicy," Cherish

said, laughing, "and stop your complaining. Wash your face and hands before you come to the table. It's about time we started to teach the baby some manners."

"Better march right over here, Juicy," Sloan said solemnly, splashing water on his face. He touched his fingers to his jaw reminiscently. "You haven't seen Cherish in a temper yet . . . I have!"

Her face reddened and she raised her eyes to meet Sloan's devilish gaze.

"Golly, Sloan," Juicy retorted. His tone was peevish but his eyes danced merrily. "Yore gonna have ta take a strap to 'er, or she just might git to thinkin' she's the queen bee 'round this place."

Sloan's mouth twitched. "Watch out she doesn't sting you, Juicy," he said gleefully.

Pure happiness swept through Cherish. Entranced, she had watched the transformation as day by day the stern-faced man she had met in the wilderness became more and more relaxed and carefree.

True never entered into any of the teasing. He always stood back and watched, though his long serious face cracked into a grin every once in a while. Cherish knew that he liked her. He was always kind and patient and helpful, but there was an aura of sadness about him that made her want to weep. Sometimes in the early evening hours she saw him walking along the riverbank and wondered if he was thinking about his dead wife and children.

* * *

The days fell into a pattern. Cherish was seldom alone with Sloan except at night in her narrow bunk. Although he and Juicy often teased her, Sloan seldom made any gesture of affection toward her in front of his friends. The atmosphere in the cabin was warm and friendly, and Cherish was happy . . . happier than she even dreamed that she could be.

They worked from dawn until late evening, Cherish in the cabin and looking after the little girl, who was becoming more and more precious to her as the days went by. Orah Delle, on her part, was so attached to Cherish she seldom left her side. The men worked outside. The new cabin was finished and furniture was being hewed from rough wood. The clay mortar in the stone fireplace was being slowly seasoned.

The last of November was approaching. The warm spell they had enjoyed after the preseason blizzard vanished, and the days became increasingly colder. When the men were not working on the furniture for the new cabin, they chopped wood. This was stacked in a long wall between the two cabins, where it would be convenient to both.

In the evenings, Cherish knitted. Juicy and Sloan were content to sit and watch her and tease her gently. When she was bothered by the teasing, or acted as if she were, the needles flashed faster and faster.

When she made a mistake and had to pull it out, they laughed heartily.

True was always busy, either whittling toys for Orah Delle, or making fancy combs and hairpins for Cherish. Of late he had begun making bullets in the evenings. Cherish liked to watch him, for he was as particular about it as she was about her knitting. First he shaved the lead into a broken iron pot he had found in the Shawnee town and set the pot on the hot coals. When the lead melted he ladled it out into the bullet mold. The shining stream of hot lead fascinated Cherish. Actually, it didn't look hot at all, but silvery cool.

"Ye'd find out iffn ya touched hit," True told her when she mentioned that to him.

"Oh, I know it's hot, but it looks so pretty—not as if it could hurt you at all."

When the bullets cooled, True turned them out, took his knife and trimmed the roughness off. As a final step he rubbed them with an old piece of deerskin worn slick. He went about the work slowly and easily, taking care that each one should be just right. He loved making things with his hands and took pride in the finished product.

Each evening, sitting before the fire, Sloan held Orah Delle, playing with her before lulling her to sleep. It was plain that he adored the child. His face was never stern when he held her. She jumped boisterously on his lap, demanding attention—which he was glad to give. She laughed enchantingly at him when he romped with her.

One evening, Juicy produced a mouth organ. To Cherish's utter amazement he began to play the old English ballad, "Greensleeves." It was a song her mother had taught her and she began to sing, softly at first; then, as her confidence grew, her clear sweet voice filled the room. When the song ended the men sat as if spellbound until Sloan nodded to Juicy. He raised the harmonica to his lips and played the song again. Sloan sang it in French, watching Cherish's eyes go dreamy and her lips curve in a soft smile.

"That was lovely. Thank you," she said, and smiled with pure pleasure.

Cherish had ceased to worry about True and Juicy being aware that Sloan came to her bed. She had spent countless hours worrying that they would think less of her for sleeping with Sloan without marriage vows. What they did together, loving, comforting each other, whispering words that were sometimes silly, sometimes not, seemed so right. In her heart he was her husband, her man, and nothing would ever change that.

On Thanksgiving morning they woke to a frozen white world. The snow that had begun the night before was still falling, the flakes drifting slowly down, the wind having blown itself out during the night.

True and Juicy went over to the new cabin to

check the mortar around the stones in the fireplace, to see if it had dried sufficiently for them to build a large enough fire to keep the cabin warm. They had kept a low fire in the hearth for days, allowing plenty of time for the mortar to dry slowly. The previous night was the last they planned to bunk in Sloan's cabin. Both True and Juicy had cautioned Cherish, though, that she was not rid of them. Juicy said it would take a team of mules to pull him away from her table.

Preparing for the Thanksgiving feast, Cherish had soaked dried apples and raisins for pies, mashed cooked pumpkin and added butter and nutmeg, removed the pin-feathers and finished cleaning the wild turkey Sloan had shot. She stuffed the bird with corn pone dressing seasoned with spices she found in carefully sealed jars on the shelf. Remembering her mother's recipe for Indian pudding, she brought out the molasses, cornmeal, eggs she found stored in the cellar, butter and salt. After mixing it she added the milk, seasoned it with ginger and poured the batter in a pan to bake alongside the loaves of wheat bread.

She had been up early, firing the oven to bake the bread and pies early so that the big bake chamber would be free for roasting the turkey. She planned to use the fancy table cover she had discovered in the chest and to wear the new dress she had secretly made from the material she had found in the wardrobe. Sloan had said for her to use what she

needed, and she had chosen a soft piece of blue linsey and trimmed it with a white collar. There had
been enough of the piece left for a dress for Orah
Delle. While the men were away she changed into
the new dress and dressed the child. She first brushed
Orah Delle's hair and tied it with a blue ribbon, then
did her own, coiling it carefully and pinning it with
the pins True had made for her.

It was mid-morning when the whiplike crack of a
rifle sounded. The echoes of the shot reverberated
from hill to hill and were finally lost far down the
valley. More shots followed the first, then silence.
Cherish had just reached the window facing the river
when the door burst open. The men snatched the rifles from the slanting pegs along the wall and
grabbed True's newly made supply of bullets.

Seconds later True and Juicy, with Brown at their
heels, were out the door. Sloan turned to speak to
Cherish. He checked her pistol and placed it on the
mantel.

"Bar the door after me, then close the shutters," he
told her. "Don't open for anyone—and I mean anyone—except me, True or Juicy. Do you understand?"

She nodded numbly. "Is it an Indian attack?"

"I don't know. It could be river renegades. Just
don't open the door." He was out the door, and by
the time she slipped the bar in place and went to the
window, Sloan had rejoined True and Juicy.

Shots came from the river. The three men split up, Brown and Sloan going into the woods to the north, True loping down the hill to the river, and Juicy making his way toward the Shawnee lodge. Cherish's heart seemed to stop beating for a moment, then began to pound like the beat of a drum.

Something tugged at her skirt. She looked down to see Orah Delle staring up at her with wide, frightened eyes. Cherish had forgotten the child. Guiltily she gathered her up in her arms and crooned to her, trying to calm her.

Through Cherish's mind ran vivid pictures of all the things she had ever heard about Indian attacks—houses burning, women and children scalped or carried off screaming, men tortured to a slow, agonizing death. And Sloan was out there!

Oh, dear God, don't let anything happen to him! Please, God, keep him safe.

Sloan had shown her during the first week at the cabin how to swing the shutters, which lay back against the inside walls of the cabin, together to bar the windows. She did this now to the bedroom window and the one on the side of the main room, before returning to the window facing the river.

Clutching Orah Delle to her, she peered anxiously out the window, but she could see nothing moving. From time to time she heard scattered gunfire. When she felt she couldn't stand the watching and waiting any longer, she sat Orah Delle on a bunk, stoked up the fire and put the turkey in the oven to bake. The normalcy of the task soothed her nerves. She gave Orah Delle a piece of bread spread with molasses for a treat, then returned to the window.

She heard another volley of shots, this time close by. Once she thought she saw a puff of smoke rising from a clump of trees by the river. There were more shots nearby, then faintly she heard Juicy's booming voice shouting at someone on the river.

Having strained her eyes for so long and having seen nothing unusual, she couldn't believe what she saw when something did come into view. A woman, her blond hair streaming out behind her, a bright blue cape flapping around her legs, came running toward the cabin from the river. She was screaming hysterically as she ran, slipping and stumbling through the snow. Cherish expected to see someone chasing her, but there was no one in sight.

Cherish waited until the woman was a few yards from the house, then unbarred and opened the door. She was sure Sloan hadn't intended for her to refuse to admit someone like this poor frightened creature. The woman flung herself into the house and frantically tried to close the door, almost knocking Cherish off her feet. She seemed to be wild with fear and her screaming had frightened Orah Delle. The child was yelling and crying too, and clinging to Cherish.

The woman threw herself down on a bunk and pulled the covers up over her head. Clutching Orah

Delle to her, Cherish rushed back to the window. The shooting had stopped, and coming up the path now were two men supporting a third between them who was wounded, badly it seemed, for they were almost dragging him through the snow. Walking beside them, carrying a satchel, was another girl. A shawl covered her head and shoulders. Her skirts dragged in the snow. She was not nearly so well-dressed as the blond woman who lay sobbing on the bunk.

Cherish saw Sloan loping up from the river, Brown at his heels. He handed his rifle to one of the men and picked the wounded man up in his arms. Staggering under the heavy load, he came on toward the cabin.

Cherish began to turn from the window and suddenly turned back. Something about the man Sloan carried seemed familiar.

Then she recognized him. With a little cry, she set Orah Delle on the floor and ran quickly to unbar the door.

The wounded man was Pierre!

CHAPTER
* 16 *

Cherish opened the door and stepped quickly aside for Sloan to enter. He carried Pierre to the bunk nearest the hearth and gently put him down. The two men and the girl entered and stood by the door. Cherish closed it and went to where Sloan bent over the bunk. Her eyes flew to Sloan's face, but he was busy removing Pierre's heavy coat and was not looking at her.

The girl dropped the carpetbag she was carrying and went timidly toward them. She was young. The coat she wore was worn and thin. Her face was pinched with cold, her brown eyes were large with worry—or was it desperation? Cherish was not sure which, but being a woman in love herself, she knew instinctively that the girl was in love with Pierre and sick with worry.

"I'm Cherish. Let me help you with your coat." Cherish smiled and spoke in a welcoming, friendly tone. She helped her remove her wet shawl, then her thin coat.

"Thank you, ma'am."

Cherish clicked her tongue. "You must be near frozen. Come to the fire for a minute."

The girl shook her head, her eyes on Pierre. Prodding her gently, Cherish nudged her toward the bunk.

Remembering that she had other guests, Cherish turned her attention to the two men standing by the door. One was quite old, the other only a boy.

"Welcome," she said. "Hang your coats on the pegs and come to the fire and warm yourselves."

"Thanky, ma'am," the man said. "Name's Swanson. This here's my grandson, Farrway Quill." The boy said nothing but inclined his head politely.

"I'm Cherish." She shook hands with both and urged them toward the fire.

The blond woman in the bunk was still crying. Cherish wanted to comfort her, but each time she approached her, Orah Delle held her back. The sounds coming from the woman terrified the child.

Sloan worked quickly over Pierre. The girl was so concerned that her hands trembled as she tried to help. Cherish gently pushed her away, brought up a stool for her to sit on near the head of the bunk and put a cloth in her hand to use to wipe the snow from Pierre's head.

The door opened, letting in a blast of cold air. Juicy stomped in. Cherish went to him.

"Where's True?" she asked anxiously.

"He's a-comin' soon's he's shore the buggers ain't a-comin' back. Goldamn riffraff. I allus say, Injins ain't half so mean as river scum. How bad's Pierre?"

"I don't know. I need to help Sloan, but Orah Delle won't let loose of me. She's scared of all the commotion."

"Give 'er ta me. Come ta Juicy, lit'l tadpole. Juicy'll find ya a purty." The child went willingly to him.

Juicy stared with disgust at the woman on the bed. "What's she still blubberin' fer?"

"She was terribly frightened. She'll have to cry it out." Cherish wondered at the big, gentle man's lack of sympathy for the woman.

Sloan had removed all of Pierre's clothing and pulled a blanket up to his navel. The bullet had caught him in the side and he had lost a lot of blood. Sloan was relieved to discover that the bullet, having been fired from some distance, had been partly spent when it struck Pierre and had been deflected by a rib. There was a small hole in the Frenchman's back where the bullet had emerged.

Grateful that he didn't have to probe the wound to remove the lead, Sloan removed bits of cloth carried in by the force of the bullet. Cherish took a basin of warm water and together they washed the wound, doused it with whiskey, and wrapped Pierre's midsection with layers of bandage.

When he began to shake with shock, Sloan called for blankets and hot stones. They all worked feverishly to keep Pierre warm, for Sloan said that that was one of the dangers with this type of wound. Finally, the shaking ceased; color came back into the part of his face not covered with the heavy black beard, and he lay still.

The girl stayed beside Pierre. She appeared nervous and glanced often to the bunk where the blond woman lay. She looked so forlorn sitting there that Cherish went to her and draped a blanket over her shoulders.

"He's going to be all right. Sloan will see to it."

"Oh, I hope so. I do hope so." Tears flooded her big sad eyes. Her voice was soft and refined.

"Why don't you take off those wet shoes. I'll bring you a pair of moccasins."

"No. I couldn't let you—" She drew her feet back under her skirt.

"Of course, you can."

"No. Please—"

Puzzled, Cherish patted her shoulder and picked up the bloody linen. Vaguely she thought she should do something for the woman on the bunk, but apparently she had cried herself to sleep, because there was no sound from her now.

The room was filled with people. Cherish was grateful for the turkey in the oven, the fresh-baked bread, the Indian pudding, pumpkin, and the pies on the shelf. At least she had food for all of them. She took time to go to the bedroom to brush and recoil her hair and to slip an apron over her dress.

The men were talking by the hearth. Juicy had fed Orah Delle a sweet to calm her and she lay against his shoulder, her thumb in her mouth. The old man was talking, explaining:

"I wouldn't a brought them, mister, but I did need the coin. Me and the boy has been up against it lately. The woman was takin' a boat down river, come hell or high water. The Frenchman couldn't talk her out of it. I don't like to say nothin' against a lady, mister, but if she hadn't a flaunted herself . . . that is to say if she'd a behaved more like a lady ort to, that bunch of scum wouldn't followed us. They must a got to talkin' about her and drinkin' and set out to overtake us. We were mighty glad when you showed up. We sure was."

Mister Swanson paused and shook his head. "I'm downright sorry about the Frenchman. He'd not come, but he knowed the woman and felt sorry for the little gal. Now, that little gal's real pitiful. She's a bound gal. I don't know how long she's been with the woman, but that one thinks she owns her body and soul."

Cherish glanced at the girl beside Pierre. She had heard of bondsmen and had seen a few, but they had all been well-treated and seemed more like favored servants to the families they served. And this girl was one of those? She looked over her shoulder at the woman sleeping on the bunk; fear sprouted and her curiosity grew.

Mister Swanson reached out and put his hand on his grandson's head.

"I reckon as how I'd sooner see my grandson here dead than be bound like that poor young'un over there. Her might as well be a darkie for the way she's treated."

"Harrumpt!" Juicy snorted.

"It was a foolhardy thing I done, bringin' that woman," Mr. Swanson said. "I hope you see how it was, mister."

"I understand," Sloan said. He added, "Whatever she paid you to bring her here, I'll pay you twice that if you'll take her back."

The old man scratched his head. "I don't know about it, mister. I'm thinkin' you'll have to hogtie her to get her back on that boat. She's a corker, that one is."

"There's not many boats going upriver now."

"I be knowin' it. River'll be freezin' afore long."

"Well," Sloan said with a resigned slump to his shoulders, "you and the boy are welcome to stay here. That riffraff who fired on you are still around hoping to catch you alone on the river."

"We don't want to put you to no bother," Mister Swanson said quickly. "We can make out on the boat, long's it's tied up."

"No need for that," Sloan insisted. "You'll be our guests. We have another cabin and plenty of bunk space."

"Me and the lad thank ya. We sure do."

True came in then, and Cherish went to the door to meet him. She took his rifle and placed it on the pegs while he got out of his coat.

"I was getting worried about you. Oh, your poor face is frozen! Come to the fire and I'll get you some hot tea."

"Thanky, little purty. I sure do need hit."

True stood with his back to the fire. His face was blue with cold. He held the mug Cherish brought to him in his two hands and sipped the hot liquid slowly. The boy got up and politely offered True his chair.

"Thanky, son." True eased down on the chair. "I built up the fire in the cabin. Hit's gonna do fine. I figure we'll be needin' hit."

Sloan introduced the old man and his grandson.

"They will be staying for a while, True. They can't take the boat back up the river alone with that scum hanging around. And I doubt many boats will be coming up from the south this time of year."

"Yore welcome ter bunk in with us'uns. That's iffn the lad'll make do with a pallet afore the fire."

"We thank you kindly, but we don't want to be no burden. We got sowbelly and meal on the boat."

Sloan waved that aside. "We have plenty of grub."

Cherish brought over a platter of fresh sliced bread heavily coated with butter.

"Dinner won't be ready for some time. Perhaps this will tide you over until then."

The boy looked longingly at the bread.

"Go on," Cherish urged. "Take some."

After first looking at his grandfather for approval, the boy reached out and took the piece nearest him.

"It's been a spell since he's had bread like that, ma'am," the old man said, as if he were apologizing.

"Then he shall have all he wants and I'll fetch him a mug of milk to wash it down," Cherish said firmly.

After taking the milk to the boy, Cherish sliced more bread, buttered it and arranged it on a plate. She took it and a mug of milk to the girl sitting beside Pierre. Cherish placed the plate in her lap and handed her the milk.

The girl looked from the plate to Cherish, her eyes full of fear. She glanced quickly toward the bunk where the woman lay sleeping.

"Ma'am," she whispered, "you shouldn't wait on me. I'm her servant. She'll be . . . angry!"

"Don't worry. I'm sure she'll understand when I tell her that I insisted."

The girl shook her head. "She won't, ma'am."

"Maybe you can finish before she wakes up." Cherish waited until the girl picked up the bread and began to eat hungrily.

The men were on their feet now, having decided to

make a trip to the boat to bring up the baggage— Pierre's, the woman's, and the girl's.

Juicy handed Orah Delle, who had fallen asleep, to Sloan.

"We'uns can take keer of it. We'll see to the fire in the cabin while we're about it."

"Dinner will be ready in a couple of hours," Cherish said. "Be good and hungry when you come back."

"Don't worry yore purty little head none." Juicy grinned at her. "I don't aim ta miss out on that thar pie and them other fixin's."

The old man said, "We do thanky, ma'am."

He nudged his grandson in the ribs with his elbow. Cherish could barely hear the boy when he spoke, but she was sure he said, "Thank you, ma'am."

She felt a blast of cold air when the men went out. The snow was still falling and the tracks that had been made in it only a short time ago were no longer there.

Sloan took the child to the bedroom and tucked her into her crib. He put another log on the bedroom fire before returning to restore the fire in the big hearth.

Cherish watched him, puzzled. His lips were pressed tight and she saw a hardness in his eyes as he passed her to go to the bunk where Pierre lay. He lifted the unconscious man's eyelid and reached under the covers to feel his legs. He checked the wound to see if it had stopped bleeding. Satisfied that he could do no more for him, he came back to Cherish, took her hand, and led her into the bedroom.

He paced back and forth the length of the room several times before he stopped in front of her. She turned away from him abruptly, but not before he saw the fear in her eyes. She stood rigid, and he turned her back to face him.

"Have you guessed who that woman is?"

"I was afraid it might be . . . her."

"It's Ada all right," he spat out bitterly. "Now, the question is: what am I going to do with her?"

His obvious agitation heightened Cherish's fear. Something more was involved here than merely putting his sister-in-law on the boat and sending her back to where she came from.

"I just can't tell her to go!" he blurted.

Bewildered, Cherish stammered, "Well, I . . . I don't see why not. That is, if you don't want her here."

"Don't you see? If I make her go, she'll take the babe." Anguish was written on his face.

Cherish was momentarily stunned by the statement. Recovery was slow and accompanied by a rapid heartbeat.

"No! She has no right! She ran away and left her. She'll not have her! Hear me, Sloan." Cherish grabbed his arms. "I won't give her up!"

"She has the right," Sloan said wearily. "She can

bring the soldiers in here, take the babe and give her to the first Indian squaw she runs across, if she wants to. And there's nothing we can do about it."

It was something Cherish hadn't thought about. Anger swept through her. Her chin went up in the old expression of defiance.

"She'll play . . . hell getting her away from me!" Surprise widened her eyes. She had never sworn in her life. Then her courage wavered, and her eyes slowly filled with tears. "Don't let her take Orah Delle . . . please, Sloan!"

"Oh, honey." He touched his fingers to her cheeks and gently wiped away the tears. "I'll do anything short of murder to keep her," he said quietly. "But, I wanted you to know the situation." He turned her toward the door. "I'm worried about Pierre. I'm afraid he's lost too much blood. That poor little thing is sitting beside him. I'm wondering how he got himself tangled up with her. She doesn't seem to be his type at all."

"She's in love with him."

"Yes, I know. I wonder how he feels about her. With Ada holding her bond, it could be difficult for them."

They returned to the other room, Cherish to finish the dinner and Sloan to sit with Pierre.

"Cherish could use some help," he told the girl gently.

She stood, still looking at Pierre's motionless face. "He's so still."

"He's lost a lot of blood, but he's strong as a mule. He'll be good as new in a week or two. You'll see." Sloan spoke with a lot more confidence than he felt, but something about the girl—with her thin fingers and haunting eyes—touched him. He thought she looked like a stricken animal. "I'll sit with him. I'll call you if he as much as blinks an eyelid."

The girl approached Cherish hesitantly. She was slightly taller than Cherish, and terribly thin. Her hair was a rich brown with deep waves. Cherish thought her face would be very pretty if it had not looked so tired and worn. Rest and good food would change that. It was her eyes that drew the attention. They were two very large deep pools that seemed to hold all the sadness of the world in their depths. Her dress was faded and almost threadbare, but neat stitches had repaired it and made it wearable. Her shoes were so worn the sides had split. Cherish scolded herself that she had not insisted she take them off. She went to the other room and returned with a pair of moccasins. She handed them to the girl and smiled.

"Pierre was going to make shoes for me," she told Cherish. "Moccasins, he called them."

"Sloan made these for me. They're not fancy, but they're so comfortable and warm." She motioned to the chair. "Put them on and leave your shoes by the hearth to dry."

Cherish spread the cloth on the table and lifted the pewter plates from the shelf. The girl came to help, after first washing her hands in the basin by the door.

"What can I do, ma'am?" she asked shyly.

"First thing you can do is to stop calling me ma'am," Cherish said with a smile. "Call me Cherish."

A look of acute alarm came over the girl's face. "Oh, no! I can't do that. Mistress Carroll wouldn't allow it."

"I requested that you call me Cherish. It has nothing to do with her!" Cherish protested.

"Please—you don't understand." The big brown eyes were actually pleading. "It will make it much easier if you just let me call you ma'am."

Cherish hesitated for a moment. "Well," she said reluctantly, "if it means so much to you. But what shall I call you?"

The girl looked relieved. "My name is Katherine." Her eyes were down as if she were studying something on the floor.

"That's a beautiful name, and it suits you." Cherish glanced over at the woman in the bunk. "Mistress Carroll has been sleeping for a long time."

"She didn't sleep much at all last night. She walked up and down on the boat and worked herself into a tantrum and . . . and she's tired." Katherine's face went blank and she turned away. Cherish didn't have the heart to ask her anything more.

With two pairs of hands working, the dinner was ready faster than Cherish expected. She went to the cellar and brought up berry jam, pickled duck eggs, and pickled fish. Katherine cut the pies and sliced the bread.

The feast was being set on the table when the men came in. They went immediately to the bunk to inquire about Pierre and then to the wash bench. After washing they slicked their hair down with the comb and stood waiting for Cherish to call them to the table. The boy eyed the heavily laden table with disbelief.

"Farrway, you and your grandfather sit on this side. True and Juicy will sit on the other. Katherine, sit beside Juicy."

Katherine moved away from the table to take Sloan's place beside Pierre. Cherish gently took her arm and steered her to a place at the table.

"He's sleeping. You have time to eat," she said kindly but firmly.

"No, ma'am. I'll eat later." Katherine was equally insistent; her eyes had that pleading look again.

"Sit, gal." Juicy's rough voice boomed in her ear and made her jump. "When the lit'l 'un makes up her mind, thar ain't no sense buckin' 'er."

Katherine unwillingly sat down. After Cherish was seated the men took their places.

Sloan went to the bedroom for Orah Delle. He put her into the chair with the high legs, and Cherish tied her there with a rectangle of cloth and sat down again beside her. The child leaned as close to Cherish as she could get and tried to hide her face with her small hands, peeking between her fingers at the strangers at the table.

"Mama—"

"Don't be shy, lovey. Mama's right here beside you."

True brought the turkey to the table and placed it in front of Sloan to carve.

"Sloan, will you say the prayer, or would you rather I did?" Cherish asked.

Across the table of food she had prepared for his guests, their eyes caught. Sloan had a faint smile on his lips and pride in his eyes.

"You do it, sweetheart. This is your first Thanksgiving in your new home."

A joyous warmth spread through Cherish. He had announced to all that she was his sweetheart and this was her home. *First Thanksgiving.* He meant for her to stay here forever. With Orah Delle's hand clasped tightly in hers, she bowed her head.

"Dear God, we thank Thee for Thy goodness and for this bounty spread before us. We thank Thee for good health and loyal friends. We thank Thee for this warm cabin and for Thy protection against our enemies. We pray that Thou will extend Thy mercy to our friend, Pierre. Ease his pain and make him whole again. We ask this in Thy name. Amen."

Cherish looked up and met Sloan's eyes again and found something new. She took a trembling breath for she was sure that what she saw there was abiding love. Her lips curved in a smile, giving her heart away. Love welled up and she had to look away to keep from making a complete fool of herself.

"I never know which end of this thing to start on," Sloan said, with the knife poised over the golden-brown bird. "You're much better at this than I am, True. Why don't you do it?"

"Ya'll do real good. Jist tie inta it," True said. "Hit smells purty. Let's see iffn it tastes purty too."

All eyes were turned expectantly toward Sloan when a sweet, lilting voice called out:

"My baby! Where's my baby? Where's my darlin', darlin' little girl? Bring her to me, Sloan! I've waited so long to hold her."

Ada Carroll was sitting on the edge of the bunk, holding her hands out beseechingly.

CHAPTER
* 17 *

A silence fell over the room—a particularly tense silence. Someone took a deep breath, but no one at the table moved or spoke. Cherish's eyes sought Sloan's. He held her gaze for several seconds, then carefully placed the carving knife and serving fork back on the platter beside the turkey. Slowly and tiredly, he got to his feet.

Ada stood beside the bunk. She had thrown off the cloak. Her dress was wrinkled, her blond hair mussed, her face tear-stained; yet she was the most beautiful woman Cherish had ever seen. Her wide blue eyes clung to Sloan as if he were the only one in the room.

"Sloan, darlin', I'm home! I've come back to you and my baby."

There was another silence as she moved toward him. With an odd little cry, she stretched out her hands and stroked his arms up and down.

"I'm sorry," she said meekly. "I tried to get back

when I heard about . . . Slater. I shouldn't have married him, Sloan, when it was . . . you. It's always been you. But that's all behind me now. I'm back. And I do so want to hold my darlin' little girl."

She stepped quickly around Sloan and before he could move to stop her, her face radiant with a beaming smile, she swooped down on Orah Delle, who was sitting perfectly still for once, her spoon clutched in her chubby little hand. When the strange face appeared before her, blocking her view of Cherish, the child stiffened and then screamed in terror. Ada, disregarding the frantic movements of the tiny arms trying to push her away, continued to hug and kiss her.

Sloan was beside Ada in two strides. His big brown hands grasped her shoulders and yanked her away from the child. Cherish quickly untied the cloth holding Orah Delle to the chair and took her in her arms, snuggling the small body to her, crooning comforting words.

"The child doesn't know you, Ada. And she's frightened," Sloan said harshly. "She isn't used to seeing so many strangers all at once." He added in a more restrained tone, "Let's have dinner. We can talk about it later."

"She doesn't know me? Oh, Sloan! What have I done? My own precious little darlin' doesn't know her own mama!" Ada hid her face in her hands, the picture of utter dejection.

Over Orah Delle's head, Cherish watched the scene. What had started out to be a joyous occasion had turned into a nightmare. The men at the table had not moved a muscle since the woman had uttered her first word. Now one of them let out a breath and Cherish thought she heard him mutter, "Jesus!" She suspected it had come from Mister Swanson.

Cherish had forgotten about Katherine sitting beside Juicy, until Ada looked at her. The beautiful face hardened and the blue eyes went round with horror as if she couldn't believe what she was seeing.

"Kat!" The voice was no longer soft and appealing. "What are you doing sitting at the table with Mister Carroll and his guests. You know better than that. Why didn't you inform him of your status? How dare you fail to tell him that you are my bound girl!"

Cherish's mouth dropped. She was overwhelmed with pity for Katherine, as was everyone at the table. In all her life she had never seen anything so blatantly cruel.

"I was aware of exactly who she was, Ada," Sloan said icily. "She is still welcome at my table."

Ada's hard eyes stayed on Katherine's face though she spoke to Sloan.

"You don't mean that. You don't know anything about this girl." Her eyes swung to him, lingered momentarily, then back to Katherine. "Leave the table, Kat."

Cherish's pity for Katherine gave way to hot, blinding anger. She got to her feet in a rush, Orah Delle still in her arms, and faced the woman over the heads of the men seated at the table in stunned silence. But before she could open her mouth to tell Ada what she thought of her, Sloan spoke quickly.

"I repeat, Ada, we were well aware that the girl was your servant." He moved a chair out from the table. "Come, let's have our dinner."

"I do not eat with thieves!"

"Oh, no!" Katherine's voice was barely a whisper, but it was heard around the table.

"Ada, for God's sake, let it go and sit down!" Sloan's temper was rising and he gritted out the words.

Ada ignored him and turned accusing eyes to Katherine, who sat looking down at her plate, her hands clutched tightly in her lap.

"Six years ago Kat was tried and convicted of stealing. Uncle Robert bought her services for seven years. Deny it, Kat! Deny that you are a convicted thief!"

Katherine looked up as all the heads at the table turned in her direction. Her chin quivered, but she raised it bravely.

"What Mistress Carroll says is true. I was accused by my stepfather of stealing money from his tavern. I . . . we . . . needed the money to buy a warm coat for my mother. We had only been in the country a short while, and she wasn't . . . wasn't well."

Ada smiled cruelly. "A thief is a thief. Leave the table. Now!"

"No! Katherine does not leave this table." Cherish could contain herself no longer. "She is our guest— as you are."

Ada looked directly at Cherish for the first time. Her mouth twitched slightly and her perfectly arched brows lifted as her eyes ran up and down Cherish's body.

"Tut, tut, Sloan. You should know better than to let servants become too familiar. Your nursemaid takes much upon herself." There was a twinge of contempt in her voice.

Cherish's anger blazed anew. Her cheeks were red and her eyes sparkled with inner rage. She had never felt more like attacking someone in all her life. Her fingers itched to scratch this woman's eyes out.

"This is my home! I have cooked this dinner and the people at this table are my guests as well as Sloan's. I will not stand for your outrageous behavior a minute longer." She was breathless when she finished, and too angry to see the fleeting smiles of approval that appeared and disappeared on the faces of the men at the table.

Ada's expression never changed. She gave Cherish a contemptuous glance and turned to Sloan.

"As I said, your nursemaid takes much upon herself. I'm surprised at you, Sloan. *Her* home. *Her* guest. Oh, dear, I fear I've been away far too long. But it's not too late to change things. It will all get straightened out later, but back to Kat. We'll let her decide if it's proper for her to sit at the table and eat with decent folk, shall we? You know you shouldn't be there, don't you, Kat?"

The girl's face was drained of color, her eyes vacant pools. She looked down at her hands. "Yes."

"Look at me when you speak to me. Yes, what?"

"Yes, Mistress Carroll."

"All right, get up. You know your place—or you should by now. I don't know what's come over you, Kat. Really I don't. You've let that Frenchman go to your head."

Katherine got up from the table, her hands trembling so that she almost knocked her plate to the floor. Head bowed, she went to the far end of the room.

Giving Cherish a triumphant look, Ada went to the chair Sloan had pulled out for her and sat down.

Dumbfounded, her heart aching for Katherine, Cherish stood holding Orah Delle. The girl's humiliation was the saddest thing she had ever had to witness.

True unfolded his long lanky frame and stood. "Scuse me, little purty," he said to Cherish, his long face set in disapproving lines. "I'd ruther wait."

"An' me." Juicy's voice boomed out. The table jiggled as he pushed away from it.

"Me and Farrway would be pleased to wait and get the meal with the other gentlemen and the little lady." Mister Swanson and the boy got up and left the table.

Cherish stood silent. When she dared to look at Sloan, she saw that his jaws were clenched and a muscle jerked in his cheek. When his hands reached for the carving knife, she sat down, holding Orah Delle on her lap. She would not have been surprised if Ada had asked her to leave the table and made up her mind that if she did, she would hit her in the face with a pickled fish.

Ada didn't seem to be at all abashed at what she had done. She pushed her blond hair back from her face and smiled at Sloan.

"Now this is the way it should be. You and I . . . and our darlin' baby." She completely ignored Cherish's presence and didn't seem to notice that Sloan paused in his carving. "I do so love the white meat, Sloan. Remember the turkey shoots we had back home?"

Sloan didn't answer and Ada chatted on. "I'm going to rest and get acquainted with my baby. She's going to love her mama. I know now I was too anxious and scared her, but I have been through so much. You'll never know how much I've had to endure and how I regretted having to go back to see

Uncle Robert before he died. But he didn't die, Sloan. That's the sad part. I got stuck there. He wouldn't let me come back. Oh, how I grieved when I heard my darlin' Slater was gone."

Watching Sloan's hands, Cherish saw him grip the carving knife until his knuckles were white. He made a vicious jab at the meat with the fork and continued to carve.

Heartsick, her stomach in such an uproar she was sure it would reject any food she tried to put into it, she prepared Orah Delle's plate and handed the child her spoon.

"I'm going to call my baby Lillian. Orah Delle sounds like the name of some backwoods child. Don't you think it would be fitting to call her Lillian, Sloan? Lillian, after my mother. She so wanted me to marry you instead of Slater. But she would be pleased to know she had a grandchild sired by a Carroll." Ada beamed at the child, ignoring the fact that she was sitting on Cherish's lap. "Lillian looks more like you than like Slater. She could be . . . yours, Sloan."

Cherish didn't miss the little hesitation and glanced quickly at Sloan. He slammed the knife to the table so hard the plates bounced, and Orah Delle whimpered in alarm.

"Her name is Orah Delle, Ada. Orah Delle. Slater named her after our grandmother. Her name will remain Orah Delle." His eyes were cold, his face tight with fury. He was struggling to control himself, and the quiet that came over him made him more dangerous than if he were shouting.

Ada's eyes opened wide. She looked surprised.

"Orah Delle? Well, I never gave it a thought that you would want to name her that, but if that's what you want, Sloan, I guess I'll just have to—"

"Slater, Ada. Slater!" Sloan's voice was deadly quiet. "It's what Slater wanted. He named his child Orah Delle."

"Yes, of course. And you wish to abide by Slater's wishes." Ada spoke soothingly as if to a child.

For Cherish, the meal was a nightmare. She never knew how she managed to get through it. She gave all her attention to Orah Delle, and the child ate happily with someone feeding her.

Ada ate daintily, eating only the slice of turkey breast and the bread. She sniffed disdainfully at the pickled fish, the duck eggs and the Indian pudding. Katherine stood behind her chair and fetched tea when she raised her hand.

Occasionally, Cherish would hear the men talking at the end of the room. True's tangy voice reached her suddenly. He was trying to calm Pierre, who had awakened.

"Yo're gonna be all right, Pierre, iffn ya don't git too rambunctious an' break open the hole them varmints put in ya. Ya already bled like a stuck hog."

Sloan left the table without excusing himself. He went to the bunk where his friend lay.

"The shot went into your side and out your back, Pierre. I don't think it did any real damage, but you've lost a lot of blood and will have to lie still. You can't afford to lose any more."

Pierre's voice was weak when it came and he spoke in French. Sloan answered in the same language. He came to where Katherine stood behind Ada's chair, took her hand and pulled her to the bunk. Pierre lifted his hand up toward her, then it fell limply to the bed. He closed his eyes wearily and spoke to Sloan again in French.

"It will be done, *mon ami*. Sleep now and don't worry."

As soon as Sloan turned Katherine loose she rushed back to stand behind Ada. Sloan took Orah Delle from Cherish.

Ada's eyes glittered and her lips twitched in that odd way again.

"Your friend is wasting his time," she said softly, her voice purring, sensuous. "Uncle Robert gave Kat to me. I hold her bond for another year. If she doesn't serve me well, I can have it renewed for another seven."

Holding the babe in his arms, Sloan looked down at her. When he spoke his voice was quiet, sad.

"I don't think I realized until now just how evil

you are, Ada. I doubt that you've got a decent unselfish bone in your body."

Ada got up from the table, totally composed and smiling. She went to Sloan and brushed her fingertips lightly along his cheek and over his lips. It was a possessive, tender gesture that filled Cherish with dismay and rage.

"Not evil, darlin'. Just practical. A woman alone must be practical."

Ada sat in the fur-lined chair and gazed thoughtfully into the fire. Her expression was soft and wistful, and at that moment she was incredibly lovely. So lovely, it was hard to believe that this was the same woman who had mouthed such insults only a short while ago.

Cherish took away the soiled plates and rearranged the table to make it as festive as possible. The men ate, but not as heartily as she had expected. Katherine ate hardly anything at all. Only the boy, Farrway, ate with relish, as if his young, growing body demanded it.

When the meal was over, True and Juicy, the old man and the boy stayed only long enough to be polite, then prepared to go to the new cabin. While they lingered beside Pierre's bunk, Cherish wrapped several loaves of bread, the pies, the Indian pudding and the remainder of the turkey in the tablecloth and loaded it into Juicy's hands.

"This will get you by tomorrow. I'll make more bread in the morning." She smiled. "It'll take several days before True's stew is fit to eat."

"I ain't shore it'll be fit fer the dogs then." Juicy chuckled, then sobered and put his fingers beneath her chin. "Hit were the best feed I've had in many a year, little purty. Yo're pure-dee ol' hickory, is what ya are."

"Thank you. I'll miss you," she whispered.

"Me'n True'll be jist a holler away."

"I know." Cherish saw Sloan watching her and Juicy and went to the door to say good-bye to Mister Swanson and Farrway.

True offered to come back and sit the night with Pierre. He and Sloan talked it over and decided that Pierre would probably sleep the night through, and Sloan could check on him from time to time.

Cherish put away the remainder of the food stuff. Darkness came suddenly and she lit the lamp. Sitting beside Pierre, Sloan held the sleeping Orah Delle in his arms. Cherish took her to the other room, undressed her, sat her on the chamber pot and urged her to let water. Afterward she put her in her sleeping garment and tucked her in her crib. She loved and kissed her and wondered how such a darling child could have been born to such a woman as Ada.

With the cleanup still to do, Cherish began the chore. Katherine came silently from the shadows to help her. They had been working only a few minutes when Ada spoke from where she sat by the fire, her voice cold and demanding.

"Where are my boxes, Kat?"

The girl jumped nervously. Cherish watched her with a sinking heart.

"They are by the door, Mistress Carroll." Katherine's voice was steady though her chin quivered.

"Take them to the other room. I presume that's where I'll be sleeping."

"Yes, Mistress Carroll." As Katherine passed her, Cherish could see the naked fear in the girl's eyes.

Sloan was there ahead of her when she reached the pile of boxes beside the door. He picked them up, leaving the small satchel for Katherine to carry. Walking purposefully into the bedroom, he set the boxes down heavily on the floor and returned to sit beside Pierre. Katherine stayed in the bedroom.

Perhaps a half-hour passed. Cherish went on with her work, her nerves taut, her stomach churning with tension. Ada sat in the chair by the fire, her feet and legs drawn up under her skirt, her chin resting on the heel of her hand. Presently she got up and walked slowly into the bedroom, closing the door softly behind her.

Cherish felt uneasy being on this side of the closed door with Orah Delle and Katherine on the other side with Ada. Sloan did not seem to notice that she had left the room. He sat in a chair beside Pierre, elbows on his knees, flexing his fingers tensely. Cherish hurried to finish her tasks, thinking that she might have a few minutes alone with him.

From the bedroom she could hear Ada's voice, though not what she was saying. She heard Katherine's brief, "Yes, Mistress Carroll." Then there was silence.

Cherish continued her work. Then suddenly she was jerked quiveringly alert, caught by an odd, steadily repeated sound that she couldn't identify coming from the bedroom. Then she heard a low, agonized moan, and in a moment of horrible revelation, she knew what the sound was. *The regular fall of a strap.*

In seconds she was at the door, but Sloan was already there and had thrown it open. White with a rising fury, he sprang into the room, grabbed the strap from Ada's hand and shoved her hard against the wall. In the flickering light of the candles they saw Katherine on her knees beside the washstand, dressed only in her thin shift, her skirt stuffed in her mouth to muffle her cries, her arms folded to protect her face.

Cherish was beside her in a moment, gently disengaging her arms, lifting her to her feet, murmuring:

"Oh, my dear, my dear. Oh, my dear Katherine."

She turned the girl to face her and her heart rose in her throat. Across Katherine's face, down her cheek and over her lips, was an inch-wide red welt. Her lips had already started to swell. She tried to turn away to hide her shame.

"I'm all right," she whispered frantically. "Please, ma'am, leave me be. It will only make it worse for me if you don't."

Ada was leaning against the wall where Sloan had flung her. She had a smile on her face and her eyes glittered with excitement. Sloan faced her, the strap still in his hand.

"If you ever do such a thing again, Ada, you'll get some of what you were giving that poor girl." His angry voice reverberated about the room.

"I do believe you mean that, darlin'," she purred, her face radiant, her eyes shining.

"I mean it! If you so much as lay a hand on that girl, you'll wish you hadn't."

"You're tempting me, darlin'," she taunted. "You're tempting me to see just how far you would go. Would you beat me?"

Ada was enjoying the situation she had created. Watching her, Cherish had a sick feeling in the pit of her stomach. She shuddered.

Sloan's voice changed, becoming softer—and deadlier.

"No, I wouldn't soil my hands with you. I'd just push you out into the snow and bar the door. It would only take a few hours for you to freeze to death." He tilted his head and looked at her, his eyes as cold as a frozen pond. "Don't fool yourself in believing you'd get any help from the men in the other cabin either. They'd just as soon see you drawn and quartered."

The smile left her face. "A lot of people know I'm here. A lot of people know that I've made this *perilous* journey just to get my child." She walked over to the crib where, luckily, a tired Orah Delle was sleeping. "She's the picture of you, Sloan. The 'spittin' image' as they say." She laughed. "Deny that if you can."

Sloan went to the fireplace and threw the strop in the flames. As he turned to leave the room he spoke in a commanding tone.

"Leave this door open. Do you understand?"

"Of course, darlin'," Ada said sweetly. "In case you want to come to me in the night you don't want a squeaking door to contend with. I can remember when it took much more than a squeaking door to discourage your . . . wanderings." She laughed again as Sloan charged out of the room.

Shaken by what Ada had implied, Cherish went to the wardrobe and took out a clean dress and a baglike sleeping garment she had made for herself, copying from the one the slave woman had made for Orah Delle. With her eyes, she begged Katherine to leave the room with her, but the girl only shook her head.

CHAPTER
* 18 *

C herish finished the cleanup, and when Sloan
put on his coat to go outside, she hurriedly
extinguished the lamp. In the light from the
fireplace she washed herself, used the chamber pot
and prepared for bed.

As she sat on the bunk at the far end of the room
and brushed her hair, her mind whirled with unpleasant thoughts, and her heart filled with jealous suspicion. Had there been something between Sloan and
his brother's wife? She could not believe it, did not
want to believe it. And yet, there was Orah Delle,
who was the mirror image of Sloan. And, of course,
if he'd had an affair with Ada, he would want to hide
it, would not want anyone to know that he had betrayed his brother.

How can a person be so happy one day and so
miserable the next? she asked herself. Now in the
back of her mind she fervently wished she had
agreed to marry Sloan when they met the preacher

on the trail. But, her common sense argued, a few words spoken by a stranger would not hold him if he wished to be with someone else.

Sloan came back into the room, bringing with him the taste of cold tangy air. He hung his coat on the peg and went to the washstand. After washing his face and hands, he took a long drink of water. Cherish watched him take a log from the stack by the wall and drop it on the hot coals. Sparks danced about merrily before disappearing up the chimney.

Cherish didn't dare believe that he would come to her with Ada in the next room, but she hoped that he would, and, by doing so, reassure her, driving the ugly thoughts from her mind. He stood with head bent for a long moment, the picture of utter dejection, then crossed the room to where she sat on the bunk and held out his hand.

He led her to the fur-lined chair, sat down and pulled her down into his lap. Cherish sighed contentedly, worry pushed to the back of her mind for the moment. She lay perfectly still against him and let the pleasure of his warm body, his scent, the safety of his arms flow through her. Nothing else mattered but this. Nothing at all.

He leaned his cheek against her hair and slipped his warm, rough hand inside the sleeve of her robe to caress the smooth skin of her back.

"You were wonderful today. I was proud." His words came out on a breath of a whisper.

"It was . . . difficult."

"I know." He kissed her forehead, his lips lingering there.

"I've never met anyone like . . . her."

"You should be grateful for that."

"I am. Oh, Sloan, how long will she stay?"

"I don't know, love. If a boat comes upriver before the freeze, I'll put her on it, if I have to break both of her legs."

"And if not, she'll be here all winter."

"I'm afraid so."

"Couldn't she stay in . . . the other cabin?"

There was a moment of silence before he spoke. "If I insist that she move over there, she'll take the babe just for spite. Not that she wants her."

"Orah Delle would be frantic. It would be terribly frightening for her. She's not used to strangers. And, I don't think Ada knows how to take care of a baby. Katherine might, if Ada would let her."

"Ada not only doesn't know how, she doesn't want to learn. Give me some time, sweetheart. I'll work something out."

He kissed her nose, then her lips. She moved her arm up and around his neck and clung to him.

"Sloan," she whispered, "I can hardly stand the way she treats Katherine. Can't we do something for the girl? I'm sure she's in love with Pierre."

"He loves her too. He told me so and asked me to

look after her. He called Ada a sow. To a Frenchman that's about as low as a woman can get."

Cherish could feel his chest move against her breasts when he chuckled.

"I can hear him saying that. It would be funny if it weren't so serious."

"We'll not have much time alone now. Let's not waste this time talking about her. Kiss me, sweetheart."

Her mouth lifted to his. He kissed her. And if ever there had been another thought in either of their heads, it was gone the instant their mouths met and clung. Passion surged through them. He drank deeply of her sweetness before he lifted his head and gazed down at her. Cherish let out a little whimper of yearning and reached for his lips again.

He smiled down at her. Her heart stumbled and her mind went blank. His mouth came down. She opened her lips so that he could kiss her the way he had done the night before when they lay closely entwined in her bunk.

Somehow he managed to whisper her name. "Cherish, Cherish, love—"

He caught her bottom lip between his teeth and nipped it gently. Live sparks shot through her when he pinched the tight tip of her breast. Everything he did made her want more, and what she wanted now was for them to lie naked together in her bunk, and for him to fill her with his magnificence.

The ugliness of the day rolled away and was lost. In its place rose a tide of love, strong and sweet—

The moment was abruptly shattered.

"Isn't this sort of thing rather tame for you, Sloan?" Ada's voice, soft and mocking, came out of the shadows.

Cherish felt Sloan's body jerk and stiffen. "Damn!" He took a deep breath and held still.

"Where's the Indian girl? Minnie Dove? Are you tired of her already? Tut, tut, Sloan. Under the bushes and against a tree is more your style than this." She laughed, a false tinkling sound. "When you get tired diddling the nursemaid, you know where you can find someone more accomplished . . . someone who *knows* what you like."

Sloan hadn't moved, hadn't turned his head, hadn't breathed. But his voice, when he spoke, told Cherish he was making an enormous effort at self-control.

"Get out of here, Ada."

The soft laughter came again. "I'm going, darlin'. I'm going. You'll remember what I said . . . won't you?"

They continued to sit by the fire after Ada had gone, but it wasn't the same. Sloan tilted her face up and kissed her soundly, not speaking.

I love you, she told him in her thoughts.

He rested his cheek against hers.

"Sweet Cherish—" he muttered.

She hoped he wouldn't say anything, because if he did she would cry. He didn't. After a while she moved off his lap and went back to her bunk.

Sickening doubts assailed her again, thoughts of what Ada kept hinting about herself and Sloan, and now Sloan and Minnie Dove.

When at last Cherish fell asleep it was to dream of a child and Sloan. This time the child had black button eyes and black braids and wore a beaded Indian dress.

She woke early. Sloan was already up, fully dressed, putting wood on the fire. The flames leaped and snapped and flickered in the darkness of the room. Cherish lay and watched him until he put on his coat and went outside. She swung her feet to the floor and dressed swiftly in the semi-darkness just as the clock finished striking for the fifth time. She lit a candle and took it to the table beside Pierre's bed.

Sloan came in with an armload of wood. "He had a restless night. He needs food."

Cherish thought for a moment. "My papa used to make a broth from fresh meat and feed it to someone who had lost a lot of blood. He called it 'meat tea.' I can make it using the meat in the smokehouse, but I'd rather have fresh."

"I'll get fresh meat, but in the meantime we need to feed him something."

"Do you think he could swallow bread, if I toasted it, buttered it and soaked it in warm milk?"

"He needs something in his stomach. We'll have to give it a try. I'll get yesterday's milk from the cellar. True will milk come daylight."

Pierre grimaced painfully when Sloan placed another pillow under his head. The big Frenchman opened his eyes and looked past Sloan to where Cherish stood with the bowl of bread and milk. His eyes clung to her.

"Katherine—?"

Cherish moved forward and bent down. "Katherine is sleeping, Pierre. How are you feeling?"

It seemed to take all his strength to say: "I'm hungry."

"Good. I'll make a strong meat broth later, but now I want you to eat this."

He made an effort to keep his eyes open while she spooned the soft bread into his mouth, but finally he gave up and closed them. He ate almost all the bread and milk before he fell asleep.

Cherish went to where Sloan stood by the mantel, gazing down at the teakettle he had swung over the flames. "Have you thought of something to do about . . . her?" she asked.

He was silent for so long that Cherish began to feel uncomfortable.

"I've done nothing but think about it the whole night through," he said at last with a deep sigh. "If she goes to the other cabin, she'll take Orah Delle with her. Another thing, she'd have to have a man over there from time to time and . . . through the night to tend the fire. And there's Katherine. I promised Pierre that I would look out for her. I don't know if he's in love with her or not, but he's concerned about her. And after what happened last night it's important that she stay here." He put his arm around Cherish. "It'll be hard on you, and I'm sorry for it. But I just can't let Ada get her hands on Orah Delle. I just can't!"

Cherish nodded unhappily. "I understand. I agree about the baby. We couldn't possibly let her go to Ada."

Sloan pulled her to him and kissed her forehead. "Thank you," he whispered.

Cherish felt a stab of guilt: how could she have doubted him? How could she ever believe that he and Ada—? But even as she asked herself the question, she knew that the suspicion was still there.

Cherish moved around the room as quietly as possible, making tea and mush, setting out bread, butter and molasses. Sloan ate silently, and when he finished, he put on his coat, took his rifle down from the pegs and left the cabin.

When Katherine suddenly appeared beside her, Cherish was so startled she almost dropped the crock she was carrying. The girl glanced fearfully toward the open door of the bedroom before she spoke.

"How is he?"

"Pierre is going to be all right," Cherish assured her. "He ate a bowl of bread and milk this morning, and Sloan has gone out to get fresh meat so I can make him a broth."

"Thank God! And . . . thank you!" She was almost weeping with relief.

"Isn't there anything I can do for you, Katherine?" Cherish asked quickly. "I don't see how you can—"

"There's nothing, ma'am. Please don't try to help me. It just makes her . . . meaner. Pierre was going to get me away from her. He would have, but now— Oh, ma'am, I think she's mad!" She slipped away and was back in the bedroom before Cherish could say more.

The morning was not as unpleasant as Cherish had anticipated. She went into the bedroom and took Orah Delle from her crib the minute she awakened and called to her. She dressed her and had given her her breakfast before Ada appeared. The woman ignored Cherish as if she weren't there and ordered Katherine to serve her meal.

Holding Orah Delle, Cherish went to sit beside Pierre in order to get as far away from Ada as possible. It was obvious to Cherish that Ada had taken special pains with her appearance that morning. Her dress was a soft, finely woven wool that fit snugly at the waist and flared out behind her when she walked. Cream lace edged the high neck and the cuffs that hugged her slim wrists. At her throat was a cameo pinned to a dark-blue velvet ribbon. Her blond hair was piled high on her head, with finger curls cascading down over her ears to frame her face.

She was the loveliest woman Cherish had ever seen. An agony of apprehension seized her. This woman who was so beautiful was also cunning, sly, unscrupulous, and—Cherish was sure—determined to have Sloan.

Katherine stood behind her chair again while Ada daintily picked at her food. She complained about the tea being too strong, and the mush being too thin. The bread was doughy and the butter old, although it had been churned the day before. Cherish bristled at the criticism, then was secretly glad Ada could find fault with the food and secretly prayed that she would detest it so much she would leave.

It was mid-morning when Sloan and Juicy returned, dragging a fresh-killed deer. They dressed the animal and brought a choice cut of venison to Cherish. She cut the meat into small cubes, put it into the heavy iron pot, added salt and several dippers of water, and swung it over the flames to simmer slowly.

True came to check on Pierre and found him sleeping. He warned Cherish to be sure to keep him warm, then left again, ignoring Ada.

The men did not come in for a noon meal. The leftovers from the Thanksgiving feast would be enough for the day. Cherish knew that was not the reason they were staying away, but she said nothing and sent more bread, butter and a crock of honey over to the cabin with Sloan.

By early afternoon the broth was ready. Cherish set a mug of it out in the snow to cool, then sat beside Pierre and spooned it into his mouth. Katherine hadn't come near him all morning, although Cherish had seen her glance his way when Ada's attention was occupied. As Cherish fed Pierre, his eyes searched the room, and they lingered on Katherine's thin figure when she came into view.

He whispered her name.

Cherish bent low and murmured in his ear. "She's all right. Sloan is watching."

Pierre's dark eyes held Cherish's and he nodded, then closed his eyes. Her heart went out to him. She was sure now that he was deeply in love with the bound girl. He must feel so helpless lying there unable to shield the woman he loved from Ada's viciousness.

Ada was being pleasant. She spoke kindly to Katherine, hummed softly to herself and even moved out of Cherish's way when Cherish put bread in the side oven.

Casually she set about winning Orah Delle. She never tried to touch her, but with bribes and song and verse she finally coaxed the child to toddle over to where she sat in the fur-lined chair and lean against her knee. Then, with the cameo as an inducement, Orah Delle allowed Ada to pick her up and set her on her lap. Ada crooned and jostled her, even let her muss her hair.

Her actions seemed so completely out of character that Cherish was baffled. Judging from the look on Katherine's face, Cherish was sure this was something out of the ordinary for Ada to do.

The sight of the child and Ada together was almost more than Cherish could endure. She went so far as to admit to herself that she was jealous and scolded herself for being so petty. And then something happened to make her heart soar.

Ada was talking to the child. "Do you like to play with your mama, darlin'? Your mama will find you some pretty ribbons for your hair."

"Mama!" Orah Delle shrieked and wiggled out of Ada's embrace and off her lap. "Mama! Mama!" She came across the room as fast as her chubby little legs could carry her, seized Cherish's skirt and tried to pull herself up in her arms.

Cherish picked her up and hugged her. "I'm here, lovey."

"Mama girl," Orah Delle said and wrapped her arms around Cherish's neck and looked back at Ada.

"Yes, you're my sweet girl." Cherish kissed her rosy cheek.

"Mama rock," Orah Delle demanded, her arms

tight around Cherish's neck and her little legs about her waist.

"Mama has things to do, but we'll rock for a little while."

She started toward the rocking chair and stopped. Glancing over Orah Delle's head, she saw a look of pure hatred on Ada's no-longer-beautiful face. In a matter of seconds her face had twisted into an ugly mask. The venom that shot from her eyes froze Cherish on the spot.

CHAPTER

* 19 *

A cold chill crept up Cherish's back and her knees began to tremble, yet she looked straight into the hate-filled eyes. When Ada got to her feet and walked toward her, Cherish did not move. A fierce desire not to allow the woman to intimidate her burned in her. Although she was frightened by so much hate, she refused to allow her fear to show.

"Slut!" Ada stopped not a foot from Cherish and spat the word in her face. "The brat may prefer you now. So may Sloan, but not for long. I know him. I've known him all my life. I know what he needs in bed and out. He'll stay with you for a while. You're something new to him. He's not had a backwoods slut before. But in the end, he'll choose me and . . . our daughter."

The heat of anger melted Cherish's fear.

"Call me that name again and I'll scratch your eyes out!" she blurted angrily.

Ada tossed her head contemptuously. "You've just proved what I said. You would never fit with the Carrolls. You have no breeding."

"Breeding! If you are an example of breeding, I'm glad I don't have any."

Orah Delle began to whimper, and Cherish tried to soothe her by swaying back and forth.

"You poor silly little fool. Where did you come from? Certainly not from a respectable family. You look more like the riffraff that lives on the river. Did Sloan pick you up somewhere and feel sorry enough for you to bring you here? So that's it! I can see it in your face. You're as easy to read as you will be to get rid of."

"You may think you know Sloan, Ada," Cherish's voice shook with fury. "But in the end you will be the one to go."

"Don't count on it, nursemaid, whore, river slut—"

Cherish was so angry her eyes burned. If not for having Orah Delle in her arms she would have smashed the woman's hateful face.

"You couldn't be the mother of this sweet child," she shouted. "You're a mean, vicious woman. And if you—"

The door opened.

Sloan stood there looking from one woman to the other. Behind him stood a tall Indian brave with a somber, handsome face.

"What's going on here?" Sloan's eyes slid over

Ada, then back to Cherish, who met his glance in silence. He stepped inside, the Indian after him. After closing the door, he repeated, "What's going on?"

"She told me to go," Ada said pitiously, looking meek and innocent. "She told me to go and leave my baby."

"She did?" Sloan looked at Cherish.

Ada pointed an accusing finger. "She . . . she said you would choose her over me and . . . and our baby."

"Cherish wouldn't say a thing like that."

"Ask her, Sloan! Ask her. If you don't believe me, ask Kat. Kat! Come tell Sloan what this . . . nursemaid said."

"That isn't necessary," Sloan said firmly. "Go to the bedroom, Ada. I want to talk to Cherish."

"Of course, Sloan, honey," Ada purred. "Come, Kat. I need you to rub my back."

Cherish could have cried, but deliberately she raised her eyes to Sloan's. He looked steadily at her a moment, then turned away to remove his coat. Cherish sat Orah Delle down in a chair and gave her a piece of bread.

The Indian who had come in with Sloan had remained standing beside the door. Now Cherish was suddenly conscious of his eyes on her. Blushing, she turned to look at him.

He was tall and handsome, the color of bronze, with midnight-black hair in braids on either side of his strong-boned face. He wore deerskin leggings and fur-lined moccasins. A white fur robe was draped over his broad shoulders. His eyes were dark and fathomless. When they met hers, he did not look away.

"Cherish, this is my brother and friend, John Spotted Elk," Sloan said, coming up behind her. "John, Mistress Cherish Riley."

"I'm honored, Mistress Riley." The Indian's voice was deep and smooth. He spoke English tinged with a faint French accent. He didn't offer his hand to her, but to Sloan, who took it and shook it vigorously. "Your woman is like the morning sun, Light Eyes. Her beauty climbs across the sky to warm your heart." The dark eyes, alight with pleasure, swung back to Cherish. "My brother has chosen well."

Cherish blushed. She could not look at Sloan.

"I'm pleased to meet you, Mister John Spotted Elk. I've heard about a few adventures you and Sloan have had." Her eyes lit up with mischief and she laughed. "I don't know what to call you!"

He looked down at her solemnly for a moment, and then his face brightened with a smile. It was plain that he was fascinated by her.

"Call me John. My mother was French and refused to call me anything but John."

"That's a relief!" Cherish laughed again. "And you must call me Cherish."

"Cherishe." He gave the name a French pronunciation.

"That's near enough." Sloan was amused. "Leave your robe there on a peg and come look at Pierre."

Cherish stepped aside to let John pass. He was so tall, she felt like a child beside him. The confrontation with Ada had left her shaken, but it was almost forgotten in the pleasure of meeting Sloan's Indian friend.

John went to squat down beside Pierre's bunk. The Frenchman was awake, and it was clear the two men had a strong liking for each other. They conversed in French, in low tones, then John removed Pierre's bandages so he could examine the wound.

Sloan carried the blood-soaked bandages to a bucket of water beside the washstand while John looked closely at the wound, then leaned over to smell it. Finally he nodded approval.

Cherish handed clean bandages to Sloan, then moved back out of the way so they could wrap Pierre's midsection with the linen. When they had finished, John knelt beside the bunk and continued to talk to Pierre. Sloan joined her at the worktable.

"We're taking Pierre to the other cabin so True can look after him," Sloan told her.

She was surprised at that. "Do you think it's safe to move him?"

"I think so. It isn't that you haven't done a good job caring for him. It's other things. He has to be washed and he has to . . . relieve himself. And, well, he wants to go. He thinks it would make things easier for Katherine."

"It might at that," Cherish agreed. Then, wishing to ease the tension between them over what had passed between her and Ada, she said: "Sloan, about . . . Ada . . . what I said was—"

He cut her off. "We'll not talk about it now. I can imagine what Ada said to you. But try not to irritate her . . . please." To her utter amazement, he walked away.

Cherish sat quietly, her heart heavy, while they prepared to move Pierre. John Spotted Elk went out and returned with a litter. He put this on the floor alongside the bunk. After wrapping Pierre in a heavy fur robe, and being careful not to break open his wound, they gently lifted him to the litter. He lay with his eyes closed, weary from the exertion.

Cherish felt John Spotted Elk's eyes on her again. She was used to being looked at, but there was something about the intensity of the Indian's dark gaze that made her immediately aware each time his eyes found her. Not looking at him, she went to where Pierre lay and knelt down.

"I'll look after Katherine," she whispered. "Don't worry."

His eyes opened. He whispered weakly: "Tell her . . . I love her, *chérie*."

Her eyes brightened with tears. She kissed his whiskered cheek. "I'll tell her."

When she stood, Sloan and John were looking at her curiously. She smiled at them.

"Good-bye, John." She held out her hand.

He scarcely touched her fingers before releasing them.

"Not *good-bye,* Morning Sun." His eyes held hers for a long moment before he bent to pick up the litter.

As she held the cabin door open for them, Cherish noticed smoke coming from the Shawnee lodge and horses tied under the trees. Indian women were moving supplies into the lodge. She looked at the broad back of John Spotted Elk. These must be his people. Before closing the door, she looked at the women again and wondered if one of them was Minnie Dove, John Spotted Elk's sister.

Cherish hated being alone in the cabin with Ada and Katherine and decided busy hands were the best solution. She tied Orah Delle in the high chair and moved her close to the table so she could play with the small animal figures True had carved and polished for her. For the next couple of hours, Cherish worked, keeping her mind as blank as possible.

She made another batch of bread and set it aside to rise. She scrubbed the workbench and the trestle table, put cabbage and bacon in the pot to boil. She changed the bed linen on the bunk where Pierre had lain and rolled his clothes and personal things into his heavy coat, leaving the bundle by the door for Sloan to take to the other cabin.

In all this time, she hadn't heard a sound from the bedroom. When Ada came up behind her and spoke, Cherish was so startled her heart jumped.

"Well," Ada said. "I trust you've learned your lesson and know your place."

Don't irritate her. Sloan's words popped into Cherish's mind and she didn't answer. Instead she went to the contraption True had made for her to set beside her chair. It was a three-legged tripod supporting a deerskin bag. She took her knitting from it and, ignoring Ada completely, began to knit.

Ada went on talking. "So John Spotted Elk and his sister are moving into the lodge. That will make it handy for Sloan. And you, nursemaid? Have you ever fornicated with an Indian? That John Spotted Elk is an attractive stud. He's half-French, you know. I bet he'd be a demon in bed. I'd like to try him. I'm sure he wouldn't say no. But then Sloan could never say no, either."

Cherish's silence did not bother Ada. She wandered about the room and talked about the things she and Slater and Sloan had done when they were young . . . how the two brothers had vied for her favors.

"Slater was always jealous of Sloan. And Sloan was randy as a billy goat." Ada laughed as if remembering. "He wasn't at all discreet in his affairs. I caught him with one of my friends and just for spite I married Slater."

Ada went to the window. "Minnie Dove has had her eye on Sloan since the day he came here. She's the chief's daughter, you know. I've caught them together more than once . . . swimming naked in the river, lying under the willows—"

Cherish tried to close her ears to the words, knowing that the woman was deliberately trying to provoke her. What she said about Sloan and the Indian girl cut into Cherish like a knife. Oddly enough, it also bothered her to think of Ada with John Spotted Elk.

The day passed with dreadful slowness. Cherish wanted to put on her shawl and go out into the fresh air, but she was afraid to leave Orah Delle and Katherine alone with Ada. Ada made sure that Cherish and Katherine didn't get a chance to speak to each other. She knew that Katherine was anxious to hear about Pierre, and Cherish suspected that Ada was enjoying prolonging Katherine's anxiety as long as possible.

The evening was disastrous as far as Cherish was concerned. She felt uncomfortable sitting at the table with Sloan and Ada while Katherine stood behind Ada's chair. She would have preferred to wait and eat with the bound girl, but she wouldn't give Ada satisfaction by demoting herself to the status of a servant.

Cherish ate sparingly, tending to Orah Delle's needs and listening to the trivial chatter between Sloan and the woman who wanted him. She was baffled by Sloan's attitude . . . and disappointed. He talked with Ada about people and places they both knew, making no attempt to draw Cherish into the conversation. Although she laughingly coaxed Orah Delle to eat, Cherish's spirits sank lower and lower. As soon as the child finished the last bite, she took her from the table without as much as a word to Sloan and went to the bedroom.

After washing the child, she dressed her for bed, then sat with her in the rocking chair before the fire. Ada had taken over this room she had enjoyed. Her robe was draped over the end of Cherish's bed, her boxes lined the wall, her brushes, combs and mirror sat on the table beside the wardrobe along with a selection of perfumes and powders.

Cherish tried not to allow her thoughts to dwell on Sloan and Ada, only on this small bundle she held in her arms. This baby needed her to stand between her and the mother who did not love her, but only wanted to use her to get the man she lusted for. When Orah Delle was asleep, Cherish tucked her into her crib, gently kissed her rosy cheeks and reluctantly returned to the other room.

Sloan and Ada sat in the chairs before the fire. Katherine was sitting at the workbench with a plate of food. When Cherish began to clear the table,

Sloan brought the heavy copper kettle from the fireplace and poured hot water into the basin for her. She murmured "thanks" without looking at him. He replaced the kettle and sat down again, picking up the conversation with Ada. At that moment, Cherish would have enjoyed tipping the water over both of them.

Katherine finished her meal and moved to help Cherish, but Ada's voice stopped the girl.

"Kat, I need you to mend the shawl you tore on the boat coming down. I will want it tomorrow, so you must work on it tonight." Her tone was sweet, as if she were talking to a friend. The hypocrisy of it turned Cherish's stomach. Her gaze flew to Sloan to see if he had noticed, but he was staring into the fire.

Cherish took unnecessarily long with the cleanup. The two before the fire disturbed her almost more than she could endure. When she finished, she lit a candle and, knowing it would irritate Ada, carried it into the bedroom, where Katherine was trying to mend the shawl by the light of the fire.

"It's foolish for you to have to sit in here doing that by the light of the fire. You'll strain your eyes." She spoke loudly enough to be sure her voice carried to Ada. After she put the candle down, she leaned over to whisper:

"Pierre asked me to tell you that he loves you. He thought it would make things easier for you if he went to the other cabin. He'll find a way to get you away from her. Don't worry. I'm happy for you, Katherine. Pierre's a good man."

"Thank you," Katherine murmured, tears glittering in her eyes.

Cherish squeezed her hand, then returned to the other room and picked up her knitting.

"Do you remember when your father caught you and me and Slater swimming naked in the creek, Sloan?" Ada's voice was light, and there was such a spiteful gleam in her eyes as she looked at Cherish. Cherish was amazed that Sloan didn't see it. She almost hated him when he laughed.

"Yes, and I remember the feel of the willow switch on my bare backside."

Cherish's stomach churned. Ada was working to re-establish the relationship she and Sloan had had as children. Chaining him to the past would make it more difficult for him to cast her off in the future.

Ada's trilling laughter filled the room. "Just the other day I was thinking about the first time Mama let me wear a lace chemise. It was so pretty and didn't hide much. The first chance I got, I put on my wrapper and ran to find you and Slater so I could show you. You made me think you didn't want to look, but you and Slater each got an eyeful. Was it you who wanted to touch my breasts or was it Slater?"

Sitting by the table, knitting furiously, Cherish wished fervently the evening would end.

Finally, Ada stood, stretching her arms up over her head, moving her body seductively. Going to Sloan, she trailed her fingers lightly along the side of his face.

"This has been nice, Sloan, darlin'. It reminds me of the times you and I and Slater used to sit and talk. I'm looking forward to more evenings like this." She twirled around as if she were dancing. "Goodnight."

The silence was deep when she left the room. Soon she was talking loudly, but kindly, to Katherine, making sure the two people in the other room would remain aware that they were not alone. Every now and then she would come to the doorway and call out something inconsequential to Sloan.

Cherish put away her knitting, blew out the candle, and went to the bunk at the end of the room, the one she had occupied the night before. With her back to Sloan, she undressed and slipped into her nightclothes. Taking down her hair, she left it hanging in a cloud about her shoulders and got into the bed. She pulled the covers up to her chin and lay stiff with misery.

Only the candle on the mantel was left burning. Sloan got up and pinched out the flame. Cherish held her breath, although she knew he wouldn't come to her until all activity in the adjoining room ceased, if he came at all. He sat back down, stretched out his long legs and leaned his head against the back of the chair.

Anger at Ada for her scheming beat through Cherish. She wanted to cry, but the tears wouldn't come. She lay dry-eyed, staring into the orange flame of the fire across the room.

Later, as she lay in the void between sleep and wakefulness, he came to her. She felt his hand on her breast.

"No, Sloan," she said firmly. His hand went rigid and dropped away from her. He eased himself off the bunk, and she heard his bare feet padding across the floor and the squeak of the ropes as he lowered his weight onto the other bunk.

Only then did she realize what she had done. She had allowed Ada to drive a wedge of suspicion into her mind, so that she had failed to use the only weapons she had: her love for him and the comfort he received from her body. She had not only hurt him, but herself. She moaned softly in despair, longing to call him back to her, but she dared not, afraid he would reject her.

She wept at last.

CHAPTER
* 20 *

Sloan behaved as usual the next morning. As Cherish prepared breakfast, he talked easily about John Spotted Elk and the Shawnee who had moved into the lodge.

"They may be here a month and they may stay until spring," he said in answer to Cherish's question. "I'm glad they're here. There's a lot of unrest among the tribes this winter, and the river renegades seem to be getting bolder."

"I was surprised to hear John speak such good English."

Sloan smiled. "His French is just as good as his English, and a lot better than mine, although my mother was French also. John's mother was well educated and she persuaded the chief to send John to school in Pennsylvania, besides teaching him herself."

"How did she happen to marry John's father?" Cherish asked.

"I don't know how old Chief Running Elk came to marry her. I'm guessing that she was a captive and he bought her from another chief, but I'm not sure. They were probably married according to Indian custom. From what John tells me she was content with her lot."

"I think it would be hard to adjust to a whole new set of rules and customs."

"Maybe she adjusted out of necessity. Sometimes whites are not kind to a woman after she has been captured and lived for a while with the Indians."

"I've heard that," Cherish murmured, then asked: "How did you and John become such good friends?"

Sloan grinned. "It took a while. He was on the council that made the decision to let me have this land. In fact, he helped persuade them to agree to it. He believed that I could be trusted not to open up the land to a rush of settlers who would force his people farther west, away from their hunting grounds." He carried the heavy teakettle from the fireplace to the table and poured the hot water in the crockery pitcher to make the tea. "That was four years ago. We've hunted together, fought together, and one time almost died together when we were captured by the Hurons. We learned to like and respect each other."

"Well, I'd think so . . . after all that."

Ada came in. Katherine scurried along behind her. Ada was wearing a light, revealing wrapper over a nightdress that showed the upper part of her breasts.

Her blond hair hung loose about her neck and shoulders. She looked seductive, which was her intention.

"Mornin', Sloan."

"Mornin'."

She smiled prettily. "How's my darlin' baby this mornin'?" She held her arms out to Orah Delle, and when the child cringed, she sighed dramatically. "It just breaks my heart . . . that my baby doesn't know me." She sat down at the table. "Get my tea, Katherine. Oh, my, what I wouldn't give for some grits like Mammy Vinnie used to make. I heard that she died. That . . . Frenchman told me. Poor Vinnie, she hated it here anyway."

Sloan ate his meal without speaking. Cherish fed Orah Delle. Katherine served Ada and then stood behind her chair. When Sloan finished, he put on his coat.

"Sloan—" Ada rose quickly from the table and went to him. She circled his arm with her two hands. "It's so crowded here. Why don't you open up the other cabin and let the nursemaid take care of the baby over there. It's going to be a long winter—"

Cherish felt her heart thump painfully while she waited for Sloan's answer.

He looked down at Ada for a long time, then loosened his arm from her grasp.

"Cherish and Orah Delle stay right here in this cabin, Ada. If you want quiet you go over there, but Orah Delle stays here. Do I make myself clear?"

Ada sighed prettily. "Darlin', you always were so stubborn. I was afraid you'd say that. Well, where are you going now?"

"I'm going to see about Pierre."

"Hurry back . . . will you?"

As soon as Sloan was out the door, all pretense was over. Ada turned on Katherine.

"Come fix my hair, you lazy slut. That is, if you can get your mind off that damned Frenchman. I wish to hell they'd killed the interfering bastard."

Cherish turned her head and closed her eyes until the two women left the room. Ada's behavior continued to shock her, yet she marveled at the woman's ability to switch from one personality to the other so quickly. *The gall of that woman to suggest that she and Orah Delle move to the other cabin!*

Ada was determined to have Sloan. Would he be able to hold out against her? And if he tried to send her away, would she take Orah Delle?

To keep occupied, Cherish got out the butter churn, made a quick trip to the cellar, poured the accumulated cream into the churn, and began to work the dasher. She kept Orah Delle entertained by singing little tunes to the rhythm of the up-and-down motion.

Sloan came in with a fresh bucket of milk to be strained. He set it on the bench and left again with the two water buckets. He returned with the water, went out again and came back with an armload of wood. Each time he lingered a few minutes, as if he wanted to say something to her. Ada was in and out of the room on the pretext of picking up something or returning something, and he remained silent.

Later, with Orah Delle playing happily on the floor and Ada and Katherine in the bedroom, Cherish stood before the window and brushed her hair. Looking out toward the Shawnee lodge, she saw a girl come out and stand waiting at the corner of the building. She was young and dressed entirely in buckskin. Her hair was raven-black and parted in the middle. Two long braids entwined with brightly colored ribbon hung down over her breasts. Cherish knew instinctively that the girl was Minnie Dove, John Spotted Elk's sister.

Cherish was about to move away from the window when she saw Sloan coming from the other side of the lodge. The girl moved around so that he had to pass within a few feet of where she stood and waited. She must have called out to him, for he stopped and waited for her to catch up. They talked, and Cherish saw her tug pleadingly at his sleeve. Finally Sloan allowed her to lead him to the back of the building, but still where Cherish could see them. Once there, the girl threw her arms around Sloan in what looked like a passionate embrace.

Shaken, her heart aching, Cherish could not make herself turn away.

Sloan tried to free himself from the girl's embrace.

When he finally succeeded and held her away from him, she appeared to be pleading with him. She broke away, angry now, and tried to hit him. He pushed her aside, and she ran to the front of the lodge and disappeared.

Cherish didn't know what to think about the scene she had just witnessed. Had Sloan encouraged the Indian girl, played with her affection, then cast her aside? It didn't seem likely a girl would declare her love so openly without some sign that her affection was returned.

Later, with Orah Delle tied in her chair and playing happily with her wooden toys, Cherish put on Sloan's old coat and stepped outside to get an armload of kindling. She came face to face with John Spotted Elk. Startled, unsure what to say, she smiled.

He was a tall, handsome man. She felt dwarfed beside him. He wore a buckskin shirt with the tail outside and belted at the waist. Fringed leather pants and knee-high moccasins encased his legs. Two thick braids hung over his shoulders to his chest. His deepset, licorice-black eyes looked intently into hers. He stood silently, seemingly unaware of the cold.

"Had I found you first, you would be my woman." He reached out a hand and lightly touched her hair. "Morning Sun. Morning Sun." He repeated her name softly. "You are very beautiful."

Cherish stood still, her eyes locked with his. She was not in the least afraid.

"You, too, are beautiful, John Spotted Elk."

"We would have made beautiful children."

Her eyes twinkled. "I've not seen a red-headed Indian."

He smiled. "It would be a sight to see, would it not?" His smile faded. "You are Light Eyes' woman. If ever he is not there to protect you, I will be."

"I am most grateful that you take responsibility for your friend's woman."

"Walk with care, Morning Sun. The woman within your lodge is a serpent." He turned and walked away.

She watched him until he entered the lodge, then went back into the cabin, wondering at his words.

The noon meal was on the table and the tea poured when Sloan came in. Like magic, Ada appeared and, as usual, monopolized the conversation. Cherish had so much to think about that it was a relief not to have to converse with them. The scene was a repeat of last evening's meal, and she longed for it to be over.

Sloan tried to catch her eyes as he put his coat on to leave again, but she avoided him. She heard him tell Ada that he'd not be back until suppertime. Cherish knew that would be well after dark.

Ada and Katherine returned to the bedroom, leaving Cherish with the washing up and other tasks. When they were finished she sat in the rocking chair with Orah Delle. She was determined to get out of the house this afternoon, if only for an hour. While rocking she planned. She would put the child to sleep in her own bunk in the main room with a chair to guard the side to keep her from falling. She would ask Katherine to watch her. Not even Ada could object to that.

She rocked the baby until she was sleeping soundly, then settled her in the bunk. Gently she brushed the dark curls from the chubby cheeks and tucked the covers around her. Feeling better now that she had a chance to get out for a while, she slipped her feet into her moccasins and tied them securely about her ankles. Wrapping her shawl over her head and about her shoulders, she took the blanket she had worn on the trail from the foot of her bunk and draped it over her head, then walked with determination to the bedroom door.

Ada was lying on her bunk. Katherine was sewing by the fire.

"I'm going out for a while, Katherine. The baby is asleep. Will you keep an eye on her, please?" Not waiting for an answer, or for Ada to object, she walked quickly to the door and let herself out into the crisp, cold air.

One of the places she wanted to go was to the barn. It was a joy to see the milch cow. She was so big, gentle and warm. But first she wanted to visit Pierre. She hoped that Sloan would not be there. She wasn't quite sure how she was going to respond when they met at last out from under Ada's watchful eyes.

It was wonderful to be out in the fresh air. There was a little wind and it stirred the snow restlessly. She looked around for Brown. Usually the dog came running when he saw her, but he was nowhere to be seen.

At the door of the new cabin, she rapped, and she heard True yell:

"Come on in. Figured hit was ya a knockin'," he said as soon as she opened the door.

"How is Pierre?"

"Must be doin' a'right. He been complainin' 'bout thin's. Sleepin' now."

"This is the first chance I've had to come see him—" Cherish's voice trailed. She stood just inside the door. "I just thought I'd run over."

"Ya holdin' up a'right?" True's long face took on a worried look.

"I'm doing my best," Cherish laughed nervously.

"Hit's a pity she come is what it is. Her ain't worth one hair on yore purty head, to my way of thinkin'."

"Well, thank you, True. Guess I'd better go. I've missed you and Juicy." Feeling her eyes begin to tear, she opened the door and hurried out. She stood for a moment and then slowly walked toward the barn.

The snow was soft, easy to walk in, and didn't come up to the top of her moccasins. She was glad the barn was to the rear of the cabin, for she wouldn't be so likely to be seen. A meeting with Sloan was the last thing in the world she wanted at the moment.

She reached the barn and opened the heavy door just a crack and slipped inside. It was larger than it appeared from the outside and was divided in sections. One part was for the cow, which eyed her dreamily while chewing its cud, and there were three stalls for the horses Sloan hoped to bring out from Virginia someday. Loose hay was piled around the sides of the barn for warmth.

Cherish went into the corner to lean against the animal's side and pat her bony back. She heard a rustling in the hay and thought perhaps there might be a barn cat. But as she walked out of the cow's stall to investigate, she gasped in surprise.

Standing between her and the door were two men. She thought immediately of the trappers, Mote and Seth, who had hounded her along the Kentucky River. She could tell at a glance that these men were the same type, and that they were here to do her harm. Before she could make a sound, a rough hand was clapped over her mouth. She struggled with all her might, but, hampered by the blanket she wore, she offered little resistance.

"This ain't the gal," one of the men said.

"This'n purtier."

"What we gonna do?"

"We come to get a gal, and this'n'll do jist fine."

Cherish was more frightened than she had ever been in her life. How could this be happening so quickly and so close to the cabin?

Sloan! Sloan! Please come!

Almost out of her mind with fear, she struggled. The man holding her swung her roughly about. His hand left her mouth, but the instant it did, the other man filled it with a dirty rag. Cherish gagged as the rag was tied tightly in place.

Now that she was silenced, the men looked her over closely. One lifted the blanket and ran his hand down over her breast. She struck out at him and he grinned. It was an evil thing to see. Both men were fairly young, their faces scarred from many fights and their eyes bloodshot and watery from either drink or lack of sleep. They wore the clothing of river men: heavy woolen coats with knit caps on their heads. Cherish suddenly realized that they must be the renegades who had followed Mister Swanson's boat; the men Ada had teased, the men who had shot Pierre.

"We got what we come fer. Let's go. I took to the river to git outta barns, and here I be stayin' in one most of two days and a night jist to get a gal." The man who spoke had two front teeth missing. He spit through the gap. "Iffn them Injin bastards found ol' Finger and the boat, we're gonna be sittin' in shit up to our necks."

"'Aven't you got no con-fee-dence, 'Arry?" The

other man had a Cockney accent that betrayed the fact that he was British. "The bloody boat 'n' Finger'll be there."

"If he ain't, I'm a makin' 'im a new asshole."

"And if he is, 'Arry, I be gettin' the wench first."

"Open up the winder back thar. I'll tie up the gal's hands."

Cherish's heart quaked with fear. She hadn't realized there was a way to get out of the back of the barn. Her fear gave her strength and she began to struggle anew. Finally the man with the missing teeth put his hands over her nostrils and cut off her air. She slumped long enough for him to bind her hands under the blanket.

"She's a fine-bodied wench," the Cockney said. "Spirited too . . . I likes 'em fightin'. I'll go up and over. You boost 'er through."

He went through the opening, and Cherish knew this was her one chance. Quickly she brought her knee up between her captor's legs. The heaviness of the blanket and the man's coat softened the blow and only made him angry. His fist lashed out and connected with her jaw. Lights flashed before her eyes and she knew no more.

CHAPTER

* 21 *

Sloan sat on the buffalo robes that had been placed in a circle around the fire in the Shawnee lodge. John Spotted Elk's father, Chief Running Elk, passed the ceremonial pipe to Sloan, who drew the sweet tobacco smoke into his mouth before passing the pipe to John. The father, who was greatly loved and respected by his son, was very old. They sat in silence, and soon the old man was nodding sleepily before the fire.

"Why has your brother's wife returned?" John Spotted Elk asked when his father had at last fallen asleep, his chin resting on what had once been a strong and powerful chest. His son would not have dishonored him by speaking of these things which he did not understand in his presence.

"She says she's come back for the babe," Sloan replied slowly.

John Spotted Elk smiled without warmth. "She lies."

"Yes, I'm afraid so. She has no love for the babe," Sloan said sadly.

"What will you do, Light Eyes? She wants to be your woman."

"I know that."

"You said Morning Sun was your woman."

"I have not wed her in the white man's ways."

John Spotted Elk snorted with disgust. "You've taken her to your blanket. Is that not enough?"

"For me it is."

"And for her?"

"She says she loves me."

"Send the yellow-haired woman away."

"If I do that, she'll take the babe."

John Spotted Elk looked thoughtful, then said, simply, "I will kill her."

Sloan looked up quickly. "No, John. That is not my way. I have a plan to send her downriver."

"It would be easier to kill her, than send her downriver. She is worthless."

"I'll give her money and send her to New Orleans. She likes fancy places, and she may go. It will give me time to get a paper saying that I am the child's guardian."

John Spotted Elk puffed solemnly on the pipe before speaking. "It would be good for you to get the paper."

Running Elk's wife came and draped a robe about the humped back of her sleeping husband. She was fat and her broad face was pleasant. Her hands lingered on the shoulders of the old man. She was Running Elk's third wife and John's stepmother. He smiled fondly at her as she moved away.

When they were alone again except for the sleeping man, John laid the pipe down in front of him. His expression was unreadable, but Sloan knew him well enough to know he had something on his mind.

"I have a desire to talk of my sister."

Sloan nodded and waited.

"It is embarrassing to me, Light Eyes, that she pursues you. Her white blood is strong. She is possessed with the wish to marry a white man—be like a white woman."

"Your sister is very beautiful," Sloan said earnestly.

"She is young. She has not yet learned the foolishness of such a wish."

"If she went to the white man's village, she would be desired by many white men, but she would not be happy with the white man's way."

"I have told her that."

"Here, she is the daughter of Chief Running Elk and the sister of a great warrior. There she would be just another Indian maid."

"To be shunned by people of class."

Sloan ignored the bitterness in his friend's voice.

"I have given thought to Minnie Dove. I would like her to become friends with Morning Sun." Sloan used John's name for Cherish deliberately. His eyes twinkled. "It would be a thing to see."

John Spotted Elk failed to see humor in the situation.

"It would be best that Morning Sun know that Minnie Dove is . . . determined to have you for her man."

"We would take care to not leave them alone for a while. I will talk to Morning Sun. I will tell her of Minnie Dove's desire to wed a white man, and I will ask her to discourage it by teaching your sister the white woman's ways."

"I do not understand."

Sloan chuckled at the puzzled look on his friend's face.

"I will ask Morning Sun to lace Minnie Dove in a tight corset, put tight shoes on her feet, and make her sit still for hours while her hair is arranged. Above all, she must insist Minnie Dove take a tub bath every day."

John laughed. "Light Eyes, your way may indeed restore her pride in her Indian blood."

"She is young enough yet to be molded, my friend," Sloan said. "She will be what she was meant to be—a beautiful, proud Indian maiden."

John Spotted Elk smiled broadly, his teeth flashing in the failing light of the fire. He dropped a hand on Sloan's knee.

"My brother, you bring me hope. Would that I had

spoken sooner. But tell me of the woman, Morning Sun. She is fair to look upon."

Sloan's face clouded. In a quiet, husky voice he answered: "I first saw her kneeling beside a stream in the woods. I thought she was a vision that I had conjured up from a dream in my head."

"She is indeed beautiful."

"The most beautiful woman I have ever seen. Because of my experiences with beautiful women, I would prefer her not to be so fair."

"You think she will betray you?"

"No. It didn't take long for me to realize that she was no ordinary beautiful woman, but one with courage, pride and determination. On the trail, I grew . . . fond of her."

They were quiet then. John Spotted Elk studied his friend's face in the soft glow of the firelight. His eyes narrowed.

"You are only fond of her?" he asked, so seriously that Sloan glanced curiously at him.

"I am troubled, John. She may very well be my dearest possession, but I want my heart to be free." Sloan's eyes filled with sadness. "I don't want my heart to break if she should leave me. I don't want my thoughts and dreams and happiness to depend on a slip of a girl. You see how it is, my friend?"

John Spotted Elk leaned back, picked up the pipe and puffed on it, then handed it to Sloan.

"You think of your brother." His dark eyes met Sloan's light ones and he held the gaze.

"My brother loved Ada all his life. He lived to be with her even though he knew that she was a selfish, deceitful woman. He believed the babe would change her. When she left him and the babe, it killed him."

"In my village she would be cast out . . . stoned. Not even a wolverine deserts her cubs," he added.

They sat quietly and smoked. Sloan's thoughts were of Cherish and how he missed the sweet intimacy they had shared before Ada arrived. John Spotted Elk broke into his thoughts.

"I would speak to you about Morning Sun."

Sloan looked at his friend and nodded his head ever so slightly.

"I want you to know that my white blood calls out to her, but I am wiser than my sister. Your woman would not be content with the Indian way, and I would not see her unhappy."

For some reason unknown to him, Sloan was not surprised. "I am honored that you speak of it to me."

"She will bring you great joy if you open your heart."

"You cannot command the heart to open, my friend. It will open when the time is right."

"I understand."

"It is good to know that, should I be killed, Morning Sun would have a protector."

"I would guard her life as if it were my own ... as I would yours," John said gravely.

Sloan got to his feet. "It is late. I want to stop by and see Pierre, so I will leave you." Sloan held out his hand. "I know where there is a salt lick. A deer can be found there if your people need meat."

John Spotted Elk's face broke into a smile. "We will hunt on the morrow."

On the way to True's and Juicy's cabin, Sloan thought about what John had told him. He was attracted to Cherish, and being the man he was, he had felt duty-bound to tell him. Sloan had sensed his interest when John and Cherish had met. Now he found himself wondering if Cherish might not also be drawn to the tall, handsome Shawnee. His heart gave a queer lurch at the thought.

Life had been difficult for her since Ada's arrival; nevertheless, Cherish's rejection of him the night he went to her bunk had hurt. Tonight he would go to her again, he decided, and tell her of his plan for Ada.

The cabin smelled of new wood, sizzling meat, and tobacco smoke. True was whittling, as usual, and Juicy was entertaining Farrway with some wild tale. The boy sat big-eyed in rapt attention. Mister Swanson was grinning, his rough hands working the stiff fibers of a rope he was repairing.

"*Mon Dieu*, Sloan," Pierre said weakly. He was cleanshaven and had a fresh haircut. "I am glad to see you. Tell these hide scrapers, I can take no more broth. Meat is what I need. Meat!"

"Tell them yourself." Sloan laughed. "I've not known you to keep your mouth shut when you had something to say."

Pierre rolled his eyes in disgust and mumbled to himself.

"I jist don't know about Pierre no more, Sloan," Juicy said. "He warshed in the summer. I know he did, 'cause I seen it with my own eyes. We had to tote water so he could do it agin. Do ya reckon he's sparkin' a gal?"

True snorted. "Ain't no gal worth her salt have anythin' to do with a bow-legged Frenchie."

"Don't know 'bout it, True." Juicy scratched his whiskered chin. "He could get out that thar squeeze box and play her a tune. Could even sing her a ditty."

"Sing? Him? Heard him onc't. I done thought somebody's scalded a cat."

Pierre took the teasing with good grace. He looked younger without the beard, and his eyes were getting some of their old sparkle back.

Sloan grinned. "You're better off than me, Pierre. You've got three old goats and a kid. I've got three women and a babe in my cabin."

Pierre scowled. "One of them is a bitch, Sloan. A she-devil." His voice shook with anger.

"I know, and I promise you that when Ada leaves it will be without Katherine," Sloan said firmly.

"Oui, oui, Sloan." Pierre sank back weakly, plainly relieved by the promise.

"How's the little purty doin'?" Juicy asked.

"She's doing all right."

"She be lookin' right peaked." True had a worried look on his face.

"She's not said anything about being sick," Sloan said with a frown. "She needs to get out some. I'll see to it tomorrow."

True unfolded his long, lanky frame from his chair and motioned to Sloan, who followed him to the back door. Brown lay there with his big head on the floor, his nose to the cold air blowing in under the door.

"I'm afeared Brown here is ailin'. He won't eat no meat an' don't walk no straight line no more either. He kinda staggers like. I be thinkin' that thar Injin arrow did somethin' to his head."

Kneeling beside the dog, Sloan felt a stab of fear. Brown had been with him a long time, had saved his life more than once, had led him and Cherish through the blizzard to the cabin and safety.

"Did he go out at all today?"

"Onc't ta do his needs. Wanted back in."

"What can we do, True?"

"Wal, I figur' ta wait till mornin' an' see. Hit could be thar's nothin' we can do. Could be pus from the sore is pressin' on his brains. I ain't knowin' 'bout splittin' his head ta let it out." He shook his head. They all had a fondness for the big brown dog. "We best not do nothin' yet."

It was dark when Sloan left the cabin. The wind had come up and was swirling the light snow on the ground. It had started to drift into piles, and he kicked his way through it thinking that trouble came in bunches. God, he would miss that dog! First thing in the morning, he would get John over to take a look at him. If True was right, well, he didn't know if anything could be done; but if there was a way to help, John would know about it.

Sloan was jarred from his thoughts. Over the sound of the wind he heard a babe crying. He frowned. Was Orah Delle sick? The child's plaintive wails were loud and continuous. He quickened his steps and then broke into a running walk. He couldn't remember the babe ever crying in such an agonized way except for the time she'd had the earache. True had eased the pain by blowing his warm breath in her ear.

Alarmed now, Sloan hurried to the cabin and pushed open the door.

Ada was sitting by the fire, her hands over her ears. Katherine was walking the floor with the crying child in her arms. Sloan took off his coat and reached for the babe. Orah Delle cuddled against him, her small arms around his neck. He talked softly to her. Her crying stopped and she lay hiccuping, her tearful little face pressed to his neck.

"Ma . . . ma. Ma . . . ma."

"Thank God!" Ada got up from the chair. "My head is splitting from listening to that child bawl. I must say, Sloan, your little nursemaid has a nerve to leave us with a crying child all afternoon. I wanted to have my hair washed, but Kat has been walking the floor with that bawling infant, and even that wouldn't shut her up."

"Where is Cherish?" A cold circle of fear was forming around Sloan's heart.

"How should I know?" Ada said angrily.

"Where is she?" Sloan demanded.

"Probably in the barn, rolling in the hay with John Spotted Elk, or out in the woods with some other Indian. Who knows what a whore—"

"Shut up!" Sloan shouted. His loud voice scared the baby. Orah Delle hiccuped and began to cry again.

"Ma . . . ma. Ma . . . ma."

"Now, now, baby. Mama will come," he crooned and patted her back. "Katherine, where is Cherish?" He tried to speak calmly in order not to alarm the child.

Katherine looked at Ada before she answered. Ada lifted her arms in a gesture of resignation.

"She put the baby to sleep right after the noon meal, sir. She came to the bedroom door and said she was going outside. That's all I know."

"Was that all she said?" Sloan's anxiety showed in his voice.

"She asked me to watch the baby. Ah . . . she had wraps on, sir."

Sloan looked at the clock and paced back and forth for a moment. His mind tried desperately to grapple with what Katherine had told him. Orah Delle, exhausted from crying so long, had fallen asleep. He carried her to the bedroom, placed her in her crib and tucked the covers about her. Returning, he picked up his coat and jerked it on.

"Katherine, watch that the babe doesn't kick off her covers. I didn't put her in her sleeping bag."

"For heaven's sake, Sloan," Ada said impatiently. "You're not running out to look for that little baggage? I warn you. You may not like what you find!"

"What do you mean by that?" he demanded.

"You're not the only handsome man in this settlement. Anyway . . . it's just what she wants—you to come looking for her."

"Goddammit, Ada!"

"Don't shout at me . . . honey," Ada said, and sniffed prettily. "You know it scares me when you shout."

"Shitfire! Stop play-acting. Cherish has been gone for more than four hours. Can't you get it through your thick, stupid head that she would never go and leave the baby for that long?" Sloan shoved his fur cap down on his head and took his rifle from the pegs.

"Sloan, honey . . . don't go—" Ada came to him and tried to put her arms around him.

"Get away from me," he snarled, shoving her aside and rushing out the door.

A half-hour later the settlement had been thoroughly searched. Sloan, True, Juicy, Mister Swanson, John Spotted Elk and four of his braves had gone over every foot of ground in and immediately around it.

The men were gathered in front of the cabin to decide what to do next when Sloan remembered something. He had milked the cow that morning thinking to relieve True of the chore, and besides, he had been up earlier than usual. At the time he had noticed a smell in the barn that he hadn't been able to identify. With more pressing problems on his mind, he had dismissed it.

"Who searched the barn?"

"She ain't thar, Sloan," Juicy said. "I looked in ever' crack an' cranny."

"Did you notice a different smell while you were there?"

"Can't say as I did."

"Animal smell?" John asked suddenly.

"I don't know, John. I don't think it was that or the cow would've been nervous. Could have been my imagination."

The Indian waited until Sloan finished speaking,

then took off at a trot for the barn. Sloan and the men followed.

Sloan held a torch while John Spotted Elk examined the hay scattered about the floor of the building. He sniffed until he found the place where the two men had hidden themselves when Sloan had gone in to milk the cow. Carefully reading the signs, his sharp eyes missing nothing, John plucked a thread from a rough board by the shuttered rear window.

Outside, circling the barn on his hands and knees, John found traces of track, although the wind had swept the area clean of snow. Abruptly, he got to his feet and trotted into the woods. Sloan waited anxiously. In a minute or two John was back.

"Two men have taken Morning Sun. One man carries her. We must go."

Sloan turned to True and Juicy. "Get the babe and take her to your cabin. Keep her with you until I return. Take Katherine, if she'll go. Ada will be difficult, but pay her no mind. And True, do you think Brown is up to tracking?"

True shook his head. "He be bad off."

Sloan looked down at his feet. "Do what you can for him."

"Ya ain't to be worryin'. We take keer of the babe," Juicy said grimly.

John Spotted Elk spoke to his braves. One of them removed the tomahawk from his belt and handed it to Sloan, then trotted back with the others toward the Shawnee lodge.

"Could hit be Hurons?" Juicy asked the Shawnee.

John's lips lifted in a sneer. "No Indian leaves such an easy trail to follow, but I told my braves to be on guard. River man got Morning Sun."

"Oh, my God! That sweet little gal!" Mister Swanson said hoarsely. "We can take the boat and—"

"No. I go. Light Eyes go," John said firmly. "She his woman."

True spoke. "Hit's best. John an' Sloan. They'll get her."

"But iffn . . . iffn . . ." Juicy sputtered.

"We'll get her, Juicy," Sloan spoke calmly, although his insides were tied in knots. "You and True look after things here."

"We'll do hit, Sloan. Bring back the lit'l purty."

CHAPTER
* 22 *

When Cherish regained consciousness, she was lying on her back. The rag had been removed from her mouth and someone was washing her face with snow. She sputtered and spit. When she rolled her head, it felt as if it would explode. Her stomach roiled and she gagged.

Memory came rushing back, followed by pain in every bone in her body and even worse . . . black despair. *Would she ever see Sloan and Orah Delle again? Would she ever hear Juicy call her the little pretty?*

"Ya've come to. Open yore eyes, gal." A hand circled her throat with strong fingers.

Cherish kept her eyes closed, hoping they would think she had swooned.

"Open yore eyes, I say, and don't ya let out a peep. I'm gettin' tired a foolin' with ya."

Hurry, Sloan. I can't hold out much longer.

Suddenly she felt a hand go up under her skirt.

290

Terror knifed through her. Her eyes flew open. Her vision was blurred, but she could see the face that loomed close to hers—the face with its broken nose and loose lips—the face of the man who had hit her.

"He, he, he," he chortled. "I knowed it. I knowed ya was playin' possum."

The foulness of the man's breath made Cherish gag. She struggled and tried to turn her head. Two hands curled around her forearms and jerked her to her feet. Her head whirled and her stomach churned. She feared she would be sick. She managed to control her stomach, raise her head and focus her eyes.

"Please . . . " she whispered.

"I ain't a carryin' ya another step, gal. Ya make up yer mind ta walk or I aim to slit yore gullet right here an' now." The man jerked her and pain shot through her head. "What's it ter be?"

The pain in her head was almost unbearable, but she managed to answer. "I can walk."

Harry was pleased with his success. He looked over his shoulder and spoke to his companion.

"Didn't I tell ya she'd walk, Beecome? Didn't I tell ya that?"

"Ya told me, ya stupid, stinkin' whore's son," he muttered under his breath, then louder, "Let's go. Them Cherokee is long gone. We been a 'unkered down here fer more'n an hour. My bloody ears is a freezin' off."

The broken-nosed man gave Cherish a push. She

stumbled and would have fallen had he not grabbed her shoulder.

"Keep goin'," he snarled.

Somehow Cherish managed to keep putting one foot in front of the other. Her jaw hurt. The pain was so severe that she was afraid it was broken. She wondered how much longer she would be able to endure this torture. Into her dulled mind drifted the thought that these men were utterly ruthless and she would probably die, but not before these cruel animal-like dregs of the human race did unspeakable things to her.

Sloan, Sloan. Where are you?

Her brain cleared and she thought for a moment of the tall bronze Indian. Would he be concerned about her? Would he be able to follow the tracks over the frozen ground?

She made up a game to keep her feet moving and to keep herself from going mad. Sloan would come for her. She prayed he would come. With each step the words pounded in her head. *Sloan will come. Sloan will come.* The words became so imprinted in her mind she began to mutter them aloud.

"Sloan will come. Sloan will come."

The man behind her gave her a vicious shove. She fell to her knees and was unable to get to her feet. He seized her by the shoulders and yanked her upright.

"Quit yer blasted jabberin' an' walk. I ain't a-tellin' ya agin."

Darkness came. They pushed on through the eerie woods, where the trees stood like tall silent giants. Cherish thought they must have walked miles and miles from the settlement in the bend of the Ohio. They moved through a gully where the snow was so deep it came up over the tops of her moccasins and chilled her legs. They climbed over rotted logs and took a path where the ground sloped upward away from the river. At this place the brush was thick and the frozen branches clawed at her face. With her bound hands beneath the blanket, she was helpless to ward off the stinging blows.

The man called Beecome stopped. "Ain't we 'bout there, 'Arry?"

"Over an' through that thar clearin' is the place. The breed'll be a waitin' fer us. He'll signal ol' Finger ta brin' up the boat."

"The wench'd better be worth the trouble we took ta git 'er," Beecome complained. "That settler ain't gonna take kindly to this'n bein' took. She's family, she is."

"How ya be knowin' that?"

"She ain't no doxy. That's how I know. The other'n now, that bloody bitch was so 'ot she 'bout set the tavern afire." Beecome blew on his hands to warm them. "I been thinkin' on it. I'll be bloody glad to be gittin' to the boat."

"Don'tcha worry none. The winds come up and

blowed our tracks out. Think 'bout crawlin' between this'n's legs. That's what I been a thinkin' on."

Revulsion convulsed Cherish's stomach and it heaved. There was no way she could hold it back. She bent over to allow its contents to spill out, moaning with pain as she opened her jaws.

"I don't like pukin' women," Beecome said angrily.

"She ain't sick-sick. But I ain't keerin' if she is. I'm gonna have me a fine time with 'er."

"Yer just a stud, 'Arry. A bloody stud. Ain't ya got nothin' on yore mind 'cept shovin' it in a woman?"

"Ain't nothin' better to be havin' on my mind or shovin' it in, either." Harry's laugh was nothing more than a dry chuckle. He poked Cherish in the back with his elbow. "Huh, gal?"

Cherish turned her head painfully and stared at the two men with utter loathing. She hated them with every fiber of her being. Somehow this gave her strength and she plodded on, more determined than ever to stay alive and endure until Sloan came for her.

Beecome continued to complain. "We ort to waited and got the other'n. This'n won't last. The other'n's been tried. I was wantin' to give 'er what she bloody well asked for. Flippin' her skirts, shakin' 'er arse—"

Harry stopped and turned. "If yer a wantin' the other'n, go get 'er. I say we be lucky to get outta thar with our hair. Them Shawnee ain't ta be messed with. Iffn not fer them comin' we could'a burned out that settler and took all three of them women. They'd brin' a good price at the Injin slave market up along the lakes."

"Is it what yer goin' to do with this'n?" Beecome asked.

"Finger an' the breed'll have a say. Could be we'll keep 'er till she's wore out."

Cherish listened. Then she heard a small whimpering sound and realized it came from her. She heard an evil chuckle and knew it came from Harry.

They came to a clearing and waited a few minutes before Harry gave a signal. It was a poor imitation of a hoot owl's call. The men moved about restlessly while they waited. Harry called again. Beecome pushed Cherish against a tree and held her there with a hand against her chest. He muttered obscenities against the cold, against Harry for getting him into this situation, against Cherish.

At last, from a distance, they heard an answer to Harry's call.

Harry laughed. "Tol' ya. Didn't I tell ya they'd be here? Didn't I tell ya?"

Beecome grinned with relief and Cherish's hopes faded.

The snow on the ground made it easy to see the silhouette of the man when he came through the trees. He moved slowly, and in the heavy fur robe he looked like a great shaggy bear.

Beecome cursed him under his breath as he approached.

"Goddamn greasy Injin! Smells like a bloody boar's nest, he does."

Harry walked a short distance to meet him, but the bear of a man ignored him and kept on coming until he stood near the tree where Beecome was holding Cherish. His putrid odor radiated like an aura around him. She turned her head away in an effort to breathe sweet, clean air.

"Come," the man said, his voice guttural. "We wait for Finger."

"Come where, ya stinkin', bloody redskin?" In his agitation Beecome seized Cherish's arm and shoved her to her knees. "Ain't Finger here?"

"Finger come. We wait."

Harry laughed, trying to break the tension between Beecome and the Indian. He pulled Cherish to her feet.

"Come on, Beecome, let's git 'er on down thar." He stood back and waited for the Indian to lead the way.

"'Ow long'll it be 'fore Finger gits 'ere?"

Beecome was irritated. What had seemed to be a good idea when they were drunk had been soured by the failure to capture the boat with the blond bitch on it, the long wait in the barn, the taking of the wrong woman, and the long cold trek in the snow. The whole thing was going to end up wrong, he was sure of it.

"One, maybe two hour. We wait in cave."

"Two hours!" Beecome stopped and confronted the half-breed.

"Finger take boat to middle of river when Cherokee come this way. Boat drift down two, three mile. Finger pole boat back. Send me up shore to tell."

"'Ow far's the bloody cave?" Beecome growled.

"Not far. Build fire, cave warm." The man who resembled and smelled like a bear turned and waddled on down the hill toward the river.

For the first time since she had been abducted, Cherish allowed the tears to come. The pain in her head and in the arm Beecome had twisted when he shoved her to the ground, the agony in her jaw from the blow from Harry's fist were nothing compared to the pain in her heart. She had been living on the hope that Sloan would come for her. Now the chances of his finding her had faded to almost nothing.

The half-breed led them down the hill, then up a short incline and around a large boulder. They entered a shallow cave. In the back, behind a pile of cut brush to shield its light from the river, burned a small campfire.

Harry pushed Cherish in ahead of him. She cowered like a frightened animal against the wall. Her terror-filled eyes welled with tears again and she closed them tightly. Horrifying scenes danced behind her closed eyelids.

Oh, God. Let me wake up. Let all of this be a terrible dream. If not, please let me die quickly.

Still complaining, Beecome demanded food from the half-breed. The Indian threw him a bag and Beecome sat, his back to the cave wall, and chewed the dried meat.

Something nudged Cherish's leg and her eyes flew open. Harry stood looking down at her, running the tip of his tongue over his loose lips that spread in a wolfish grin when he saw her expression.

"Yer a looker!"

Cherish's throat was dry with terror, and when she spoke the words came out in a voice she didn't recognize as her own.

"You touch me and . . . and my man will kill you!"

"Yer man ain't here, missy." Harry's voice was husky and his breath was coming faster. "I got ter see more a what I got." He laughed as she struggled, and he pulled her toward him. He continued to laugh when she kicked him, and moved away easily when she tried to butt him with her head.

"Easy, gal. Easy. I don't want to hit ya agin. It ain't no fun a'tall humpin' a limp woman. I jist want ter see whatcha got under that thar blanket." He pulled the blanket off over her head and the shawl came with it. Her hair came tumbling down over her shoulders and face, blocking her vision, but she lashed out with her bound hands.

"Whoopsy, doopsy! Did ya ever see hair like that thar? It's like fire. She'd brin' a sack full of gold at the Injin market."

Harry made an inarticulate sound in his throat and gave her a push that sent her sprawling to her knees. She stayed there, her long, tangled hair shielding her face. Hands reached down and hauled her to her feet. Her hair parted and she looked into Harry's leering face.

"I ain't a waitin' fer ya much longer, gal." Then, in a quick movement that caught her by surprise, he ripped open the front of her dress.

Cherish cried out and tried to cover herself.

"I said I was gonna look at what I got." Harry viciously ripped her dress again and it hung down to her waist. Only her bound hands kept it from falling around her ankles.

Sobbing with terror and shame, Cherish tried to run, but he grabbed her hair and jerked her about to face him. He wrapped her hair around his hand and, twisting it up tight, held her head tilted up to him.

"Ain't ya ever gonna learn, *slut?*" Then, in a gentler tone, his face coming closer to hers, he said, "Ya'll like it, gal. Jist wait till ya see it. I got a thin' in my breeches what'd put a bull to shame."

Beecome laughed uproariously and slapped his hand against his thigh.

"'Ear that, Breed? 'Ear that? I seen what he got. It ain't nothin' but a little old bitty worm."

Dazed with pain, Cherish never heard what was said. The grotesque face close to hers no longer looked human to her. When she realized that two other figures stood beside Harry, their mouths open with lust, spittle running from the corner of the dark lips of the half-breed, she felt a scream build in her throat.

Harry released her hair and she fell back against the wall of the cave.

"Looky thar at them titties."

Cherish heard the words through a mist of pain and humiliation.

"I've seen bigger titties on a nanny goat," Beecome snickered.

"Go on, touch 'em," Harry invited.

Cherish's eyes glazed with fear as the rough fingers curled about her naked breasts.

"No! No!" she sobbed frantically. "Please . . . don't. No!" She twisted and turned in a desperate effort to get away from her tormentors.

"Shut up!" a voice growled, and fingers found the nipple of her breast and squeezed viciously.

A thin shrill scream tore from her throat. The walls of the cave seemed to sway inward as waves of agony blackened and numbed her mind.

"Said, shut up!" A slap across her face sent her reeling, only to be pulled up for another slap that bounced her head off the wall. Her screaming stopped and was replaced by groans of pain. She waited, eyes closed, for the next attack.

An odd gurgling noise caused her to open her eyes. She saw Harry hanging in front of her, his mouth wide open, his hands clawing at his throat where his blood was spurting. Blood seemed to be everywhere. Warm and sticky blood covered her arms, shoulders and breasts.

She was mad. She had to be mad.

The motion, the grunts, the mouth hanging open. The weight of Harry against her—and the blood. Something snapped in her mind. Her face turned a ghostly white amid the masses of tangled red hair. She screamed and screamed until she whirled through a black void, spinning dizzily into oblivion.

CHAPTER
* 23 *

Consciousness returned slowly. Cherish heard groaning and, yielding again to darkness, drifted away.

When next she awoke and opened her eyes, it was to see Sloan and John Spotted Elk sitting calmly before a heap of glowing orange coals. Their faces were shadowed, and she struggled for some semblance of sanity, thinking that she was not alive, or if she was, she was dreaming and recoiling from reality.

She sank again into blessed darkness.

The third time she fought her way to consciousness moaning and sobbing wildly with terror. She screamed Sloan's name over and over, and suddenly he was there, his arms around her, holding her, his reassuring voice in her ear.

"I'm here, Cherish. You're safe now. Don't cry, sweetheart. You're safe with me and John. Don't cry." He murmured the soft comforting words.

"Don't . . . don't let them—" She sobbed and clung to him.

"I won't let them hurt you. They'll never hurt you." He held her and stroked her hair.

It was several minutes before she grew still. She raised her tear-stained face, her eyes darting about the cave.

"Have they . . . gone?" she asked fearfully.

"Yes, my sweet, they're gone. It's over now. John and I will take you home."

The shame and humiliation of what she had endured returned and she began to tremble anew. Fearfully she looked down, expecting to see her torn dress hanging to her waist, but it was pulled up over her body and her shawl was wrapped around her. Two strong arms were holding her against a broad sheltering chest and a strongly beating heart.

"I . . . went to the barn to see the cow. They were there, waiting for Ada, I think. They talked of the woman on the boat—"

"Shhh . . . don't think about them."

"I didn't know how you'd ever find me, but I knew you'd come!"

"I couldn't have found you in time without John." He held her away from him and smoothed the tangled hair from her face. His face showed lines of worry and fatigue.

John Spotted Elk was sitting only a few feet away, but it was impossible to see his face clearly in the dim light of the fire. Cherish left the warm comfort of Sloan's arms and slid over to him. Taking his hand in hers, she placed it against her cheek.

"I'll never be able to thank you enough, John."

The Indian removed his hand from hers and placed it behind her head. Ever so gently he drew the shining head to his shoulder. When it rested there, he stroked her hair.

"You do not thank me for breathing, Morning Sun. You do not thank me for seeking rest when my body is weary, or for filling my belly when hunger is upon me. I came to you as I do these things. I will always come to you if you are in need. We will speak no more about it."

Cherish thought his voice the most beautiful she had ever heard. She raised her head and looked into his dark face. His eyes gleamed.

"We will speak no more about it," she repeated.

Sloan wrapped the blanket around her. There were still portions of the night that her weary, confused mind blanked out, and she was content to let it be so. She was exhausted. The pain in her jaw was not as acute, but there was a sour taste in her mouth. She remembered that she had been sick while coming through the woods. She didn't want to remember anything unpleasant, but at the same time she seemed compelled to ask questions.

"How did you find me so soon? I don't think we

were in the cave long, though it seemed like an eternity."

She looked at John Spotted Elk, but it was Sloan who answered.

"John sets a fast pace." Sloan's lips twitched in a half smile when he looked at his friend, but John was staring stoically into the fire.

Hesitantly, Cherish said, "There was another man coming. A man named Finger."

The silence lasted so long that she was wondering if she had voiced the statement or only thought she had.

Finally Sloan said, "He came."

In spite of her tiredness, Cherish's mind was beginning to clear. She gazed into the sputtering campfire and wondered at the miracle of her rescue. She had lived through a horrible nightmare. Never as long as she lived would she forget the instant glimpse she'd had, before blackness took her, of John Spotted Elk behind Harry drawing his knife across his throat, of Sloan, cords of his neck standing out, lips skinned back, tomahawk in his hand, and the bloody dead bodies sprawled one atop the other.

She wanted to go home; and yet, now that her reason had returned, the barrier between her and Sloan had also returned. Quietly she accepted the fact that her place in Sloan's life would always be what he had intended it to be when he met her on the trail: a nursemaid for the babe and, if she were willing, a companion for his bed. When she had accepted his offer, she had expected no more. He had not asked her to love him and could not be blamed for not loving her wholeheartedly as she yearned to be loved.

The cabin now was home, and she thought of it, the babe, True and Juicy, with longing.

As if in answer to her thoughts, Sloan began preparing to leave the cave. Cherish got to her feet and pulled the shawl up over her head. Her legs were weak and shaky, and when she moved she felt suddenly dizzy. She doubted her ability to walk the long distance back to the cabin, but she resolved to try. Then, a pain knifed through her and she leaned weakly against the wall, hoping the men would not notice her distress. Mercifully, it passed.

Sloan took her arm and led her out of the cave, keeping himself between her and the ravine that ran alongside the river. They walked down the incline and had reached the level ground when the second pain struck her, almost bringing her to her knees. She stood swaying until it passed, trying to hide it from them.

"What is it, Cherish?" Sloan peered anxiously into her face.

"A cramp." She smiled weakly. "It'll pass."

Cherish walked on, determined that whatever it cost her in pain and weariness, she had to keep up. She lost all sense of direction as she concentrated on putting one foot in front of the other. Her head felt light and empty and there was a buzzing in her ears.

Suddenly her insides were tearing apart. She gasped and clung to Sloan's arm as she doubled over.

"What's the matter? Cherish, sweet— What is it?" Sloan's arms were around her, holding her. John turned and trotted back to them.

Frightened, she gasped, "I don't know. Pains . . . in my stomach."

John touched her face with a gentle hand. Beads of perspiration stood out on her forehead. He bent and picked her up in his arms. Her eyes closed wearily and her head fell back against his shoulder. John's piercing black eyes looked directly into Sloan's as he walked past him.

Sloan followed. "You have the right, my friend," he said under his breath.

As soon as John Spotted Elk picked her up, Cherish fell into an exhausted sleep. But she slept intermittently. The sharp pains she had experienced had subsided into pulsing pains that started in her lower back and extended all the way around her middle. At times they were so severe she moaned.

She lapsed into a semiconscious state. From time to time she was transferred from one pair of arms to another. Both held her tenderly, but the pace remained the same. Once she knew she was being carried by Sloan, for when a groan escaped her, she heard his voice.

"Try and sleep, love. We'll be home soon."

Home. The small log cabin she shared with him had never seemed so much like home as now.

Around and around her confused thoughts wandered—to Sloan, to Orah Delle, to True and Juicy, and to John Spotted Elk. He was a special man. She felt an affinity with him, as if she had known him in another life. He was strong, yet gentle. She could have loved him—

Now the terrible cramps drove all other thoughts from her mind. She tried to recall when she had last had her woman's time. It was while she was with Roy and the Burgess family. The first time she had lain with Sloan was during the blizzard—how long ago?

No! No! She could feel the warm sticky discomfort between her thighs. Oh, dear God, not that! Oh, please, please, God, let them hurry. If they should have to help her, it would be the final humiliation.

She began to cry softly.

Sloan carried Cherish into the cabin, past the two startled women and into the bedroom. John Spotted Elk parted from them at the door.

"I go for my father's wife," he said. "She will know how to care for Morning Sun." He took off in an easy loping run for the Shawnee lodge.

Ada followed Sloan into the bedroom.

"What's wrong with her? Where has she been all this time? Fine nursemaid you have, Sloan. That's blood on her dress. Don't put her on my bed! Do you hear me? Sloan!"

"Shut up and get out of here, Ada. Katherine, bring warm water and come in and close the door."

"She'll do no such thing!" Ada stood in the doorway, her hands on her hips. "Kat will not wait on your doxy! I've told you that before, Sloan. Kat is mine—mine! She takes orders only from me."

Sloan's face went white. The strain of the night's ordeal had stretched his nerves almost to the breaking point. He grabbed Ada by the arm and roughly jerked her aside.

"Do as I say, Katherine!" he roared. "You make one move to interfere, Ada, and so help me I'll break your neck."

"Would you, darlin'? Would you, really?" She smiled up at him and rubbed her breasts against his arm. Sloan shoved her away. Her expression changed instantly. "Your dirty old friends came and took my baby. I'll have the soldiers on them. They had no right to take her out of here."

"They had every right because I told them to. You're not fit to even touch that babe and you'll never have her. Get that through your stupid head!" He grabbed Ada's shoulders and gave her a vicious shake.

From where she lay on the bed, Cherish could see through the blur of her tears the smile on Ada's face. She was looking at Sloan with pure lust, wanting him to hurt her, loving the way he was manhandling her. The sight was embarrassing to Cherish. And then embarrassment turned to disgust toward both of them.

Sloan pushed Ada into the other room and came back to Cherish. He knelt down beside her to remove her shawl. She pushed his hands away.

"Please . . . please!" she cried. "Leave me alone! I can't stand anymore—" Between sobs she pleaded, "Please. Just go and leave me alone."

The hurt and confused look on Sloan's face was gone by the time Katherine came in with the copper kettle and a supply of towels.

"Do what you can for her." He stood and looked down at the girl who meant the world to him. She had turned her face away and refused to look at him. He left the room, closing the door behind him.

Gently, Katherine undressed the weeping girl as if she were a child. When the blood-stained garments were removed she pressed a pad of clean cloth bandage between her legs, washed her thoroughly with the warm water and slipped a clean nightdress over her head.

"You poor little thing," she crooned. "You poor sweet girl. What did those evil men do to you? You're worn out, is what you are. Mister Carroll is worried sick about you."

Cherish continued to cry, pressing her fingers to her eyes as if to hold back the weight of tears that pushed for release against a barrier of despair. She no longer cried aloud, but silently, inwardly, the dry tears of hopelessness. Finally she exhausted herself and drifted to sleep.

She was awakened by the sound of Sloan's voice in the other room. He spoke sharply to Ada and she replied with a purr in her voice that made Cherish cringe with disgust.

The door opened and a fat, round-faced Indian woman and a slim young girl came into the room. Katherine backed away from the bed as the woman and the girl came to the bunk and looked down at Cherish. The girl was beautiful. Her fine-boned features were perfectly formed. Her dark brows looked as if they had been painted on her face with a fine brush. They arched over large brown eyes with flecks of gold in their velvety depths. Her skin was flawless, her mouth soft and red.

The girl spoke. "My brother, John Spotted Elk, sends our father's wife, Falling Leaf, to you, woman of Light Eyes." The girl's face was without expression, yet there was a resentful note in the tone of her voice.

Through the fog of her emotional turbulence, Cherish recognized the girl. She was Minnie Dove, the girl who was in love with Sloan. A wave of pity for the girl overwhelmed Cherish. Minnie Dove's chance of having her love for Sloan reciprocated was even more hopeless than her own.

"Thank you for coming," Cherish said. "I don't know, but I think that I'm only having a bad . . . woman time."

Minnie Dove translated for Falling Leaf in a soft melodious voice. The pleasant-faced woman listened and nodded her head. Then with a quick movement she swept the blanket from Cherish and flung up her nightdress. She took the pad from between Cherish's thighs, examined it and returned it. Cherish's cheeks flamed. She dared not look up at the woman. Falling Leaf spoke to Minnie Dove, who turned to Katherine.

"Falling Leaf wish to see dress and blanket."

Katherine looked puzzled and glanced toward the pile of soiled clothing she had left beside the washstand. Falling Leaf's eyes followed hers; she went to the pile and carefully unfolded the torn bloody dress and the shift. She found what she was looking for and took the soiled garment to the light from the window.

Her eyes were sad when she came back to the bed. When she spoke to Minnie Dove again her voice was low and sorrowful. She spoke long and elegantly. When she finished she stood at the end of the bunk, her arms folded over her ample bosom.

Minnie Dove looked down at Cherish for a long moment before she spoke.

"Falling Leaf say seed planted in woman of Light Eyes stay only a short time. White woman's body not strong enough to hold seed, and it wash away in the flood of woman's sickness." Minnie Dove stopped speaking abruptly.

Falling Leaf looked at the Indian girl as if expecting her to continue, but Minnie Dove was silent, staring coldly at Cherish.

Cherish was not surprised by Minnie Dove's words; they told her what she had suspected. She was, however, surprised at the girl's hostility.

"It saddens me to lose the seed," she said slowly. "And it saddens me that you and I are not friends, Minnie Dove. I have heard of the great beauty of Minnie Dove, sister of John Spotted Elk. Now I see with my own eyes that what I heard was true."

A flicker of surprise passed across the Indian girl's face, and she looked at Cherish with new interest.

"Who tell you this?"

"The one you call Light Eyes. He says that you are not only beautiful, but a woman of great intelligence. The men in the new cabin have also told me of your beauty. Can we not be friends? You and I could teach each other many things."

Minnie Dove lifted her head proudly and folded her arms across her breasts. Looking down her nose at Cherish, as if she were a queen addressing a loyal subject, she said coolly:

"I will think about your wish."

"Thank you," Cherish said gravely, "and thank Falling Leaf for coming to see me."

The two women left the room. Katherine covered Cherish with the blanket.

"Oh, ma'am, I'm so sorry," she murmured. "You were starting a baby and now it's gone."

Cherish closed her eyes. "Katherine, dear," she said wearily. "Please don't call me ma'am ever again."

She settled herself more comfortably in the bed and drifted off to sleep.

CHAPTER

* 24 *

Sloan was restless, frustrated and anxious. Frustrated because he could not understand why Cherish was behaving so strangely toward him, and anxious because he feared she might have suffered an internal injury.

A wave of depression washed over him at the thought of her refusal to let him comfort her. He experienced once again the hurt he had felt when she pleaded for him to leave her alone. What a blind fool he had been not to tell her that he loved her long ago!

His heart filled suddenly with an overpowering protectiveness. She had been through so much, this slip of a girl. She had given her love freely, asking nothing but to live here with him and the babe, refusing even to take his name because she didn't want to bind him to her if he didn't love her wholeheartedly as a man should love his wife.

He looked up as Minnie Dove and Falling Leaf came out of the other room. He glanced at Ada sulking in the chair by the fire, then followed the Indian women outside where they could talk privately.

"Wife of Chief Running Elk, I thank you for coming," he said, speaking in Shawnee.

"My husband commanded it."

"I am worried that Morning Sun has suffered a grave injury."

"Light Eyes, I feel great sorrow. The seed you planted in your woman is no more. It was not strong enough to take root and grow."

She had been pregnant with his child. Of course! Why hadn't he thought of that?

"And Morning Sun? Will she be well again?"

"She is young. She will sleep and grow strong."

"Strong enough to bear other babes?" He tried to keep his voice from sounding anxious.

Falling Leaf's fat face wrinkled into a smile.

"Plant your seed, Light Eyes. You will have many sons."

Feeling heady with relief, Sloan smiled back and placed his hand on her shoulder.

"With my gratitude goes my wish and Morning Sun's that you and Chief Running Elk have many moons of good health."

Through all this Minnie Dove stood a short distance away, her arms folded, her chin tilted, her face turned away from him. Sloan went to her.

"My thanks to you, too, Minnie Dove, for bringing

your father's wife and using your skills to translate
her message to Morning Sun."

She looked at him. "My brother commanded that I
come. He is much taken with your . . . woman," she
added spitefully.

"I know that. I am grateful that she will have a
protector if I should be struck down."

"He may take her and go far away."

"He'll not do that and you know it. He is an hon-
orable man."

"Yes," she snapped. "But is Morning Sun an hon-
orable woman?"

"I would stake my life on it."

"If that is so, you do not value your life!" she
sneered. "It is known that men think with the thing
beneath their breechcloth."

"If your brother heard you speak so, he could take
a switch to your legs."

"He is not here, and you will not tell him," she
said confidently.

"No, I'll not tell him. But enough of that. I talked to
John Spotted Elk about you. He thinks it would be wise
if you came to my lodge and let Morning Sun teach you
ways of the white woman. I will command her to prepare you for the day when you go to the white man's
lodge as wife to a white man. She will not refuse."

Eyeing him contemptuously, Minnie Dove raised
her chin a little higher.

"You need not command, Light Eyes. I, Minnie

Dove, princess of the Shawnee, have already made plans for Morning Sun to teach me the ways of the white woman. I will go to her and we will talk." With her head held at a haughty angle, she walked away. Falling Leaf, after a shy grin at Sloan, followed.

A smile lit up Sloan's eyes. "The little devil," he murmured. "How did Cherish manage that?"

Ada's temper had never been worse. As soon as Sloan entered the cabin carrying a pot of stew True had prepared, she confronted him.

"Sloan, I want to talk to you. I demand that you go to that cabin and bring my baby back here. I will not have her with crude, dirty, ignorant men. They know nothing about taking care of a child."

"They know more than you do. She *knows* and *likes* them. She doesn't know or like you." Sloan hung the pot on the hook and swung it over the low-burning fire.

His words went over Ada's head. She continued as if he hadn't spoken.

"I'm ordering you to bring my baby back here. I have decided to go back to Virginia, and I'm taking her with me. Do you hear me, Sloan?"

"I hear you. I could have heard you if I had been outside. But you're not taking Orah Delle . . . anywhere. Now, do you hear me?"

"You'll see. Just as soon as a boat comes upriver,

I'm going, going, going! You can't stop me. I'm going and taking that baby. I want money, Sloan. I want Slater's part of the money your father left. As Slater's wife, I'm entitled to it. Uncle Robert said I was entitled to it. Or did your dear, *righteous* papa leave it all to you? I wonder what your dear, *righteous* papa would think about your backwoods doxy, the trollop you got off a riverboat, or did she wander in out of the woods? The slut who has been spreading her legs for your fine Indian friend."

Ada was walking the floor, bitter, unkind words pouring out of her mouth, her face flushed with anger. Sloan stood by the fireplace and watched her. *How could Slater have loved this woman?*

"I will not stand to be treated like this, do you understand? I will not! I will not! How dare you keep that whore here. Are you going to get rid of her?" She paused and looked at him. He said nothing, and she continued to pace back and forth.

"I would have married you and lived in this godforsaken place with you. What do you think of that? You could have had me and my baby. But, no. You had to take up with a bitch, a backwoods split-tail who doesn't even know the correct way to hold her eating fork.

"Well, Uncle Robert said you would have to give me money. He married again, you know, married a pious, church-loving, boring stick of a woman. Caleb Graham's widow. I never liked her and she liked me even less." She whirled around and went to the window. "I just don't understand why you came to this place, Sloan. Just because you didn't like your Tory neighbors, you flounced off to this . . . wilderness. Slater would be alive if you had stayed in Virginia. You know that, don't you?"

Ada turned and waited for Sloan to deny what she had said, but still he said nothing.

"It's your fault he's dead. All your fault. And now you want to cast out his wife and her baby. No, that's wrong. You want to cast aside his wife and take her baby from her. You're a bastard, Sloan, that's what you are. A son-of-a-bitch!"

She stopped her pacing and stood in front of him. Her hands were clenched into fists, her eyes wild.

"Well, say something!" she shouted.

He responded quietly. "It wouldn't be any use saying anything to you, Ada, while you're like this. I suggest you calm down, and we'll talk about it later."

"Later! Later! Later! You never had time for me, did you? But I got to you through Slater. Your precious little brother loved me! Me! You know it, too, Sloan. He worshiped me. Do you know what I told him? I told him the baby was yours. What do you think of that? I told him that you seduced me. That's what I told him." She laughed hysterically, her head back, her hands on her hips.

"Guess what he did. He hit me. It was wonderful. It was the first time I ever got any action out of him.

He was always so *sweet,* so *gentle.* He made me want to puke!"

Sloan wanted to strangle her. He held his hands behind him to keep them from reaching out and fastening around her neck. She was waiting for him to make a move, and he was determined not to let her provoke him into doing something he would regret. He forced himself to smile.

"Slater didn't believe a word you said. He told me after you left him and the baby. I made him see that it would have been impossible for me to father the child. I wasn't within a hundred miles of you for a month before and after the child was conceived. And, Ada, Slater believed me."

He put out his hands then and pushed her away from him. She went to the bunk at the far end of the room and sat down. She leaned back against the wall and closed her eyes. Her hands were folded in her lap, and she looked as if she were falling asleep.

Sloan realized then that Ada was dangerous. He had to get her out of his house, away from Cherish and the baby. He didn't know what he could do about Katherine. He would talk to Pierre about that. Pierre could figure out what to do.

Katherine had stayed in the bedroom with Cherish throughout Ada's outburst. She came silently into the room now and began setting the table for the evening meal.

"How is she?" Sloan asked anxiously.

"Asleep." Katherine, her face turned from Ada, gave him a reassuring smile.

Going to the bedroom, Sloan added more wood to the fire, then went to look at the sleeping girl. He gently touched the back of his hand to her pale cheek, then left the room quickly. Ada was curled up on the bunk with her face to the wall.

Sloan and Katherine ate the stew, he at the table, Katherine in the chair by the window. Not knowing if Ada was asleep, they didn't speak. When they finished, Katherine took the bowls to the workbench and Sloan carried the heavy copper teakettle from the fireplace. While he was pouring the water in the dishpan, he leaned close to Katherine.

"Stay in with Cherish tonight. Bar the door."

She looked at him with large frightened eyes and nodded.

The night passed slowly. Sloan sat in the fur-lined chair with his legs stretched out, his head resting against the high back. From time to time he got up and put another log on the fire. As far as he could tell, Ada had not moved since she had thrown herself down on the bunk. There was an eerie quietness in the cabin. Although Sloan felt a creeping uneasiness, his eyes burned, and he had to hold them wide at times to keep them open.

This was his second night without sleep.

Along toward morning, he dozed. He didn't know

if he had slept a minute or an hour when, suddenly, he came instantly awake. Ada was standing in front of him. Her hair was hanging around her shoulders, her face looked as young and innocent as it had years ago when they were children in Virginia.

"Mornin'." He forced himself to speak calmly. He stretched his arms and yawned, never taking his eyes off the woman.

"Mornin'. Did you sleep there all night?"

"I guess I did." He put a log on the fire and stoked the coals until the wood caught. "Are you hungry? I'll have tea ready in a little while." He filled the copper teakettle from the water bucket.

Ada sat down in the chair he had vacated, her eyes closed, her hands folded, her feet crossed.

When the tea was steeping in the pitcher, Sloan went to the bedroom door and knocked gently.

"Katherine," he called softly. He heard the bar lift from the door, then it was opened. Katherine was fully dressed. He glanced at the bunk where Cherish lay. "How is she?"

"She slept all night."

"She was worn out. Come have some breakfast."

Katherine followed him into the other room.

More than an hour later, it was full daylight, and Ada had not moved from the chair. Katherine picked up her sewing and moved near the window. After tending both fires, Sloan put on his coat. Ada opened her eyes and watched him.

"Ada," he said, "I'm going to get Slater's cabin ready and tomorrow you are going there. You will be brought food and wood for the fire. As soon as I can arrange it, you will be escorted down the river to New Orleans, or upriver to Virginia, whichever you choose. I'll see that you have money to live on, an allowance paid to you quarterly."

She looked at him with a fixed stare. He couldn't tell by her expression if she approved or disapproved of his plan for her. She said nothing, only stared at him through half-closed eyes.

"I'll be back soon, Katherine. I need to see about the babe."

Katherine looked fearfully past him to where Ada sat, then raised pleading eyes to his.

"I'll be back soon," he said reassuringly.

CHAPTER

* 25 *

When the door closed behind Sloan, Katherine waited, tense and afraid, for Ada's temper to erupt, but she sat quietly for a long while. Suddenly her foot began tapping the floor. It rapped faster and faster, harder and harder, until at last she jumped to her feet and started pacing about the room.

"Did you hear what he said? Did you?" she demanded in a voice that shook with rage. "Did you hear him tell me he was moving me to Slater's cabin?" Katherine didn't answer and Ada whirled to come toward her. "Pay attention to what I'm saying or I'll . . . slap you. Did you hear him say that?" Katherine nodded. "He's going to move me out of here because of that . . . that backwoods slut!"

Katherine was terrified. She wished fervently that Sloan had not left her alone with this woman. He didn't know how violent she could be when she was in a temper. If not for the defenseless girl sleeping in the other room, she would have run out of the cabin. But she didn't dare leave Cherish at the mercy of this madwoman. Clasping her hands together, Katherine waited to see in which direction Ada's temper would turn.

"I asked you a question, Kat. Did you hear me?"

"Yes, Mistress Carroll."

"You would like to see me put out of here—out in the cold, wouldn't you? You hate me! Yes, you do. Don't deny it. You hate me, I know you do. Don't you, Kat? Because of me you can't get under the sheets and diddle with that Frenchman. That's what you want, isn't it."

"No . . . ma'am."

"Don't you lie to me, you . . . bitch!" Ada came toward her, her hands knotted into fists, her arms swinging back and forth, her body swaying from side to side. "You hate me! Say it or I'll slap you till your eyes rattle!"

"No, Mistress Carroll. I don't *hate* you," Katherine said as calmly as her trembling lips would allow.

"No, Mistress Carroll," Ada mimicked. "I owe you something, Kat. You disobeyed me. I owe you something for serving that . . . that . . . slut in there!"

"Mister Carroll ordered me—"

"You don't belong to *Mister* Carroll. You belong to me. You know that, don't you? You are mine! Mine!" The shrill voice beat against Katherine's eardrums.

Ada wheeled about and went into the bedroom, the heels of her shoes tapping on the bare wood floor.

Sweat broke out all over Katherine's body and her heart pounded in fright. She fought to keep her fear from forcing her to flee the house. Oh, God! Don't let her beat me again! I won't take it . . . I can't take it! I'll fight her even it if means I'll never be free of her. If it means I'll never be with Pierre. Oh Pierre! What am I going to do?

Cherish!

Katherine jumped up and went to the bedroom door. Ada had opened her trunk and was tossing things out onto the floor. She found what she was searching for and turned with a small rawhide riding whip in her hand.

At that moment, Cherish awoke and sat up in bed. Ada's eyes went to her, then back to Katherine. She began to smile and slap the whip against her thigh.

"Ada!" Katherine said loudly. "About what you asked me—"

Ada's attention went immediately to the bound girl and she started toward her. "What did you call me? Kat, I don't know what's the matter with you. That Frenchman put you up to this, didn't he?"

Katherine stepped away from the doorway. As soon as Ada entered the room the frightened girl called out to Cherish.

"Shut and bar the door!"

Ada's eyes were on Katherine, who had darted around to the other side of the table.

"I never gave you permission to call me by my first name. Only my friends, my dearest friends, have that honor. You're nothing, Kat. You're lower than the slaves on Uncle Robert's plantation. I'll have to teach you your place."

Katherine was trembling so hard she could barely stand. The bedroom door remained open. Why hadn't she run in there and barred the door? She had thought only to draw Ada away from Cherish. Now Ada was between her and the door.

The sound of the outside door of the cabin opening set a flood of relief through Katherine. She spun about, expecting to see Sloan. The Indian girl, Minnie Dove, stepped quietly into the room and closed the door behind her. She moved to the center of the room and stopped, sensing the tension.

Ada stood near the bedroom door, the riding whip still in her hand. Her attention turned immediately to the Indian girl, who hesitated, uncertain about trying to pass the woman who blocked her way to the room where Light Eyes' woman lay.

Seeing the pretty young girl in the soft buckskin dress, Ada suddenly transferred all her hatred to Minnie Dove.

"How dare you come into this house uninvited!" she hissed venomously.

Minnie Dove raised her head proudly. "I was

asked to come here by Morning Sun, the woman of Light Eyes."

"Have you decided to share him between you? A dirty half-breed Indian and a backwoods slut." Ada's voice rose, echoing through the room, through the cabin.

"I have come to see Morning Sun," Minnie Dove said firmly.

"Get . . . out!"

"Morning Sun asked me to come."

"Get out! Get out!" Ada was shaking uncontrollably now. Her lips were drawn back over her teeth and she looked like what she was: a woman possessed.

"I will not leave because you tell me to go. I will leave only if Light Eyes or Morning Sun tells me." The Indian girl's beautiful face showed not a trace of fear as she looked straight into Ada's wild-eyed stare.

"You . . . dirty . . . dog-eating . . . slut! You . . . stinking whore!" Ada screamed her insults and advanced on the girl. Minnie Dove moved back toward the fireplace. Her action was not one of retreat, but a reaffirmation of her intention to stay.

Ada's face was a mask of fury. Saliva ran from the corner of her twitching lips. The hand holding the riding whip drew it back over her shoulder.

"Stop it! Stop it!" Shocked out of her fear and into

action, Katherine moved quickly to Ada and took her by the shoulders, shaking her. "Please . . . stop!"

Strengthened by her anger, Ada swept Katherine from her, flinging her aside so that she crashed against the wall. The half-crazed woman advanced on Minnie Dove, screeching a shrill stream of obscenities.

"Indian dog . . . dirty whore! He won't think you pretty when I finish with you—"

The whip rose and fell across Minnie Dove's face. Katherine heard the plop as she tried to get to her feet. The blow was repeated. She heard the whistle of the whip as it lashed through the air, the sickening plop as it landed on the girl's soft flesh.

Minnie Dove was stunned with surprise and pain when the first blow fell. The second blow, following so closely behind the first, caught her cheek and neck. She turned—to protect her face and to find something with which to defend herself. Her outstretched hand closed about the handle of a two-edged skinning knife as the whip fell across her back.

Infuriated that she should be treated like a dog by this white woman, she spun about. Ada raised her arm again, her eyes glazed with hatred and madness. As the whip began to fall toward her, Minnie Dove darted in and plunged the knife into Ada's chest.

The blond woman hung there for a second, her ꞊rised eyes looking directly into the dark furious eyes of the Indian girl, then she slowly sank to the floor.

Katherine gazed at the scene with horrified fascination, the world tilting crazily. A scream from behind her brought her back to sanity. Cherish swayed in the bedroom doorway, her eyes blind with horror, her knees buckling as she started to fall in a faint. Katherine caught her and they both eased to the floor just as the cabin door was flung open.

Sloan stood there, grim-faced and stunned, staring at the tableau in front of him. It seemed minutes, but could have only been seconds, that he stood frozen before John Spotted Elk and Juicy appeared behind him. Quick strides took Sloan across the room to where Katherine sat holding Cherish.

"She's all right," Katherine told him.

He breathed then and went to kneel beside Ada, who lay on her back, the handle of the knife protruding from her chest. Her eyes were open and staring and her hand still clutched the whip. A pool of blood was forming on the floor around her. With a tug Sloan removed the knife and tossed it aside. He got to his feet slowly, his bewildered mind trying to understand what had taken place in the short time he had been away.

Juicy went to Cherish and lifted her in his arms. Katherine, wild-eyed and sobbing, stood by, holding the unconscious girl's hand.

"Come, gal. Come now," Juicy coaxed. "Come

help ol' Juicy with this little purty." He carried Cherish into the bedroom and Katherine followed, keeping her face turned away from the body on the floor.

Minnie Dove had not moved from where she had been standing when Ada attacked her. She stood stoically, holding her head high, ignoring the pain from the angry welts that crisscrossed her face. Blood trickled from her chin and strands of her hair stuck to the cuts on her neck. John Spotted Elk stood beside her. Together they faced Sloan.

"I killed the woman, Light Eyes," Minnie Dove said calmly. "I am not a dog to be whipped. I am not a slut, a whore. I came to see Morning Sun. This one—" she nodded toward the body on the floor— "gave me insult, told me to go . . . beat me. I will not be whipped by a white woman. I am Minnie Dove, daughter of Chief Running Elk, sister of a proud warrior. I will not be shamed for my Indian blood. I am Shawnee."

John Spotted Elk stood proudly beside his sister. Sloan looked from one to the other as he spread his hands in a gesture of regret.

"I am more sorry than I can ever say, Minnie Dove, for the insult you suffered in my lodge. I should never have left the cabin. I know now that the woman was mad." He looked sadly at the man who had been his friend for many years. "I hope this will not affect our friendship, John."

"The deed is done, Light Eyes. My sister is a true

daughter of Chief Running Elk. She can walk with pride. We value your friendship and that of Morning Sun. We will not speak of this again." John turned and ushered his sister out the door. Together they walked toward the Shawnee lodge.

Sloan stood with his head bowed, leaning against the warm stones of the fireplace. The possible consequences of what had happened had just penetrated his numbed mind. Ada's uncle was bound to make an inquiry about her sooner or later. It would be best to send a dispatch to him as soon as possible. What could he say without bringing the awful truth out in the open? Finally he decided he would simply write, *Your niece sickened and died.* It was true to a certain extent. Ada's mind had sickened, and she had died because of it.

Juicy wrapped the body in a sheet. He hadn't liked the woman, but now he felt a certain pity for her.

"I'll take 'er to Slater's cabin," he said. "But first I'll take the gal to Pierre. She's real tore up, an' Pierre'll take keer of 'er. You'd best go see 'bout the little purty. She's come outta it an' is cryin' some."

"Ada didn't strike Cherish . . . or Katherine?" Sloan asked, sudden anxiety making his voice sharp.

"No, no!" Juicy's booming voice was reassuring. "They be a'right. Ya see ta the little gal and git some sleep. Swanson an' me'll make a box for this 'un. An' don't go worryin' none 'bout the babe. Ol' True's been watchin' o'er 'er like a mama hen."

Katherine, dry-eyed and composed, draped a shawl about her shoulders.

"Sir," she said hesitantly, "the Indian girl didn't do anything to cause Mistress Carroll to turn on her."

"I know. I'm sorry I left you alone with Ada. I didn't realize she was so violent."

"Her uncle made her leave Virginia because of her temper, sir. She . . . beat one of his horses something awful. She hit the poor beast in the face and put out its eyes. Mister Robert had to shoot it. He was very angry and . . . just packed her off."

"What about you, Katherine? Why did he send you away with her when he knew what she was like?"

"She wouldn't go without me. And . . . she never whipped me until after we left. I had less than a year to serve her and I would be free. Do you understand why I had to . . . had to let her do what she did?"

"You're free of her now," Sloan said wearily. "Free to go to Pierre. We'll take care of your bond papers. Don't worry about them."

Suffering the weariness of both mind and body, Sloan walked slowly past his brother's dead wife lying wrapped in the sheet and ready for the grave. He went into the bedroom and closed the door.

He wanted to be with Cherish. He needed to be with her.

Suddenly he was desperate to know if it could ever be as it had been between them before Ada came. No, not just the same. This time he would hold nothing back. This time he would tell her, his beautiful Cherish, that she was his love, his life. That he had only begun to live the day he met her on the banks of the Kentucky River, that his heart was bound and tied . . . that his future, his happiness, depended on her. Only her.

He would insist that she marry him when the first preacher reached the settlement in the spring.

"Cherish?"

At the sound of his voice she opened her eyes—wide, smoke-fringed, sky-blue eyes set in a pale face surrounded by flame-colored hair.

"Sloan?" she whispered. "Minnie Dove? She was so . . . brave—"

"She did what she had to do."

"I'm . . . sorry. She was . . . the babe's mother."

"Ada gave birth to her. You, my love, are her mother." He was kneeling beside her. His tired, anxious face was close to hers.

"Is she with True?"

"Yes, he's taking care of her. Are you all right?"

"I'm all right. But you look so tired." Her fingers touched his cheek, rough with several days' growth of whiskers. He captured them and held them to his mouth.

"I am tired, but more than that . . . much more than that . . . I need you! I need you!"

The unexpected words filled her heart with joy.

Encouraged to go on by the tender look in her eyes, the sweet smile on her lips that were tantalizingly close to his own, he continued.

"I have never been so frightened in all my life. When I discovered you were gone, I was so afraid I had lost you. I prayed that I'd get another chance to tell you how important you are to me . . . how much I need you. I need you for . . . me."

He buried his face against her shoulder and was very still.

"I knew you would come for me." Her hand moved to the back of his neck, and her fingers caressed the thick dark hair. "I was so scared, but I kept telling myself over and over, 'Sloan will come. Sloan will come.' And . . . when I needed you the most, you were there."

With his face against her, breathing in the warm scent of her, Sloan knew the first peaceful moments since the day Ada arrived. He could feel the quiet measured beat of her heart, and he knew that if that beating should stop, his world would end.

The minutes slipped away. After a while he raised his head and studied her face. He stroked her hair and draped a strand behind her ear. He traced her straight brows with his fingertip and touched the dark circles beneath her eyes. His thumb caressed the hollows in her cheeks.

His hand trembled.

Feeling it, Cherish was convinced of the truth of his words: he needed her as much as she needed him.

"Everything will be all right, Sloan." Her voice was tranquil and infinitely tender.

He searched his mind for the right words to say.

"There's so much to explain. So much."

"It can wait."

"No. Not all of it." He shook his head, his eyes caressing her. "I need to tell you how much I love you. My heart is bound and tied and held in these small hands." He brought her fingers to his lips. "I'm so sorry I didn't tell you before now. I don't think I knew how to say the words."

Cherish stared into his eyes. Was she dreaming? Could it be that her longing to hear just these words had made fantasy stronger than reality? This was a side of him, a vulnerable side, she had not seen before. He was always so strong, so positive, so sure of himself. She never expected to ever see him so humble.

"Oh, my dear!" She lifted her arms to encircle him and draw him down to her. "I've waited so long to hear you say it."

He lowered his head to reach her mouth, his lips moving sensuously against hers, their tenderness releasing a response in her that she had always before held in check, fearing her love was not returned. But now . . . now there was nothing to hide, to fear, and she ached with the need to show him her love.

Her response brought a deep moan from his throat, and he gathered her close.

"I love you so much, so much." He was trembling as he put her from him so he could look into her face. "Sweeting, after what you've been through, I must be careful. It would kill me if I hurt you."

Her mouth curved in involuntary delight at his remark. Gently she touched his face, her eyes full of love for him. Her smile was radiant and her face held nothing but tenderness.

"Don't be afraid to hold me. I'm much stronger than I look."

He smiled a little and touched her lips again ever so gently with his. It was the sweetest kiss Cherish had yet received. They were silent for a while, gazing at each other. Then she whispered:

"There's room for you."

"I was hoping you'd say that." His tired face creased in a smile, the dimples showing in his cheeks. He kissed her again, not so gently this time. "I've missed our nights together."

"I couldn't . . . with Ada here."

"I hated her for keeping us apart."

"Don't think about her. She was . . . sick."

"I hope Slater knows . . . the reason she acted as she did. She broke his heart."

"He knows, my love. We have his child. We'll tell her about him when she's old enough to understand."

"Ah, love. I want to hold you, sleep with you in

my arms. I thought that I might never lie beside you again. When I saw that scum with their hands on you, I wanted to kill them. John made me wait until the time was right. I hope never to have to go through such a night again!"

"Don't think about it," she urged. "It's over."

"I want to tell you so many things about me and Slater and . . . Ada. But not now. I'll wait until you've rested. Now I want to lie beside you and hold you. Are you sure you're all right?" He smoothed the tumbled, shimmering hair back from her face.

"I feel wonderful!" She laughed. "Glorious! If I felt any better, I would . . . would swoon."

She lifted the covers. He stood and quickly removed his clothes.

"Get some sleep," she said as he slipped into the bed and gathered her close. "Tomorrow we can talk and you can tell me everything. Then, in a week or two," she added shyly, "you can plant another seed."

EPILOGUE

*I*n the spring, Cherish, Sloan, Orah Delle and the other residents of the settlement waved good-bye to John Spotted Elk and Minnie Dove as they departed for the Shawnee summer camp. The violence at the beginning of the winter had drawn the group into a close family-like unit.

Cherish and Minnie Dove had become friends—more than friends. The fondness they felt for each other was more like the affection between sisters. Minnie Dove gradually became reconciled to her way of life and no longer wished to live in the "white man's lodge." She confessed to Cherish that she was looking forward to another meeting with Black Fox, the brave her brother had picked to be her husband months ago. She had rejected him at the time, viewing him with the eyes of her white blood.

John Spotted Elk visited the cabin often. His gaze would often linger on the girl he called Morning Sun. Seeing this, Sloan felt a sadness for his blood-brother, whose white blood "called out" to Cherish and whose anxiety had been as great as his own the night she had been taken by river renegades.

Brown went into convulsions on the night Cherish was taken and was mercifully put out of his misery by True, who couldn't bear to see the animal suffer. He was buried beside Sloan's cabin. Sloan and Cherish wept unashamedly when they stood for the first time beside the grave of the faithful dog who had led them through the blizzard to safety.

Ada was buried on the hill beside her husband. True carved a marker for her grave as he had done for Slater's:

ADA ELIZABETH CARROLL
1754–1779
25 YEARS OLD

Slater's cabin was now Katherine's and Pierre's. The English girl had bloomed like a winter rose. Pierre idolized her. Like Cherish and Sloan, they were waiting for a preacher to come along and marry them, but as they were expecting a baby before the end of summer, Pierre laughed uproariously whenever they spoke of it.

"*Mon Dieu,* Sloan," he said, patting Katherine's protruding abdomen. "We will tell heem my little *chérie* swallow a pumpkin seed."

"Stop teasing me, Pierre," Katherine retorted. "You'll say no such thing!" Then, wistfully, "If that preacher doesn't come soon, I'll have to stand behind the door during the ceremony."

Pierre's laughter rang out and he hugged her to him.

"No, no, my little one. You stay by Pierre, even if you hold *two* babes in your arms."

Mister Swanson and his grandson decided to stay in the settlement and ferry supplies for Sloan; and so another room had to be added to the new cabin. Both True and Juicy had taken a liking to Farrway, much to the relief of the old man. He had been worried that he might die before the lad was able to fend for himself.

When the last Shawnee canoe was around the bend and out of sight, the group by the shore straggled back up the path toward the cabins.

"I'll miss Minnie Dove," Cherish said wistfully.

"They'll be back in a few months, sweetheart. Besides, you still have me," Sloan teased.

She tilted her head back, her eyes sparkling.

"Yes! Yes, I have you. Oh, how I do love you, Sloan."

With his arm about her waist, they moved on up the slope toward the cabin. He stopped and kissed her and kissed her until Orah Delle tugged at his hand.

"Impatient child," he scolded gently, his eyes warm with happiness. "Let me kiss your beautiful mama."

Cherish took the child's other hand and they walked on swinging her between them. Sloan stopped once again and brushed Cherish's hair with his lips.

"No regrets that you didn't let Pierre take you back to Virginia?" he asked, his eyes twinkling with mischief.

"None," she assured him firmly, turning her head to meet his lips. Her heart soared as it did each time he declared his love.

He held her to him with his free arm. "I couldn't bear life without you. Fate was kind when she let me meet you on the banks of the Kentucky. I pray each day she will be generous and let me keep you by my side . . . always." His voice was husky with emotion.

Cherish loosened her hand from the child's grip and wound her arms about his neck. Raising her lips to meet his, she whispered:

"Not only in this life, my love, but . . . beyond."

ALMOST EDEN
coming from Warner Books October, 1995

Dear Reader Friend,

Many of you have asked me to write the story of Maggie Gentry and Babtiste Lightbody, the fey woods sprite and the French/Indian scout. Light was introduced in WILD SWEET WILDERNESS, Light and Maggie in ANNIE LASH. ALMOST EDEN, is their story.

Maggie was Light's world. He loved her more dearly than life. Together they journeyed from the Mississippi River to the Rocky Mountains at a time when few white men had made the journey. Light built a home for his love on a mountain top in Colorado. They later became the great-grandparents of Lorna who lived on Light's Mountain in WAYWARD WIND.

Light and Maggie's love story became a legend in the Rocky Mountains and was passed down from generation to generation among both the Indian and the Wascium.

I am always grateful for your comments about my stories. Through your letters I have improved my craft and made lasting friendships. My address: Dorothy Garlock, c/o Warner Books, 1271 Avenue of the Americas, New York, NY 10020.

Dorothy Garlock

INDIAN PUDDING

(1828 recipe)

1 cup (not quite full) molasses, 1 cup (not quite full) corn meal, 1 egg, 1 heaping spoonful of butter or fat, salt, ginger or cinnamon to taste, all beaten together. Full quart sweet milk put on to boil and these ingredients stirred in. Take from fire and add not quite a full cup of cold milk. Pour into pan onto lumps of butter. Bake one hour. Extra good.

(Modern recipe)

4 cups plus 2/3 cup milk
2/3 cup yellow cornmeal
3/4 cup molasses
2 eggs, beaten
1 tablespoon butter
1/2 teaspoon salt
1 teaspoon ginger or cinnamon

Preheat the oven to 275° F.

Heat 3 cups of the milk in the top part of a double boiler over boiling water. Mix 1 cup of milk and the cornmeal. Stir into the hot milk. Combine the molasses, beaten eggs, butter, salt, and ginger and add to the cornmeal and milk mixture. Cook over low heat until the mixture thickens slightly. Remove from heat and add the remaining 2/3 cup milk. Pour into a buttered 2-quart casserole and bake for 2 hours. Serve warm or cool with whipped cream. Makes 8 servings.